MORE PRAISE FOR *FIRST BLAST*

"McCormack is an expert in the art of quiet treachery, in creating the fine unassuming line which sheathes a knife, in the shadowy craft of luring us into the torture chamber we secretly can't resist, beckoning us to act on the desire to revel in the truly sadistic . . . A damn good read." *The Vancouver Sun*

"*First Blast* is an ingenious celebration of human solemnity... a book artfully written for the thinking person, and that means each and every one of us." *The Globe and Mail*

"There's a fairy-tale quality to *First Blast*, a Brothers Grimm for grown-ups who like an intelligent read with a bit of snap, crackle, pop . . ." *The Georgia Strait*

"[McCormack] is one of a kind . . . a unique literary voice . . . *First Blast* celebrates the priority of imagination. It's completely accessible and non-stop entertaining." *The Calgary Herald*

"Engrossing . . . [McCormack] is a crackling good story-teller with an uncanny ability to expose the macabre underbelly of human nature." *The Record* (Kitchener/Waterloo)

"McCormack's beautifully written account of one man's search for redemption and some sort of answer to it all is a great read." *Eye Weekly*

"McCormack's postmodern metaphysical puzzle is also a marvellous yarn. It spins out in picaresque segments, each distinct, vivid, funny, and full of sighs and wonders." *Quill & Quire*

"One of Canada's foremost

"McCormack's prose, on a purely sentence level is always unerring, often stunning . . . *First Blast* is a novel that expertly sets its sights on an impressive assortment of truths."

Books in Canada

"An impressive book, one that treats the reader as an intelligent, thinking creature, without being obtuse . . . *First Blast* is a solid novel by a confident writer, moving smoothly and strangely through a man's life and mind and his various disasters."

The Ottawa X Press

"The power of invention is a rare thing and McCormack has tonnes of it . . ." *See Magazine*

"McCormack writes beautifully . . ." *The Leader Post* (Regina)

"Reading McCormack is like wandering through a mansion with each room crammed to bursting with strange and terrible objects suggesting mysterious lands and arcane philosophies . . . this novel is a pleasure to read and to read again. The story and the stories within reveal additonal subtleties with each new visit."

The Edmonton Journal

"*First Blast* is a fun-house ride of a novel; an amusement park of childish nightmares and fears . . . an imaginative novel, straddling the twilit world where dream and reality merge and linger . . . A novel of bizarre fantasy and imaginative, gothic terrors made casual, *First Blast* is a grown-up fantasy novel that will amuse any lover of the unusual, the supernatural and the paranoid."

The Telegraph-Journal (St. John)

PENGUIN BOOKS

FIRST BLAST OF THE TRUMPET AGAINST THE MONSTROUS REGIMENT OF WOMEN

Eric McCormack was born in a small village in Scotland. He moved to Canada in 1966 and attended the University of Manitoba. Since 1970 he has taught English at St Jerome's College in Waterloo, Ontario, specializing in seventeenth-century and contemporary literature.

FIRST

of the

Blast Trumpet against *the* Monstrous Regiment *of* Women

Eric McCormack

Penguin Books

PENGUIN BOOKS
Published by the Penguin Group
Penguin Books Canada Ltd, 10 Alcorn Avenue, Toronto,
Ontario, Canada M4V 3B2
Penguin Books Ltd, 27 Wrights Lane, London W8 5TZ, England
Penguin Putnam Inc., 375 Hudson Street, New York,
New York 10014, U.S.A.
Penguin Books Australia Ltd, Ringwood, Victoria, Australia
Penguin Books (NZ) Ltd, cnr Rosedale and Airborne Roads,
Albany, Auckland 1310, New Zealand

Penguin Books Ltd, Registered Offices: Harmondsworth,
Middlesex, England

First published in Viking by Penguin Books Canada Limited, 1997

Published in Penguin Books, 1998

1 3 5 7 9 10 8 6 4 2

Publisher's note: This book is a work of fiction. Names, characters, places and incidents either are the product of the author's imagination or are used fictitiously, and any resemblance to actual persons living or dead, events, or locales is entirely coincidental.

Manufactured in Canada.

Canadian Cataloguing in Publication Data

McCormack, Eric, 1938–
First blast of the trumpet against the monstrous
regiment of women

ISBN 0-14-026683-6

I. Title.

PS8575.C665F57 1998 C813'.54 C96-932440-5
PR9199.3.M42378F57 1998

Part of this novel has appeared, in a different form,
in *Gates of Paradise*, ed. Alberto Manguel.

Original title page photograph by Hans Neleman/Image Bank

for Nancy

Note on the Title

John Knox (1513–1572) was the author of the original *First Blast of the Trumpet Against the Monstrous Regiment of Women*. The phrase is now often misapplied: “Regiment” here has its old sense of “rule, magisterial authority,” and has no connection with the later sense of “large body of troops” (Margaret Drabble, ed. *The Oxford Companion to English Literature*, 1985).

First Blast *of the* Trumpet against *the* Monstrous Regiment *of* Women

Prologue

No BOOK'S WORTH reading that doesn't offer some information of practical use to the reader. That's what Harry Greene, steward of the SS *Cumnock*, told me. I think my Uncle Norman might have agreed, too. Once, on the Island of St Jude, he showed me a jar containing a scorpion he'd trapped. It was a brownish colour, the size of my hand.

"Come with me," he said.

He gave me a can of kerosene to carry and we went out to a bare area in the garden. He poked his finger into the soil and made a little circular ditch about nine inches in diameter and an inch deep. He filled the ditch with kerosene and lit it, making a ring of fire.

"Now watch this," he said.

He took the lid off the jar and dropped the scorpion into the middle of the ring. It immediately tried to scuttle away. The flames stopped it. It tried again, and again, and again. No matter where it went, the flames drove it back.

The scorpion stopped and crouched for a while in the middle of the ring. Then it raised its sting and slowly lowered it onto its own back. It gently felt around for a crevice in its scales, inserted the sting, paused and jabbed itself.

It went into a trembling frenzy, then it shuddered once or twice more, then it died. The flames still blazed around it.

"See?" said Uncle Norman. "A scorpion would rather sting itself than die with its sting unused. I read that in a book."

What if a book revealed maybe the most sought-after piece of practical information any human being could ever want? I mean, the location of Paradise on this earth—its exact co-ordinates: latitude and longitude, and a description of how to get there.

I undertake to reveal that information. The location's straightforward enough. What you may have to go through to get there isn't. In my journey, I experienced things few, if any, other inhabitants of this earth have ever had to undergo.

But before I get into all of that, I want to give a piece of advice: *Be very careful about putting your nightmares into words. Not only can you NOT get rid of them that way, but the words only give them another, more concrete kind of reality. So you might well end up with double the terror.* That's one piece of advice I don't think I've changed my mind about. Not long ago, I would have added another one to it: *Never trust anyone you know well. You may love them. But you can't trust them.*

Now, the promise made, the warning given, I'll begin at the beginning of the journey—the moment of my birth.

Part One

Birth and Death

The faces fade, and there is only
A sort of meaning that comes back
Donald Justice

Chapter One

It happened in Stroven, one of those little mining towns deep among the Upland hills. Little town after little town, squat hill after squat hill (squat because they'd been flattened by millions of years), it was hard to tell one town or one hill from another. Each town was linked to the next by tortuous roads that followed the traces of ancient paths that came before them.

A few miles south of Stroven lay Carrick, and not far west of that, Muirton, and a little south-west of that, Cumner, then a little south-east, in a valley, Patna. And on and on—Rossmark, Lannick, Taymire, Gatbridge—town after town, each one with grey buildings and low hills. There weren't many trees. The thick forests that used to grow here were cut down and dragged thousands of feet below the earth to hold up tunnels in the coal mines. The coal was all that was left of even more ancient forests.

Most of the mines are closed now; but at one time they bulged at the edge of every little town, like a tumour. There would be a scattering of grimy sheds and smouldering slag heaps. The mine elevators looked like Ferris wheels, and rose higher than the town halls, or the church steeples. These elevators plunged the miners deep into the earth, or whisked them back up into the daylight—a grey daylight under grey skies. Grey skies and biting winds were the rule among these hills.

But on the day of my birth, the last day of June, the skies weren't grey, and the wind didn't whine across the moors. All that spring in the Uplands, the weather had been unusual. In April the days were warm. By May, hot. No one could remember such a sunny June.

I was born near midday, and the birth, though it was a month premature, could be called successful—in the sense that I was successfully born, in the front bedroom upstairs in the big house. The large, raw hand of Midwife Findley snapped against my buttocks and I howled as I was supposed to.

But my passage through the narrow birth canal had been a rough one, for I didn't make the journey alone. I came with a sister. We exited together, head first (though my head was slightly in the lead, making me the elder by a few inches). Our arms and legs were tangled together. In fact, our bodies must have been so close together for so long in the womb that each of us had made an imprint on the other. Midwife Findley had to prise us apart. "They're stuck together like a package of sausages," she said. A dark purple stain in the shape of a triangle marked the upper body area, from nipple to nipple to belly-button, of both me and my sister. The shape looked vaguely like a dog's head, or maybe some kind of rodent.

The purple stain stayed with me all my life.

It wasn't that Stroven didn't have a doctor—his name was Doctor Giffen—but births were reserved to the midwife. So Midwife Findley had come across her fair share of strange births in the Uplands, mainly babies with extra limbs, or not enough of them. The very night before my birth, she'd delivered a boy without any skin for the

McCabes, who already had ten children. The boy was fortunate enough to die quickly, all the blood seeping out of him on contact with the air.

Midwife Findley was relieved that today's tangle of limbs wasn't some monster, but two normal children. She'd separated them, slapped them, they'd issued the desired howl. All was well.

All through the final hours of the labour, an unlit cigarette dangled from her lips. Now, after the births of me and my sister, Midwife Findley lit it and looked her patient over. The midwife was relieved, and she knew her relief must be nothing next to how my mother must feel after a labour that had lasted almost twenty-four hours. Childbirth, to Midwife Findley, was the ultimate torture: the slow splitting in half of the body. Yet this young woman had neither howled nor whimpered. She lay now on the bed in the big upstairs bedroom, silent and pale—my mother, Sarah Halfnight. She was almost as much a newcomer to Stroven as I was to this world.

I received my name the following week, on the first Saturday morning in July. A hot morning. In weather like this, when the sky was clear and blue, the granite walls and slate roofs of Stroven, which were perfect camouflage under normal conditions, looked out of place—as though a black-and-white set had found its way into a colour movie.

That morning at half past eight, about twenty adult townspeople in groups of two or three sweated their way along the cobblestone street that led to the Square, which was really a patch of grass, some small trees and a few wooden benches around a war memorial. Two sides of the Square contained the more impressive buildings of the town: the Bank, the Library, the Police Station, the Town Hall, the Church, the Stroven Inn. The other two sides of the Square held an array of small businesses: Glenn's Pharmacy, Darvell's Grocery, MacCallum's Bakery, Morrison's Tailor and the Stroven Café. The owners of the businesses lived in apartments above their stores.

Into this Square that hot Saturday morning came almost all the people my mother knew in Stroven. The men wore plaid caps, heavy blue suits with waistcoats, and black boots. The faces of most of them were pale, and their bodies were wiry, hunched from a life of stooping in low tunnels. The women were stocky and wore black overcoats and black felt hats. Everyone looked as though they were dressed for the usual chilly weather—afraid the heat might suddenly disappear and catch them unprepared.

They had no children with them, for children weren't welcome at formal occasions.

At the south-west corner of the Square, the group of townspeople had to step carefully to avoid another procession: a thousand hairy caterpillars dragging themselves across the hot main street on some caterpillar business. None of the townspeople could remember ever having seen anything like that.

The human procession arrived at the Church and filed inside. The shade and the cool of the granite sucked the prickly heat out of their bodies. The Church was bare. The benches and the pulpit and the altar and all the accoutrements of religion had been removed long ago, except for the words engraved in the arch above the sanctuary: AN EYE FOR AN EYE. No clergyman presided in the building any more; but people still liked rituals, and the Provosts of Stroven decided the old Church was a perfect place for the performing of the three civil ceremonies: marriages, funerals and the naming of children.

This morning, the people stood in awkward, silent

groups till a small door squealed open at the front. Provost Hawse appeared; then my mother, carrying my sister; then my aunt, carrying me. My father came last.

The Provost led the way to a circle of white marble tiles in the floor at the middle of the Church. The tiles were all that was left of an even older building. In the middle of each tile was a small blue gargoyle head. The townspeople stood on the fringe of this circle and made sure they didn't bring bad luck upon themselves by stepping on the tiles, or staring at the gargoyles.

Provost Hawse was a small, thin man. His back was stooped too, but in a different way from the miners'. He looked more like a sick rat and had little almond-shaped eyes. He wore a bronze medallion of office round his neck, and he hobbled as he walked, as though the medallion was too heavy.

My mother was taller than any of the other women. Her green eyes were clear and confident. Her age wasn't easy to tell. Her face might have been that of a very young woman who'd seen a lot; or of an older woman who'd led a sheltered life. In her arms she held my sister, fast asleep in a white, knitted shawl.

My aunt was a shorter, heavier version of my mother, with a similar face, the same eyes. She held me wrapped in another white shawl. Unlike my sister, I was awake and watchful.

As for my father: he walked last to the marble circle. He was in his mid-thirties, a plumpish man of average height. His thinning fair hair was sleeked sideways to cover his baldness. Now and then he'd pat it nervously. He hadn't removed his black leather gloves.

Everyone was quiet.

The Provost checked a slip of paper he'd taken from his jacket. He looked at my mother with his little eyes.

"You are Sarah Halfnight, the mother of this child?" His voice was loud for such a slight man.

"Yes." She spoke quietly.

"Is this the girl?"

"Yes."

The Provost again checked the slip of paper, then looked at my sister. He put his veined hand on her forehead. She already had a head of silky brown hair.

"By the power vested in me, I name this child..." He looked again at his paper, "...I name this child...Johanna Halfnight."

My sister had opened her eyes when he touched her head. Her face slowly contorted and purpled. She began to howl bitterly. My mother soothed her, and she sobbed for a while then was silent.

The Provost faced my aunt, who was still holding me. He seemed puzzled. He checked his paper again then turned to my father.

"You're the father—Thomas Halfnight?"

My father nodded.

"Then the father must hold the male child at the naming," said the Provost.

My father was about to say something when my mother spoke.

"We've agreed my sister, Lizzie, should hold him."

Provost Hawse's face was a maze of tiny intersecting lines. He looked into her unflinching green eyes for a moment, then shrugged his thin shoulders.

"So be it," he said.

He looked at his piece of paper again. Then he put out his hand. It was light and dry on my forehead, like a spider. I shut my eyes.

"By the power vested in me," he said, "I name this child Andrew Halfnight."

Everyone was silent. I opened my eyes again and saw the Provost stuff the paper into his pocket. He looked round the assembly.

"It's over," he said. "The ceremony is ended."

And that was how I received my name.

Chapter Two

THE TOWNSPEOPLE WENT back outside. The heat made even the familiar unfamiliar. The usually delightful smell of fresh bread from MacCallum's Bakery was now mingled with the smell of something slightly putrid. Things that had year after year rotted unnoticed in these hills now made sure the townspeople couldn't ignore the fact of their decay.

My parents and my aunt and the townspeople walked back along the hot street. The morning was so still that the walkers could hear, even above their chatter, a steady hum. Masses of bees were gathering in the Square, organizing to set out and pillage the moors, where gorse and heather and wild flowers were in full bloom.

The procession soon arrived at the house rented by my parents. It was at the end of the main street, which was also the edge of the town. With its gothic front windows on either side of a heavy wooden door, and its lawns and hedges, it looked as out of place as a palace among the two-roomed miners' rows on either side where most of the townspeople lived. The house was block-shaped with four large bedrooms upstairs; downstairs, the entranceway gave onto a passageway that went past the doors of the living-room and the library and ended in the kitchen.

The townspeople could have gone round the side of the house to the backyard, but it was presumed they'd want a glimpse of the inside of the big house. They went through the front door and along the passageway. The men took off their caps, and they all, men and women, filed through quietly, looking around curiously at the grandeur of the place. Through the open doors of the living-room they could see dark leather chairs, Persian rugs, mahogany tables; as they passed the library, they could see shelves of books from floor to ceiling, more books than anyone could ever want to read. They went into the long kitchen and out through the back door into the yard, with its brown lawn and high privet hedges.

Now the women put their coats aside and the men stripped to their waistcoats. Two long wooden tables with benches on either side had already been set out. Some of the women went back into the house and came out carrying trays heaped with sandwiches and mugs of beer. The townspeople sat down at the tables. My father came out, then my mother and my aunt, who'd changed their clothes, and were carrying me and my sister. My mother now wore a long black skirt and a white blouse. My aunt had put on a plain brown dress and brown shoes. My sister and I were placed gently on the warm grass beside the tables. My mother and my aunt sat together at the table nearest the back door.

The mugs were raised and clinked together in a toast. The musician began playing. He was an elderly man, one of those who'd lost a leg at the Muirton mine disaster years before. Now he played fiddle music at gatherings like this—reels and laments, laments and reels. Each blended into the other with ease.

My father, his thin fair hair carefully in place, sat on a stool at the head of the second table. He wore the same double-breasted black suit and elegant black shoes he'd worn to the ceremony. He hadn't taken off his gloves. They were made of black leather and glistened in the sun. He didn't eat or drink. Some of the men tried to draw him into conversation, and he nodded a few times, that was all.

After a while, my mother signalled to the fiddler and he stopped playing. She stood up. The townspeople were silent.

"I just want to thank you all," she said in her deep, calm voice. She had a smooth, unlined face. Perhaps she'd avoided smiling. Perhaps she hadn't found much to smile at. "I don't want to make a speech. Just to thank you for being here today and thank you for making newcomers such as us welcome in Stroven. Now please enjoy yourselves."

She sat down and the guests applauded her words by banging their beer mugs on the tables.

My father applauded her words, too, his gloved hands clumping against each other. Then he stood up, and the guests thought he wanted to make a speech, too. But he didn't. Instead he walked over to where my mother sat.

"Sarah, I'd like to hold the babies," he said.

The townspeople were watching. The birds, even the insects, seemed to have fallen silent. My mother looked at him for a while; then she breathed deeply and rose from the table. She looked down at her two babies on the grass, considering. I was wide awake, gurgling and waving my arms. But my mother bent and picked up my sister, Johanna, who was still asleep wrapped in her shawl. My mother cradled her in her own arms for a moment, looking into the little sleeping face. Then, decisively, she held her daughter out and placed her in the outstretched arms of my father.

"Thank you," he said. His plump face, which before had seemed sullen, was transformed by a smile. He looked down at my sister in his arms, then around at the guests, smiling at them all. He looked down at my sister again, examining her sleeping face, talking to her like a new father.

"My beautiful daughter," he said, "my beautiful little daughter," over and over again.

Now he wanted to show her off.

"Isn't she beautiful?" he said to the townspeople nearest, bending to let them see his little girl. "She's so beautiful." He said this even to the men seated at the tables; they agreed uncomfortably, for "beautiful" was not a word the miners used in these Upland towns.

Gradually, the guests relaxed again and the general chatter began, and the clanking of mugs, and the fiddler played another reel. But my mother didn't take her eyes off her husband. Nor did my aunt. Nor did some others of the Stroven women who must have sensed something.

They were all witnesses.

What happened was this. My father was leaning over to give Jane MacCallum, the Baker's wife, a better view of my sister's face. The knitted woollen shawl began to slip on the shiny leather of his gloves. Several of the women seated at the table, alarmed, stretched out their hands to help. My father clutched tighter to stop my sister from falling.

Crack! The distinctive and sharp sound, like the snap of a whip, was heard by everyone, even above the babble of conversation and the whine of the fiddle.

Everything stopped.

My mother jumped up from her seat and rushed over to where my father stood. She took the baby out of his arms. The little green eyes were wide open now, just as though my sister were awake. A trickle of red oozed between her soft lips.

My mother slumped to her knees, holding her baby to her. My father, standing before her, slowly raised his gloved hands to cover his face. One of the guests, Jamie Sprung, got up from the table discreetly. He walked quickly to the side of the house where there was a gate leading to the front. He didn't take time to open the gate, but leaped over it and ran along the hot street to the Square. He came back with Doctor Giffen, who took the baby from my mother. He put my sister on one of the tables and performed his examination. Then he pronounced what those in the garden already knew: that she was dead. Even her flexible baby ribs hadn't been flexible enough—they were crushed, and the jagged ends had pierced her tiny lungs.

The idea of death by crushing wasn't strange to these townspeople. For generations, Stroven miners had been killed this way in cave-ins deep under the earth. But they were shocked that it should have happened to a baby, my sister; and that it should have happened above ground, in a garden, on a sunny day.

Chapter Three

AFTER THE DOCTOR examined the baby, my father, Thomas Halfnight, left the garden and went into the house. My aunt followed him; she tried to talk to him even though she herself was distraught. After a while he left the house. Some people in the town saw him go along the street, past the Square, towards the sheep path that runs east into the hills. The gaunt shepherd Kerr Lawson was up by the sheep pens practising his bagpipes (the townspeople preferred their sound at a distance); he saw my father disappear into the hills.

It was the next morning before anyone went looking for him.

At dawn, four men headed for Hadrian's Bridge, a Roman bridge that arched over a one-hundred-foot-deep gorge. At the bottom was a stream, famous for its fat trout.

The four men had an idea this was where they might find my father. They arrived at the stream by seven o'clock. One of them was Jamie Sprung, the man who'd gone for the Doctor the day before, an agile man in his mid-twenties with sharp eyes. Always, there was an eagerness about him: his whole body seemed tensed as though ready to break into a sprint at the slightest pretext. Now, he was the first to notice the black specks in the sky, like spots in the eye of the morning sun. He pointed them out to the others.

"Crows—over there."

The birds were milling around in the sky a half-mile up the gorge, at a place where the stream narrowed to rush under the bridge.

When the men got there, it was Sprung who saw, directly beneath the bridge, the naked body of my father sprawled on the rocks, the upper half of him out of the water. Crows were everywhere, pecking, pecking, pecking at him the same way they pecked at the carcasses of drowned sheep.

The men threw rocks at them and they scattered, shrieking.

Sprung was first to scramble down the steep bank. He waded into the fast, knee-deep water. My father's neck was at an impossible angle, and the birds had already made a mess of him. They'd taken the eyes and the plump flesh of the face and chest. All that was left of his right arm was a bloody stump at the elbow.

The birds were squawking, wheeling around in the air above.

The men lifted the body out of the water. On the bank, they wrapped it in a tarpaulin groundsheet and dragged it to the top of the gorge. Among the bracken by the pathway, they saw black trousers and a silk shirt and other odds and ends of my father's clothing. They considered putting the clothes back on him, to make him decent. But no one was willing, in the end, to make such intimate contact with the mutilated body. They stuffed the clothes into the tarpaulin beside the body.

In this way, they carried my father back down to Stroven.

By the time the finders of the body arrived back in the town, many of the townspeople were standing in the glare of the morning sun waiting to see them carry their load along the main street, through the Square and down to my mother's house. The four men were sweating and tired from their efforts, but no one offered to help them. They had, by now, their own living cloud cover—swarms of blowflies enticed by the smell of death.

When they reached the big house, the men entered without knocking. They went along the passageway into the kitchen and laid their burden on the table, a deal kitchen table nicked and scarred by long service to the meat-chopper.

My mother and my aunt, who'd been watching their approach from the upstairs bedroom window, came down into the kitchen. They stood by the open door, looking at the body. When the men saw them there, they stepped aside and took off their caps.

"We found him under the Roman bridge," said Jamie Sprung to my mother.

The kitchen was full of the buzz of flies that had followed

the men inside. My mother swayed against the door-frame. Then she came forward and loosened the tarpaulin so that my father's face and his torso were exposed.

"The crows," Jamie Sprung said. "They made a mess of him."

My aunt came forward too. The skin of my father's face was whitish blue, the eye-sockets were raw, the cheeks had been torn away from the bone. The blood around the stump of the arm was congealed.

My mother and my aunt stood looking at the body, while Jamie Sprung waved the flies away with his cap.

The inquiry into the death of my father was very brief. It took place around the deal table of my mother's kitchen one hour after the body had been laid there. Present were: Jamie Sprung and the other three men who'd found it; my mother and my aunt; Doctor Giffen; and Constable MacTaggart.

Doctor Giffen said the cause of death was a broken neck as was very obvious from the angle of the head. My father must have plunged one hundred feet from the bridge onto the exposed rocks. The other mutilations were the work of the birds.

"The only anomaly," Doctor Giffen said, "is the right arm." He pointed to the stump. "See where the arm's been removed here, where the humerus joins with the radius and the ulna." The doctor looked uncomfortable as he tried to explain to my mother. "You can see where the crows have been pecking at the flesh. But the bone has been cut by some human instrument. In fact, it's been sawn off. Crows are smart, but not that smart. These saw marks are quite recent. It's hard to say whether they were made before or after death. We'd have to call in a specialist, or send the body to the City."

Everyone was silent. My aunt was watching my mother, who eventually spoke.

"Please," she said. "Can't we leave it alone? He's dead. He didn't want to live. What's done is done."

The doctor looked into those green eyes, then looked away and nodded his head quickly at Constable MacTaggart.

"Certainly," the Doctor said, "this business of the arm isn't important so far as the cause of death is concerned. Falling from a height—that's what killed him."

Constable MacTaggart was a scrawny, hawk-nosed man who'd represented law and order in Stroven for thirty years, and knew how to handle these local problems with the minimum of fuss.

"Let's get the death certificate signed, then," he said.

Jamie Sprung spoke to my mother.

"If you like, we'll go back up and see if we can find the rest of his arm," he said.

"No, don't do that," she said. "There's no need to do any more. You've been very kind." She looked at Doctor Giffen, Constable MacTaggart, Jamie Sprung and the other men. "You've all been very kind."

Only women attended the funeral service, though men carried the coffins to the graveyard: two black mahogany coffins, one large, one small.

As the funeral procession passed through the Square, I was in someone's arms at an upstairs window. The women of Stroven, of every shape and size, followed the black-curtained hearse, marching four abreast, in slow time, like a regiment in mourning. They wore the uniform of the Upland women: long black coats, black headscarves that lay low on their foreheads and flat black shoes. I could see among them Midwife Findley and the women who'd been at the reception in the garden: Mrs Glenn, the Pharmacist's wife, and Mrs Darvell, the Grocer's wife, and Miss Balfour, the Librarian, and Mrs MacCallum, the Baker's wife, and Jenny Morrison, the Tailor, and Mrs Gibson, the owner of the Stroven Café; and mixed in with them, some of the miners' wives: Mrs Blythe, Mrs Mitchell, Mrs Haworth, Mrs Thomson, Mrs Harrigan, Mrs Kennedy, Mrs Holmes, Mrs Bromley, Mrs Cummings, Mrs Hewson, Mrs Browne and Mrs Thornwayne. At the rear of the column, two women marched abreast. One of them was tall, one short. The tall one carried a long staff with a silken pennant fluttering from the top. It had writing on it that was hard to read, because the banner was constantly shifting in the breeze. When these last two women passed below the window, my heart lifted, for I knew they were my mother and my aunt, and I loved them more than anything in the world. But as they passed, their heads and the heads of all the other women turned and they looked up at me. Their faces were the faces of strangers, and even though the sun was shining, it might have been the middle of the night, for their eyes glared like the eyes of wolves caught in headlights.

But it wasn't the middle of the night; it was broad daylight, and the sun shone on the women, and on Stroven, and on the noose of hills around them. And it shone and it shone as though it would shine for ever.

Chapter Four

THOSE FIRST DAYS of my life hiccup through my mind like an old black-and-white movie. Not that I really remember them. I heard about them only once, much later, and in a very general way. But I suppose the mind can't bear gaps, and my mind has filled in the details. Now, it's hard for me to tell the difference between the things I was eventually told and those I invented; they're all like memories of my own: the moment of my exit with my sister from my mother's womb; the feel of that papery hand of the Provost on my head; the heat of the sun in the garden; the laughter, the chatter of voices, the chink of porcelain beer mugs, the fiddle music; the awful *crack!*; my father's mutilated body on the kitchen table; the procession of the Stroven women to the graveyard.

When I eventually learnt about the circumstances of my birth, I was a good deal older. Only then did I understand that my mother had given me life twice: once, in the regular way of a mother bearing a child; the second time, in choosing to place my sister rather than me in the lethal arms of Thomas Halfnight, my father.

Nor was it my mother who told me the story. Any time I hinted to her that I'd like to know something about the past—even why I had that purple stain on my chest—she gave me a look that put a stop to my questions. By the time I was seven, I knew better than to ask.

Nor did any of the adults of Stroven tell me about that day in the garden, though none of those who were there ever forgot it. It was just that they believed certain things are better left untold.

The Stroven children weren't quite so discreet. For instance, they talked about my father. To them, he was some kind of legendary monster. The story of his missing arm seemed to be common knowledge amongst them. The first time I heard of it was from Jack Macdiarmid, the son of the Carpenter, during the heat of a football game in the playground.

"Hey, Halfwit!" he shouted. That was one of my nicknames, along with "Half-pint," and "Half-baked." "Your father was a cannibal! He ate his own arm and choked on it!" He laughed unpleasantly.

Another time, one of my classmates, Isabel Blythe, told me a different rumour. She said some of the other Stroven men had cut off my father's arm and stuffed his fingers down his throat.

I'd no idea where these stories came from. But they caused me a lot of anguish. In history classes, whenever we came across the topic of cannibalism, I felt everyone was looking at me. The image of my father devouring his own arm gave me my first nightmares, and was part of my version of my life till I knew better.

I never told my mother about the stories I'd heard. If I had, she herself might have told me the truth about my father. She might have told me I once had a twin sister. I wonder what difference it would have made to me if I'd known these things sooner. Would I have become the man I am now if my past had been revealed to me when I wanted to know it? Would its impact on me have been the same? Perhaps and perhaps not. I'm not so sure the chronology of our emotional lives is all that linear.

At any rate, I was still ignorant about these earlier occurrences in my life.

I was now ten years old, a small boy for my age, shy, a good scholar at Stroven school. I felt awkward about our family name, Halfnight—I wished it had been a Macsomething, or a simple Smith or Brown, or any of the other common Stroven names. I wished my past had been the same as everyone else's. But we were outsiders. One of the only things I knew about my father was that he must have left my mother fairly well off. That was why we could afford to live in the big house and she didn't seem to have to worry about money.

The house was a misfit in Stroven, too. It had been built as a place to retire in, by an old sea captain. He let it be known he'd chosen Stroven because it was far away from the sea. He lived alone in the big house, like an exotic hermit. He kept on wearing his seaman's uniform, and he had as little to do with the townspeople as possible.

But he didn't live long. In his first winter in Stroven, after a December storm, he was found leaning over the front gate, dead. He was dressed in his oilskins and sou'wester and still clutched a telescope in his hand. Some of the townspeople believed he'd forgotten where he was—that he thought he was on deck, trying to navigate his ship through the final gale.

After his death, the house was rented intermittently, mainly by mine managers. And lastly, not long before I was born, by my parents. I loved my mother deeply, though she was not an easy mother to love: in addition to not being much of a talker, she didn't like to hug or be hugged. Displays of feelings seemed to be, for her, a sign of weakness. And yet I could never be sure if that was what she really thought, or what she thought about anything, for that matter. I had the impression it was as distasteful to her to reveal the contents of the mind as of the bowels.

"The unspoken words inside your head," she told me once, "may seem very wise. But as soon as they come out of your mouth, you realize how foolish they are, and it's too late then to call them back."

She didn't work, but volunteered to spend a few afternoons each week visiting the sick wives of miners. These women admired her. And she wasn't without male admirers such as Jamie Sprung, the finder of my father's body. He was a miner and a bachelor, and he made a point of dropping by the house regularly. He'd cut the lawn and do odd jobs, and he'd come some evenings for dinner. Sometimes he was still sitting with my mother by the fire when it was time for me to go to bed. One morning, I rose early enough to look out of my window and see him scurrying down the pathway from the house before anyone in town was up and about.

All that stopped when the War began. Jamie Sprung was conscripted into the navy. He drowned along with six hundred others when his ship, on a warm starless night, struck a mine in mid-ocean ten thousand miles from Stroven.

If my mother mourned his death, I didn't notice.

"One man in my life is enough," she would say from time to time.

I wasn't sure whether this was meant to be flattering to me, or not.

Chapter Five

A CHANGE CAME OVER her in the September after my eleventh birthday. She was coughing a lot, and I thought she'd caught a cold. I noticed how much paler than usual she looked and how much less she ate. That cough persisted, day after day, week after week—a dry, hacking cough that racked her body. Once or twice I asked her about it.

She made it plain that illness was among those things better not discussed.

So I remember very clearly the morning she broke that rule. It was a late November morning. A bitterly cold Upland wind had left the tips of the hills frostbitten.

"I've an appointment with Doctor Giffen this morning," she said, as I was leaving for school.

The fact she told me even this much worried me all day. So when I came home from school that afternoon, I was anxious to know what had happened at the Doctor's. Naturally, she said nothing about it for the longest time. When dinner was over, we sat by the fire reading. After a bout of coughing, she spoke.

"Andrew," she said. "Doctor Giffen says I've to spend more time lying down. He seems to think that'll help get rid of this cough."

Doctor Giffen took to dropping by each day, and often he'd be with my mother when I came home from school. He was a small man who always dressed formally in a grey pinstriped suit. His black hair was like hair painted onto a puppet. He had a short black beard. He had small, bright eyes. He carried with him the austere smell of ether. He didn't smile much, and when he did, it was a small thin smile, like one of those scalpels in his bag.

Once, I heard him say to my mother, after he'd examined her: "You have such lovely skin." That made me suspect he loved her, though the ether smell that was always around him seemed to me the antithesis of love.

The fact that he was small was not unusual in Stroven. Most of the miners were short men, bred like moles for the tunnels. But his beard was a different matter. He was the only man in Stroven with a beard.

It was on his advice we moved my mother's bed into the

living-room. Her bedroom, like all the bedrooms in the big house, wasn't warm enough: there were dark blotches on the green wallpaper, and blisters on the ceiling. Dampness was one of the things she needed to avoid.

My mother and I together carried her bed downstairs and set it up in the living-room midway between the big fireplace and the front window. From that day on, she spent much more time in bed, though she still got up for a few hours each day, and cooked meals for me.

While she lay in bed, she'd read the books and magazines Miss Balfour, the Librarian, would drop off on weekends. She'd sit for a while, talking, and seemed to enjoy her visits. My mother didn't say much, so she was a good audience.

Her cough wasn't going away. It left specks of blood on her handkerchiefs. She coughed more and more, day and night. My bedroom was upstairs, and the walls and the floor were thick, but I could still hear her.

A particular evening at the beginning of December is nailed to my memory. Outside, the weather sounded like a demented military band, what with the sleet drumming against the windows and the piping of the wind. She wasn't in bed, but sitting in one of the corduroy armchairs by the fire. I was sitting in the other, reading. She had a book on her knee, but she was using it as a writing desk. At one point I looked up, perhaps because I didn't hear the scratch of the pen, and I saw she'd been looking at me, I don't know for how long.

"I'm writing to your Aunt Lizzie," she said.

"Oh," I said.

She began writing again. The wind howled outside. Inside, the fire crackled, her pen was again scratching. I watched her sitting there, in her nightgown, her legs tucked under her, the book on her knee, a wisp of hair over her face.

And, suddenly, I could have wept. For at that moment, for the first time, I was struck with an awful fear that she was going to die, that she was going to leave me alone in the world. She looked up just then and her green eyes were shrewd. I tried to smile but it was too late. I knew she'd read the selfish fear in my face as easily as if it had been written on a page.

"Don't worry, Andrew," she said. "If anything happens to me, you'll go and live with Lizzie. Doctor Giffen will make the arrangements."

The fire was blazing, but her words were like slivers of ice in my heart.

At school, on the day before the winter break, I was called to the office. I knocked and the Principal came to the door. He was a tall droopy man with an oversized pale face, placid eyes, and lank brown hair that fell over his forehead.

"Ah, Andrew," he said. "Come in. Doctor Giffen's here to talk to you. I'll leave you two alone." He headed off down the corridor.

Doctor Giffen was standing by the desk. The smell of ether competed with the school's stale, institutional smell. When I came in, he wiped the edge of the desk with a handkerchief and perched on it. I stood in front of him.

"Andrew," he said. "Your mother's very ill." He spoke quietly, as he always did, though there was no one around to hear. Everything he said now had a confidential, lethal air.

"She's getting worse," he said. "She'll soon need someone with her all the time. I think I should get her a nurse. She can easily afford it. But she doesn't want a nurse. She says you'll look after her."

From his voice, I knew he didn't think this was wise.

"Yes, yes," I said. "I'll do it. I'm sure I can do it." I was thrilled to hear she trusted me that much.

"I don't know if you can," he said. "It would be hard enough even for a professional." Those little eyes were narrowed in thought.

"I can do it," I said. "Please let me do it."

He still didn't seem convinced.

"Please," I said again.

He gave out a long breath and drummed his fingers on the desk.

"Very well," he said. "We'll give it a try. For a while, anyway."

Arrangements were made for me to stay home with my mother when the school holidays were over. I understood very well that the reason for this privilege was that Doctor Giffen and everyone else thought my mother might not have long to live. But I didn't accept that. I couldn't imagine my life without her, so I simply made an act of the will that she must live. I wouldn't allow her to die. I would devote myself to her totally, like one of those saints among the lepers.

I had allies. Our nearest neighbour, Mrs MacTaggart, the wife of the old Constable, volunteered to make dinner for us each night. Mrs MacCallum, the Baker's wife, dropped off fresh bread and pastries every day. Mrs Harrigan, whose husband had died in a cave-in at the mine years ago, did the laundry once a week. Miss Balfour, as usual, brought the magazines and books, and stayed to chat.

My mother entered into the spirit of the new arrangement. Whenever she needed to walk about the house, she leaned on me. I couldn't believe how feather light she was.

She began training me for what she knew was to come.

"Andrew," she said. "If I'm going to rely on you, you'll have to learn how to do everything that has to be done."

So, as a kind of game, I learnt such things as propping her up against the bedstead, sliding the bedpan under her, emptying it afterwards. I'd rinse the cloth she used to wipe herself.

I got used to these things and was glad to do them. Anything, just so long as she didn't die.

As she became weaker, the games merged into reality. One morning I woke her and drew the blinds. I filled a bowl with warm water and put it by the bedside. I was about to leave when she spoke to me in a weary voice.

"You'll need to give me a hand bathing this morning."

She couldn't even get the buttons on her nightdress open, so I helped her and then drew it over her head. That was the first time I saw a woman's body unclothed.

She reached for the sponge and began to wash herself. Her hands were so weak she couldn't hold on to it.

"It's no good," she said. "You do it."

She lay back and I began to sponge her body. I sponged her chest, the dark nipples protruding from the flattened breasts. I sponged her belly, marvelling at the the silvery tracks across the skin.

I would have stopped at that for I was afraid to proceed.

"You're not nearly finished," she said. Her green eyes were on me.

So I soaped the sponge and carried on. She opened her legs so that I could bathe between them and down the inside of her legs.

I towelled her off and helped her turn over. I was relieved not to have to undergo the scrutiny of her eyes any more. I breathed more freely as I bathed her from head to foot. I dried her and rubbed soothing cream Doctor Giffen had supplied for the sores that were beginning to blossom as she withered.

When everything was finished, I helped her turn over again, and slid a fresh nightgown over her. She lay back against the pillows.

"Andrew," she said. Her voice was a whisper.

I was obliged to look at her.

"Thank you," she said.

The ironic glint she usually had in her eyes when she spoke to me was missing. I knew she meant what she said, and I was delighted.

It seemed at first there was no halting her decline. She became so thin I could see her ribs and shrunken muscles. Her skin was so transparent I could see the blood vessels beneath. Often I'd spend the afternoon sitting at the bottom of the bed. I'd talk as I'd never talked before. I'd tell her about mathematical problems I was studying, historical events from my school book, anything at all. She'd lie there watching me, breathing lightly, saying nothing. Once in a while, she'd be racked by a coughing fit, and lift her handkerchief feebly to her lips.

But ever so slowly, miraculously, as the weeks passed, she began to improve. Her cough was softer, less frequent. She was able to bathe herself. She could get out of bed. There were no more handkerchiefs with frightening red polka dots. Sometimes, as she padded along the floor without having to lean on me, she'd nod to me, as if to say: We may prevail yet!

Doctor Giffen, who dropped in to see her each afternoon, seemed happy with her progress.

"She's looking a lot better," he said. "Well done, Andrew. You're a good nurse."

I was happy. I let down my guard. I allowed myself, for the first time in months, to feel secure.

On a morning near the beginning of March, I woke around six-thirty. It was still dark. I lay for a while making a plan. When the warm weather came in, I would coax her to come with me on the train to the coast. She could sit on the beach for a few days. I'd heard Doctor Giffen say the salt air would help mend her scarred lungs.

When I eventually got out of bed, I shivered into my clothes and slipped downstairs into the dark living-room. She was still asleep. The embers of the fire were glowing, so I added some kindling and a few pieces of coal. The room would be cheerful for her when she ate breakfast.

Then I went into the kitchen and boiled some oatmeal. I heated the milk the way she liked it. I put the plate on the tray and took it into the living-room. I set the tray down on the chair beside her bed and switched on the light. Her eyes were open but she didn't look at me. Her face, her whole body seemed somehow to have shrunk.

I think I knew the awful truth right away, but I tried not to face it.

"Mother, I've a great idea," I said. I had trouble speaking. "When the weather warms up, we'll go to the coast and sit at the beach. Maybe you can watch while I swim. I'll collect shells for you. It'll be great fun."

Her face was grey, and her lips were twisted a little; her eyes were flat as though coins had already been laid upon them. She was quite dead.

I began to weep, as much from anger as from grief. How could she have betrayed me this way? I went crazy. I began to search the living-room, throwing open cupboard doors and drawers, searching for evidence of her treachery. It didn't take me long to find it. The narrow drawer at the bottom of the armoire near the bed was her hiding place. Rags were stuffed into it, rags spotted with blood in its various shades and consistencies, mostly dark brown, some more recent and red. I looked at her now, and from where I was, the light caused her eyes to gleam and the twist on her lips seemed to be a smile.

And suddenly I was calm, and I couldn't help admiring her for her deception. It was exactly what I would have expected of her. What strength of will she must have had to keep her condition hidden from me, and from Doctor Giffen, and from everyone else who visited her.

What could I do but forgive her?

Chapter Six

So I WENT TO HER FUNERAL, in harsh Upland weather: sleety rain and a cold March wind—perfect funeral weather. The blunt hills around the graveyard were themselves like massive burial mounds. As for the graveyard, the orderly arrangement of the plots, the symmetry of the paths, seemed to mock the chaos her death had made of my life.

Provost Hawse read the rites as the northeaster whined its lament. Doctor Giffen stood beside me. Otherwise, the gathering consisted mainly of women in black coats and fluttering black headscarves.

When the coffin was lowered into the grave, the Provost turned to me. His beaky face never seemed more at home than here in the graveyard.

"Andrew Halfnight, you may proceed now," he said.

It was my duty to throw the first clod of earth into my mother's grave. I picked up a piece of mud and tried to drop it gently onto the elegant coffin in its muddy hole. But there was no way of dropping it softly—it thudded onto the lid. Then Doctor Giffen and the women around the grave threw a barrage of clods into the grave, some of them fiercely as though they were stoning the corpse, or perhaps stoning death itself.

Then everything was quiet except for the wind's whine, and the rattle of the rain on the parts of the coffin lid that were still exposed.

In the days after the funeral, I lived with Doctor Giffen. His surgery was in the Square, next to Glenn's Pharmacy. His living quarters were in the rooms directly above. The smell of ether had worked its way through the floorboards and was on my clothes, even in the food. It pervaded my dreams. But when Doctor Giffen took me to the big house for one last visit, it was the stale smell of her sickness that rushed out to meet us.

He said he'd stay outside and I went in alone. I found a leather suitcase and packed what I needed—my clothes and a few books. The living-room was cold and clammy, the bed stripped to the mattress by the women who had come to embalm my mother. From the mantelpiece above the dead fire, I lifted the photograph of her as a young woman. She was standing in the snow with the man I knew as my father beside her. They weren't looking at the camera so much as at whoever was taking the photo. My mother was quite beautiful, her lips twisted in that ironic way that might pass for a smile.

I would have put the photograph in my suitcase, but it was too big. So I put it back on the mantelpiece. I left the house quickly, for in it, her memory was only a cold presence.

That night, I was asleep in Doctor Giffen's spare room, when the sound of loud sobbing woke me up. I didn't breathe. I listened carefully, wondering who was weeping so uncontrollably. Nothing. I could hear nothing. Then I realized my own cheeks were cold and wet. I was the one who had been weeping.

Doctor Giffen was rarely at meals, and I was glad, for he was a hard man to talk to and I never knew what he was thinking. He had instructed his maid to cook for me whatever I wished. But on the second night, he did come to dinner. We didn't talk much during it. After the dishes had been removed at the end and he was sipping his coffee, he cleared his throat.

"Your mother, Andrew. I was very..."

He cleared his throat again.

"I don't know how to say it...." He sat there for a long time, not saying anything. Then he got up slowly and left.

I understood he had been trying to tell me he loved her. He didn't know how to do it, and I understood that, too. Afterwards, even though I always felt a little uncomfortable with him, I didn't mind him so much.

He came to the bus stop with me the morning I left. It was a Wednesday, before dawn. Icy rain made the day miserable as we stood in the Square waiting for the weekly bus to the City. He held his umbrella over us. Within its enclosure the smell of ether was especially strong. If I was thinking coherently at all, it was that I was sad to be leaving the only place and the only human beings I knew. Yet at the same time, I was glad to go. He must have read my mind.

"Living here won't be easy now," he said. I knew he meant now that she was gone.

The bus appeared like a grumbling monster out of the

murk and hissed to a halt. Doctor Giffen leaned inside and gave the driver instructions about where I was to get off. Then he shook my hand formally and helped me on with my suitcase.

I walked along the passageway. There were no other passengers and the bus smelt of stale cigarette smoke. I took a seat near the middle and wiped the condensation from the window with my sleeve. Doctor Giffen was standing on the street, looking up at me. Gears crashed and the bus lurched forward. I waved to him and he waved back. He remained standing as the bus groaned its way slowly along the street.

In a minute we were out of the town, and passing the graveyard. I cleared the window again and tried to make out the area of her grave. I could see nothing but the ghostly shapes of some of the larger gravestones. My heart was empty. I felt the way an animal must feel, wrenched away from its lair.

And so, once again, in spite of everything she taught me, I began to cry. I used the camouflage of the noisy bus and cried till Stroven was far behind. I exhausted myself with sobbing, and as I fell asleep, I felt I was hopelessly tumbling with the hopelessly tumbling earth.

Chapter Seven

DOCTOR GIFFEN HAD arranged for me to stay for a few days in Glasgow till the ship was ready to sail. The Hochmagandie Hotel was in the middle of a run-down four-storey tenement by the docks. It looked like the least decayed tooth in a mouthful of bad teeth. The reception desk was just inside the entrance. The clerk was an adult, but no taller than I was, his legs were so bowed. He wore a black leather cone over his nose, and a black waistcoat that read "Hochmagandie" in faded gilt at his heart.

"You can have the room over the river. Doctor Giffen stays there when he's in town," he said. He had a way about him I'd never seen before—a city toughness.

The room itself was clean though the bedcover had ancient stains on it. In one corner was a little stall with a shower in it, and a toilet that was cracked and rusted with age. A locked door connected to the next room. From the window I could see across a wide cobbled street dissected by rail-lines, to the oily, brown river. The docks were studded with giant bollards; cranes were loading cargo into rusty freighters. Even through the glass, I could hear their clanking and screeching, and the snarling of trucks doing their business. The sky was grey with low black clouds that seemed not much higher than the cranes. Working men in dungarees and cloth caps milled around the loading areas.

I was very hungry, but the Hochmagandie had no restaurant, only a bar. So, around three o'clock, I took some money from an envelope Doctor Giffen had given me, put on my coat and went out to find a place to eat. The air was a mix of coal smoke and tar and salt water—the sea was only a few miles downriver. I found a restaurant in the next block. It was the plainest of places, with brown panelled walls. Men in dungarees sat at small wooden tables covered with plastic cloths. Tobacco smoke mingled with the smell of fried fish and chips. I ate quickly and went back outside.

I walked north towards the main shopping area of the City. Everything was new to me: dingy warehouses with small windows thick with soot; railway loading yards, their rails shining among thickets of dead weeds; narrow back alleys where discarded newspapers and wrappers were whirled along by the cold wind. The main streets, most of which ran parallel to the river, were themselves rivers of noisy traffic and unyielding pedestrians. The stores didn't interest me much—one clothing store after another, shoe shops and pharmacies interrupted occasionally by the marble entrances of banks and churches. Only the cinemas attracted me; their exotic foreign names and colourful bill-boards were like exits from an overcrowded grey hell.

On that day and all the other days I lived at the Hoch-magandie, I'd go out for dinner and then take a walk. I'd buy some rolls at a bakery for my other meals and go back to the hotel around six. To get to the stairway, I had to pass the bar. The only customers I ever saw in it were women. They'd be sitting alone at the little round tables, or on the high stools at the bar, smoking, looking at themselves in the mirror behind the gantry with its pyramids of bottles. Sometimes, one or other of those women would catch my eye through the mirror before I could look away. Their lips were shockingly red in their pale faces; their mascara didn't hide the glitter in their eyes.

On my second night in my room, I ate my rolls and went to bed around nine o'clock. I'd been asleep for quite a while when a sound woke me. It gave me a fright, for I couldn't remember where I was. Voices were coming from behind the locked door that separated my room from next door. One of the voices was a woman's, the other was a masculine rumble. I couldn't make out what they were saying, so I got up and tiptoed over to the connecting door.

Light was shining through a wide crack in the lower panel. I quietly knelt down and put my eye to it.

"Get on with it," the man was saying.

I could see him, or at least the lower part of him. He was

sitting on a wooden chair right in front of the door. He was wearing dark trousers, and beneath them I could see black shoes, and black socks with a repeated pattern—a pair of intertwined yellow snakes wrapped round an anchor.

The owner of the other voice was standing at the bed, facing the man. She was far enough away from the crack in the door for me to get a good look at her. She seemed to be one of the bar-women. Her lips were glistening red; her eyes were black slits. She wore a tight black dress.

"I'm waiting," she said.

There was a rustling, and the man leaned forward and blocked the view for a moment. When he pulled back, I saw her counting some banknotes then stuffing them into the pocket of a coat that lay on the bed. She sat down on the bed facing him and began to take off her shoes, slowly, elaborately. She slowly pulled her dress up, unhooked her stockings and rolled them off. Her legs were thin and very white.

I watched this, exactly as the man on the chair must have been watching.

She stood up and unfastened the buttons of her dress. Those slits of eyes never left the man on the chair. Her tongue wet her lips. She let the dress fall to the floor. She took off her underclothes in the same deliberate way, all the time looking at him. My throat was becoming dry.

She stood there at last, a thin woman with thin legs. Her ribs were prominent, the way my mother's were in her sickness. This woman's breasts dangled loosely, and she had those silvery streaks across her belly.

"Now?" she said.

"Come over and let's get down to business," said the man.

He rose out of his chair and moved towards the right so that I couldn't see him any longer. She followed him.

The only things in my sight now were the spars of the

wooden chair and, further away, the bed and the clothing lying on the floor.

I couldn't see the man and the woman, but I could hear them. He'd give instructions ("Move this way," "Good," "Lift your leg a little," "Put your hand here"). She spoke infrequently ("Like this?" "Ouch!" "How much longer?").

This went on for the longest time, perhaps a half-hour. And during it I was crouched by the door, breathing quietly, listening.

Then I heard him give one last order.

"Now," he said. "Stand under the light." And a moment later. "Good, good, good." And again. "Good, good, good."

Now he walked back into my view again, and this time was far enough away from the crack that I was able to have a good look at him. He wasn't undressed, as I'd expected. He hadn't even taken his jacket off. He was a big, soft-looking man with fair hair and pale blue eyes. He was carrying an open wooden box about the size of a briefcase. He set it down on the bed, folded the lid over and snapped it shut. He sat on the bed and looked over in the direction he'd come from.

"Yes, very good," he said. "You'd better clean yourself up now."

"Are you finished?" I heard her ask.

"Yes," he said. "You've done very well."

After a minute, I heard the sound of the shower where their washroom backed onto mine. Soon the water was turned off, and the woman appeared again, drying herself with one of the thin hotel towels. Her back was to me, dripping with water. She quickly put on her clothes.

"My hair's a mess," she said. "I need to put on some make-up." She went back to the washroom again, and was there for a few minutes.

Then they both left the room. I heard them open their

door, the room lights were switched off, and their footsteps creaked along the spongy corridor.

I went back to bed.

I was puzzled by the strange ritual I'd seen. Like all the boys of Stroven, I'd spied on lovers who'd gone up into the moors for privacy. And I'd heard all the schoolboy talk on the mysteries of sex. So I tried to imagine what must have gone on next door, out of my sight. I thought about it and thought about it till, exhausted, I fell asleep.

Chapter Eight

I'D BEEN IN THE Hochmagandie five days. On the fifth evening, I returned to the hotel after my walk. I was passing the front desk when the clerk called to me.

"A message," he said, handing me an envelope. I noticed he'd changed his nose-cone—tonight it was a brown leather one. "Been enjoying the sights?" He was leering at me.

I never knew what to say to him, so I just went on upstairs. In my room, I tore the envelope open and read the note inside.

Cochrane and Cochrane Shipping Line

Mr Andrew Halfnight:

SS *Cumnock* will be ready to clear customs at 12 pm tomorrow. Please board by 10 am.

I was thrilled. I packed my suitcase and read for a while, then went to bed and fell asleep in spite of my excitement.

I don't know what time it was, perhaps around midnight, that I heard voices in the next room and saw light coming through the crack in the connecting door. The nights had been uneventful since that second night.

I was suddenly wide awake. I got up and quietly took up my viewing position.

The man with the snakes on his socks was again sitting in the chair. But the woman in front of him wasn't the same woman. This time, in fact, she wasn't a woman at all. She was a girl who seemed to me not much older than myself, in spite of the camouflage of lipstick and thick mascara. She might easily have been one of the girls in my class at Stroven made up for the annual school play.

But she was much more self-possessed than any of those schoolgirls in Stroven. She began taking off her clothes, as the man in the chair instructed. She looked unblinkingly at him as she slowly unveiled a slight, hairless body with a chest as flat as mine.

The ritual began as before. The man took her out of my sight and for a while I could see nothing, only hear his voice telling her what to do. But this time, after just a minute, she came back and stood by the bed; then he appeared, and put his wooden box on the bed too.

He opened it up and took out of it something shaped like a disc. He rummaged in the case and brought out a handful of little tubes. Then he took out a brush and I understood what he was doing.

He began to paint her. Not on a canvas, but putting the paint on the girl herself. She was his model and his canvas. He began by rapidly covering all of her body in a white undercoat. Those suggestive commands I'd heard from the other night now lost their mystery.

"Turn your hip this way a little," he'd say to her; or, "Open your legs a bit more."

Soon she was entirely covered in white paint. She looked very frightening to me, an alien creature with green eyes, brown hair and pink mouth.

But he had barely begun. Now he began painting on top of the white base. He was standing in front of her, blocking my view, so I could only catch a glimpse of a blur of colours. He seemed to paint with great speed and confidence. He'd cock his head and ponder from time to time, but mainly he went at it without pausing.

After about a half-hour, he stopped.

"Now," he said. "Let's have a look at you."

He moved to one side, and I had a clear view of her.

I almost fell backwards. The girl had been transformed into a huge reptile. Her body was a mass of greens and blues and frills and warts. Her eyes were slits inside great fringed circular lids. She was the most repulsive thing I had ever seen.

"Perfect!" I heard him say. There was a long pause. Then, "Perfect," he said again.

When I'd got over my first sensation of revulsion, I could see how someone might indeed find her beautiful, she was so colourful and gleaming, as though she'd just slid out of a pond. As though the human features had been the artificial ones, and the man had uncovered the truth beneath.

"Anything else you want me to do?" she asked. A speaking reptile.

"No. You can clean yourself now," he said.

She disappeared in the direction of the shower and he bent over his box. The pipes bumped for a while, and when she came back into my sight again, she was drying herself with a towel. The paint was all gone, and so were the mascara and lipstick. Her hair was slicked back and she looked even younger than before. She put on her clothes, money was exchanged, and soon the room was empty and dark.

I went back to bed and soon fell asleep. I dreamt I was in Stroven and that I was bathing a giant lizard. All its colours were coming off on the washcloth, and as they came off, I saw that it was my mother's body underneath. The sight of it aroused me. That woke me up, and I couldn't stop myself from crying. I was shocked at how a dream had contaminated her memory. Weary and empty, I fell asleep again and slept till my dreams were shattered by the horns of tugboats announcing the beginning of the day's work along the river. And the end of my stay at the Hochmagandie Hotel.

Part Two

Voyage

A long sea passage is rather like a novel of the picaresque type. It begins with a casting off; it ends with a sailing into harbour. Nothing between these two points is certain.

J. Ballantyne

Chapter Nine

THE SS CUMNOCK LAY on the south bank of the river with its bows headed towards the sea. I'd walked past a number of dingy cargo ships on my way along the waterfront, and the *Cumnock* was as dingy as any of the others. It was shaped like a book-end, with a long, bare deck, then the wheelhouse and living quarters jutting up at the back. The wind grabbed the dirty wraiths from its smokestack and carried them ashore to melt into the city smog. The ship's hull, which from fifty yards away had at least seemed solid and seaworthy, was in fact very rusty. The plates around the bows were pocked and dented as though the ship had been tossed around by a giant dog.

The quiet rumble of the engines made the gangway tremble as I climbed aboard. An elderly sailor who didn't seem at all interested in me led me down a companionway to my cabin. It was narrow and musty, with a low bunk and a caged bulb in the ceiling. The small porthole looked out onto warehouses and sooty tenements. The enamel paint on the walls and ceiling was chipped and peeling.

As he left, the sailor mumbled that I was to keep out of the way during departure; so I stayed in the cabin and watched what was going on from my porthole. For a long time, there wasn't much to see. But around noon, the sound of the engine deepened. The gangway was hauled aboard and stevedores on the dock cast off the lines. Trembling and rumbling, the ship slowly ripped away from her berth.

Some of the stevedores on the dock stood watching, and I waved to them; but if they saw a boy waving through a porthole from the stern quarters, they didn't wave back. After a moment, they turned and headed towards one of the warehouses.

No one else, so far as I could tell, paid any attention as the *Cumnock* slowly nosed its way down the river. The dock itself soon slipped out of sight, then the warehouses along the front, the tall cranes, the shipyards, the clutter of the City. It was hard to see much beyond that, for in spite of the wind, the day had become quite foggy; so much so that the *Cumnock* began sounding its horn, making the hull shudder. Sometimes a passing tugboat or another ship on the river wailed an answer.

By three o'clock, the river was so wide that only the brightest shore lights shining feebly through the fog testified that we were still within its banks. The greyness tired me, so I lay on my bunk and must have napped a little. Around six o'clock, I woke and could tell by the ship's motion that something was different. All I could see through the porthole was pitch darkness. But I guessed from the way the hull was heaving and straining that the *Cumnock* had left the sheltered passage of the river. We were at sea.

I was starving, and wondering if I'd ever eat again, when there was a rap at my cabin door and a gruff shout:

"Dinner's ready!"

My first visit to the mess hall was an experience I won't forget. Not only because I could feel the rolling motion of the ship, by now, in the pit of my belly; nor because I sat at a table with the other passenger: an elderly woman who seemed preoccupied and who sometimes mumbled to herself in a language I didn't know, and who was dressed in an ankle-length green dress with a pattern of wilted yellow flowers; nor because I saw the crew members assembled at a long table at the far end of the mess: grizzled, elderly men who seemed very unfriendly, except for the bearded man who served the meal; nor because of the meal itself: a stewed beef that gave off a sweet smell unlike any stew made in Stroven.

These things were memorable enough in their way. But there was something else.

We'd all begun eating (in my case, pretending to eat; I picked out a few potatoes, but my hunger wasn't as strong as my suspicion of that stew) when the sliding door of the mess-room opened. At first I couldn't see whoever had opened it, for he stopped to talk to someone in the passageway and only his right foot on the raised entranceway was visible. The cuff of the trousers rose a few inches above a black shoe, showing a dark sock with a pattern of intertwined yellow snakes round an anchor. The man finished his conversation and came into the mess hall. He was a heavy, fair-haired man. He wore a uniform and had a hat tucked under his arm.

He slid the door shut behind him and without looking around went to a little table in the corner. The bearded sailor who'd served our meals got up from the long table and went over to him.

"Good evening, Captain Stillar. Now, how would you like something to whet your thirst?"

In this way I discovered that the man who was the mysterious painter of women in the Hochmagandie Hotel was also the Captain of the *Cumnock*.

The ship was steaming towards the tropics, but those first days of the voyage were anything but tropical. The skies were leaden, the winds seemed to have northern ice in them, the seas were swollen and flecked with grey crests. There was rain, rain, rain. And I was sick, sick, sick. I kept to my cabin for two days, eating nothing at all. My stomach had begun to heave during that first night at sea, and even though I emptied it totally of the few gobbets of potatoes I'd eaten, I didn't feel at all well unless I lay flat on my back.

Lying there, a little feverish, I thought what a strange man the Captain of the ship must be. And I thought about how strange it was to be on such a voyage: how time passed, hour followed hour, day followed day, but the ship might easily have been anchored just out of sight of the land, its movement only an illusion caused by the sea's motion. All of us on the *Cumnock* were like the inhabitants of a little town, except that our roots were in water. But I had learnt enough to wonder whether even towns like Stroven, firmly rooted in earth, were any more stable than this ship afloat on an endless ocean.

Chapter Ten

By the morning of the third day at sea, I was feeling a little better, but my stomach was still too queasy for me to get up. At nine o'clock, there was a knock at my door. The sailor who'd served the meals in the mess hall looked in. His eyebrows were very bushy, and his long grey hair was wild.

"Good morning," he said. "I'm Harry Greene, at your service. I've given you a day's rest. Now let's have a look at you." He was wearing a white apron and carrying a small tray covered with a cloth. He put the tray down and felt my forehead.

"God's oars!" he said, lowering his eyebrows fiercely. His strange oath made me afraid of him. "Now then," he said. "We'll have to do something about that fever."

As he was giving me some pills from the tray, I couldn't help noticing on his right forearm a multicoloured tattoo of an anchor with the words *Anchora Spei* under it. He saw me looking and told me he'd had it done just before we left port, and that the words were Latin and meant "The Anchor of Hope." He said he'd had it copied from an old book he'd brought with him. The more he talked, the less fierce he seemed. He stayed for an hour.

That was the first of many hours I spent with Harry Greene, steward and medic of the SS *Cumnock*. Even after I was well, he'd drop by once or twice a day to talk. He seemed to have all the time in the world. He'd tell me about his other voyages or about books he was reading.

I enjoyed listening to him, though at first I was cautious. I'd learnt from my mother that words weren't trustworthy. She treated them as though they were the remnants of something that might once have made sense but now were generally misleading and to be avoided.

Harry Greene, on the other hand, loved talking. His favourite time for visiting me was in the evenings after his work in the galley was done. He'd bring along his big cup of grog and sip while he talked.

I can't be sure now on which days we talked about particular things. All the days on that long voyage have blended together in my mind. But I do remember many of the things he said, they made such an impression on me.

Harry Greene grew up in Ireland; traces of the accent were in his voice still, though he'd been at sea for thirty-five years. He'd begun his career as a cabin boy at a time when many of the ships still relied on sail, either totally or as an auxiliary to their engines.

"Back then, 'twas a different life altogether," he said. "Sailors had to depend on each other. Believe me, my boy, there's no better way of getting to know yourself, or how much you can trust another man, than to be stuck out on a yardarm with him during a gale."

He said this one night, the rummy smell from his cup all through my cabin, as he was telling me about the very first voyage he made. It was an expedition to Patagonia, at the tip of South America, in search of the last of the dinosaurs.

"Our ship was the *Mingulay*, as well found a little ship as ever I sailed on. We landed on the Patagonian coast and unloaded the equipment for the expedition. But even on shore, we didn't stop being sailors. We used to sit around the campfire at night and tell stories, just the way we did in the fo'c'sle.

"One story I'll never forget was told by the Engineer. 'Twas a rainy night and the fire was blazing and bats were flitting in and out of the flames.

"This Engineer was a man from one of the northern islands. He had eyes that were milky blue.

"He said when he was a boy, a doctor and his wife and their four children came to live on the island. This doctor eventually murdered his wife, no one knew why. 'Twas most strange how he got rid of her body. He cut it up in pieces and buried parts of her in the bellies of the four children. He even buried her eyes and ears in the bellies of the family pets."

Harry Greene looked at me from under the battlements of his eyebrows.

"God's oars!" he said. "'Twas a scary story for a young lad like me to hear in that wild place. The other sailors just laughed. They said 'twas just a joke. But right then, the Engineer stood up in the firelight and pulled his shirt open. And what do you know? We could all see a big ragged scar across his belly. 'Twas himself was one of the children he'd been talking about."

The bushy eyebrows arched again.

"Yes, I heard that story on our first night ashore. I'll never forget the rain, and the bats skimming in and out of the firelight. And the scar on that man's belly."

He sighed and took a sip from his mug.

"Patagonia was the kind of godforsaken place you might have expected to find dinosaurs in. But we never found a trace of them. Later on, somebody wrote a history of that expedition. 'Twas all about the fact that we didn't find dinosaurs but there was no mention of the Engineer's story in the entire book. If you ask me, that's the problem with a lot of history books—they miss the things that really matter in your life."

He smiled at me in his fierce way.

"Now Andy, I suppose you think this is all nostalgia, eh? Sure now, I myself can't bear listening to old men looking back on the good old days and inventing feelings they never had at the time."

I didn't know what to say.

"Well, I'm not making it up," he said. "I really did love that first voyage. Every day of it was exciting."

I believed him and I envied him.

Chapter Eleven

HARRY GREENE OFTEN spoke about books. One day he took me down to his cabin just below the main deck near the crew's lounge.

He had to lean against the door to get it open, for the floor of his cabin was littered with books. They looked as though they'd once been in neat piles, but the ship's motion had toppled them; they stirred and shifted as we made our way through them, stepping in the shallower parts. The walls of his cabin had been fitted with bookshelves with little ridges in front; books were jammed into them, too. Books lay on the bunk and books protruded from under it. The washroom was open and I could see books on the floor and on the sink.

On the washroom door, there was a picture frame, but it didn't have a picture in it—just some words. I thought maybe it was an old saying:

The mind is its own place, and in itself
Can make a Heaven of Hell, a Hell of Heaven

Harry saw me looking at it.

"'Twas said by the devil himself in an old poem." His eyebrows were fierce. "But devil or no devil—I think it makes a lot of sense."

I didn't know what the words meant, or what he meant, and I couldn't think of anything to say. So I just looked around, marvelling at the number of books he had.

"'Tis my hobby," he said. "You remember I was telling you about that Patagonian expedition? Well, the ship's carpenter on that voyage was a great reader. 'Twas he who put the idea into my head. He said there's so much time on voyages when nothing happens, they're ideal for a man with a thirst for books."

So Harry Greene took up reading and had been voyaging and reading, and reading and voyaging, ever since.

"Sure there's no end to it," he said. "I soon found that out. There's an ocean of books out there. You can go from port to port without ever dropping anchor in the same berth."

His favourite pastime on shore leaves was prowling the bookstores. He'd accumulate boxloads upon boxloads of books, often on a particular subject for study on his next voyage.

"Now take this trip," he said. "I thought I'd have a try at some old books from the sixteenth and seventeenth centuries." He pointed to the tattoo on his arm. "I got this from a picture at the front of one of them—*The Faerie Queene*, 'tis called. I haven't read much of it, 'tis such a long book, and I don't think I'll be able to stomach much more now that I've got the hang of it. 'Tis mainly about damsels in distress and knights in armour. The damsels generally turn out to be smarter than the knights who're supposed to save them."

He picked up a thick book lying on the floor near his bunk.

"Have a look at this," he said, "*The Anatomy of Melancholy*. The man who wrote this spent his whole life collecting books. He was definitely a bit on the strange side. I'll tell you why: he said he knew exactly the day he was going to die, and he told everybody about it for more than twenty years. He said 'twould be on the twenty-fifth of January, sixteen-forty.

"Well, sixteen-forty arrived, and the twenty-fifth of January came. And what do you know? Not only did he not feel sick, he felt even healthier than usual. He waited all day, just in case. 'Twas no good. So, just before midnight, he went to his room and tied a rope with a noose in it round the rafter. He stood on a chair with a pile of books on it. He put the noose round his neck and kicked the books out from under himself. It didn't take him long to choke."

Harry was smiling ferociously.

"God's boat!" he said. "Now, anybody could forecast their death by that method, couldn't they, Andy?"

I didn't know what to say. I was astonished that authors could be so strange. I'd always assumed they must be the wisest of human beings.

Harry put the book he'd been holding into my hands: an old volume with leather covers. The pages were full of tiny print, and the spelling was strange. A lot of the words seemed to be written in a foreign language.

"What's melancholy?" I asked.

"Melancholy?" he said. "'Tis a kind of sadness about life. According to this book, women are the main cause of it for men. When you're older, you'll understand. The author has quotations from all over the place to back his theory up."

This got Harry going again on the topic of reading.

"Do you know, Andy, at the time that book was written, there were still people alive who'd read every single book that was in print?" he said. "Yes—everything, on every subject. They were experts in biology, mathematics, botany, astronomy, medicine, astrology, geography—anything you could name. They spent almost every waking minute of their lives reading. Some of them believed that if they studied everything, they'd find the secret of life, whatever that might be."

He reached over for a book on the shelf over his bunk. It was a thick, worn volume. "Now, take a look at this," he said. "*Mundus Mathematicus* by Johannes Morologus. He's what they call a numerologist. Among other things he believed there's a system of numbers and mathematical symbols at the back of everything that exists. According to him, if you understand numbers and the combinations of numbers, you can understand everything about life. You can even find true love by using the proper calculations." Harry shook his head fiercely. "That's the kind of thing wise men studied back then. I got this book two voyages back, and I've been through it twice, trying to figure it out. It makes me wish I'd paid more attention to mathematics when I was a boy at school."

I was only half listening, for I was still holding *The Anatomy of Melancholy*, leafing through it, trying to find some parts of it I could make sense of.

"This looks so hard," I said.

Harry glanced towards the door as though to make sure no one else was listening.

"Well now," he said, in a soft voice, "I wouldn't admit this to everybody. But I've only read a page or two of it myself. That goes for a lot of these old books. Some of the very finest books are too hard to read, but I still like to have them and to lay hands on them now and then. For good luck. Do you know what a talisman is? A book can be like that, if you ask me. You don't have to read it. 'Tis a talisman."

He went on to tell me he didn't think all books were equally valuable.

"Now, these are useful books," he said, looking around his cabin. "So far as I'm concerned, no book's worth reading that doesn't offer information of practical use to the reader. What kind of books do you like, Andy?"

I said I liked novels best. He shook his head at that and his eyebrows lowered.

"Sure now, too many people try and live their lives as though they were characters in a novel. They can't believe it when the plot goes against them. When you're older, you'll see what I mean, Andy. You'll hardly meet a woman who doesn't believe she's a character in the Beauty and the Beast story. Of course, 'tisn't all that bad for the man. No matter what he does, she'll never be convinced that her Beast is nothing but a Beast."

He held up the Morologus again.

"Then again, you can't always trust books that aren't novels. Now take Morologus. I'm a bit suspicious of him. I think maybe he wanted the world to be a magic place. He believed in a thing called the Eternal Cycle. It means people don't just have one life—they live over and over and over again. Now who wouldn't want to believe in that, eh?"

I agreed with him.

"Although, I must admit he says it's not all roses," Harry said. "There's something called the Second Self—that's your double. Somewhere in the Eternal Cycle, every human being has a double. It's possible to run into your double in one of your many lives."

"What happens then?" I said.

"Well, I'm not sure of the details," Harry said. "But according to Morologus, that's the worst thing that could happen to you. The two of you cancel each other out, and that's the end of the Eternal Cycle for both of you." He laughed. "So just you watch out, Andy. Make sure you always steer clear of your Second Self."

One afternoon after lunch, I was down in his cabin waiting for him to finish in the galley. I was rummaging through his books looking for something that might interest me. In the middle of a heap under the porthole I saw an old one with a stained leather cover. On the spine, all I could make out were the words "Blast" and "Monstrous." That attracted my attention. I opened the book, and saw the complete title—a very long title:

First Blast Of The Trumpet
Against The Monstrous Regiment Of Women

Harry Greene came in just as I was looking at it and I quickly dropped the book back on the heap. I should have asked him what it was about, but I didn't. I thought it was the most frightening title of a book I'd ever seen.

I was becoming quite accustomed to the motion of the *Cumnock*. I made myself intimate with the ship's secret places: with the engine room, where the noise was so thick I felt I could touch it; with the stinking cathedral of the main cargo hold; with the crew's lounge, where I often watched the sailors play dominoes. They looked like very old men to me.

"Why are they all so old?" I asked Harry one night after dinner, when we were standing at the rail looking out on the dark water. Funny, I didn't think of him as an old man even though—what with his beard and long grey hair—he looked just as old as the others. In fact, he must only have been in his mid-forties. But for a boy my age, that was ancient.

Sometimes, he'd sniff the breeze, which I took to be a sailor's habit. He did so now, then he answered.

"They weren't always like that. God's oars! No, not at all." He laughed sternly. "Sailors needed to be young and strong. Imagine having an old man with stiff muscles next to you when you were clinging to a spar in a storm off Cape Horn." He shook his head. "But now there's no rigging to climb, and mechanical winches do all the heavy work." The winches were located near each of the hatchways; they looked like gallows in the dusk. "They're just like old workers anywhere. They're serving out their time, waiting to be pensioned off. Most of my shipmates can hardly wait for the day. They hate the life at sea."

That surprised me.

"Why do they hate it?" I said.

"Oh well now," he said. "I think 'tis because every port they sail into reminds them of being young. When they used to do all the crazy things young sailors do. Now their bodies won't let them any more." He laughed. "Of course, some of them have been old men all their lives, and all that's happened is that their bodies have caught up to them."

He said this as though he despised such men. I kept quiet. I hoped he didn't think of me as old before my time.

Chapter Twelve

THE CUMNOCK SAILED further and further south. The skies were still overcast but the air was uncomfortably warm and moist in a way I'd never felt before. At one point, two hundred miles off the coast of Africa, a sweet, rotten smell drifted out to us on the wind. "Jungle," I heard one of the crew say. In the morning, a school of dolphins appeared and swam alongside for an hour.

The smell of land seemed to entice the other passenger, the old woman, out onto the deck. One evening, around dusk, I was standing at the rail waiting for Harry when she came out and stood just a yard away from me at the rail, looking in the direction of those distant jungles. I hadn't seen her since that first night, for she had all her meals served in her cabin.

She wasn't wearing the long dress any more. Now she had a grey trilby hat on her head, and she wore a man's blue pinstriped suit with old sweat stains under the arm-pits. What a gaunt woman she was, with a turkey neck that was brown and wrinkled, and a hooked nose. She stood silently at the rail for perhaps five minutes. Without really knowing why, I inched my elbow along the rail towards her. Perhaps because I was lonely.

She stared straight ahead, but when my elbow was close to hers, she made a low growling noise.

I quickly backed away and the growling stopped. She stood a while longer, then, without looking at me, she went back to her cabin.

When Harry came out of the galley to throw a bucket of slops in the water I asked him about the woman.

"She must be very old," I said. "Her face is so wrinkled."

"'Tis true," he said. "Her life story's written there for anyone to read." His own face was wrinkled, especially round the eyes. I'd often tried to disentangle the lines, but they were too intricate for me, and the beard covered the rest of his face.

He saw the way I was looking at him.

"Even the face of the ocean isn't easy to read," he said. "An experienced sailor can figure out what it means a lot of the time. And sometimes he'll get it completely wrong."

He threw the bucket of slops overboard, and immediately sharks began squabbling over them. In the dusk, we could see a spreading pink stain—they were biting each other as well as the scraps.

"God's oars!" Harry said. "Look at them. I surely wouldn't like to fall overboard at this time of the night."

He put down the bucket and began to talk about the old woman.

"She doesn't speak much English, but I take my time, and I find things out when I take her meals down to her. She's a widow and she's going back home to San Marco Island. She and her husband left there forty years ago and went to live in America. The island used to be a beautiful place, cut off from all the rest of the world. The reefs were full of fish, and the people were the kindest you could meet." He shook his head. "Forty years ago! She has no idea how much San Marco's changed since then. During the War, 'twas used as an air base, and the military stayed till not long ago. The reef's been poisoned with bunker oil, so there's no more fishing. The town's as bad as any slum I've ever seen, what with violence and drugs. When we call in there, our crew's afraid to go ashore. 'Tis a terrible shame."

Some sharks were still trailing the *Cumnock*, their blunt snouts raised towards us looking for more slops.

"I don't suppose," Harry Greene said, "when the widow was a young girl she appreciated how good a place San Marco was. Maybe if you're brought up in Paradise, you find it kind of dull. Eh, Andy? Paradise is always somewhere else. She thought it was in America."

The sharks dissolved into the darkening ocean.

"During all those years she was away," Harry said, "she believed San Marco was the way she remembered it. She didn't see it going down the drain."

"Why is she going back?" I asked.

"Ah, well. Her husband's dead. Her two sons are married and don't even invite her for a visit. And now she's old enough to appreciate what she didn't when she was young—now that it doesn't exist any more."

"Why is she wearing the funny clothes?"

"They're her husband's," Harry said. "It used to be the custom on San Marco when a man died for his widow to wear his clothes for a while. The islanders stopped doing that kind of thing a long time ago."

After telling me all this, Harry put a hand on my shoulder and his eyebrows lowered as they did when he was most serious.

"You know what, Andy? I'm going to make you a promise right now. If there is a Paradise on this earth, and if I ever find it, I'll let you know. It's a bit late for me. But maybe you can go there and live happily ever after. Right?"

The night after that, a very curious thing happened. Harry and I had gone for a stroll forward. Again, it was around dusk. We stopped at the rail amidships to talk. He liked it there, because it was well away from the crew, and we might have been alone on a little island in the middle of the ocean.

On this particular evening, we saw a disturbance in the sea about half a mile to port. As it came nearer, clearly visible in the dark water, we could make out a huge yellow shape. It was coming, at speed, directly at the port side of the *Cumnock*. We thought it might veer away when it became aware of us, but it didn't. This yellow creature, which was as big as the ship, and looked as ponderous, continued straight at us. Both Harry and I grabbed the rail, ready for the impact. But just as it was about to hit, the creature suddenly split into two distinctive forms, one green, one orange, and went round the ship, fore and aft. The *Cumnock* trembled gently from end to end, like a cat being stroked.

"Come on," Harry said.

We ran across the deck to the starboard rail. There we saw the green and the orange masses recombine into that great yellow shape and continue on its way towards the western horizon and the blood-red sun.

"God's rope!" said Harry. "I thought for a minute it was going to sink us, whatever it was. Isn't it strange how something that looks like a monster is really quite harmless." He looked at me sternly. "You just remember that, Andy. 'Tis often the most innocent-looking creatures that are the real monsters."

When we got back to the stern, some of the crew members who had come out on deck to see what had disturbed the ship were still staring in the direction the shape had disappeared in. They seemed scared, and relieved that it was gone.

On another one of those inseparable days, we were sitting in Harry Greene's cabin. The weather was rough and the books were stirring on the floor. His chair was like a reef in a sea of books. I sat on his bunk. We were talking about this and that, when all at once his bushy eyebrows lowered.

"Now, Mister Andrew Halfnight. Let's get down to business. Who exactly are you? Where do you come from? And why are you on this ship?"

This was the first time he'd ever asked me these questions. He was a man who preferred to talk about himself and his interests, and I understood that and accepted it. I was flattered that he should ask, so I answered all his questions as well as I could. In fact, I told him just about everything about myself.

That was the first time I ever put my life story into words. I realized then what a strange procedure that was—how different from the actual experiences themselves. Some of the experiences hadn't been at all pleasant, but the telling of them was.

At the end of it all, Harry shook his head.

"God's oars!" he said. "So you're from Stroven. What a coincidence." Then he said: "I've known sailors who came from Stroven. And Muirton, too, and Carrick, and some of those other hill towns. They were good shipmates."

Then he spoke very softly, as though it was a great secret.

"And let me tell you something else. I've visited Stroven myself."

Before I had a chance to ask him when or why he'd been there, he began to speak in a very formal voice, his eyebrows bristling.

"Andrew Halfnight," he said. "You're a good lad. Thank you for telling me about yourself."

Then, as though we'd reached the conclusion of some ritual together, he reached out across the drifting books and shook my hand.

"May life be good to you."

Chapter Thirteen

IT WAS HARD TO distinguish day from day, and the ocean had no milestones. But if I don't remember the exact order of the things that happened on the voyage, I do remember the things themselves. On one of those indistinguishable evenings in Harry Greene's cabin, he asked me more about my stay in Glasgow before embarking.

"You said you'd spent some nights in the Hochmagandie," he said. "Why did you go there?"

"Doctor Giffen arranged it," I said. "The clerk put me in the room he stays in when he's in town."

He asked me to describe Doctor Giffen, and I did.

"Sure now, I know the man," he said. "A tidy little squirrel of a man."

I smiled at his description.

"I've spent many a night at the Hochmagandie myself when we're in port. I have... friends there." He glanced at me and I couldn't help thinking he meant those women in the bar. "Captain Stillar's a regular visitor, too," he said. "I suppose you know that."

I didn't say anything, especially not about seeing the Captain through a crack in a door.

"Yes," he said. "It has to do with his painting. Sure now, didn't you know he was a painter? Come and I'll show you."

I followed him out of his cabin and we went for a long walk below decks, along a maze of passageways and narrow stairwells, moving ever forward, till we arrived outside a storage compartment low in the bows of the *Cumnock*. Harry Greene slid the door open and flicked on overhead lights that were very bright.

The compartment was quite large but had no portholes. In the middle was a metal table riveted to the steel floor, and on it were tins full of tubes of paint and dozens of brushes. The metal floor was stained with paint. An easel with a cloth flung over it was also fixed to the floor near the table. Along the walls, behind a rope lattice, dozens of canvases of various sizes were stacked facing the hull.

Harry Greene seemed very familiar with the room. He pulled one of the larger canvases out and turned it over.

"Here, have a look at this," he said.

It was a painting of a woman whose body was made to look like a lizard.

He pulled out other canvases and let me see them.

"Look," he said. "Always the same subject."

He was right. The women were of every shape and size,

and on their bodies the Captain had painted that lizard image, like a transparent costume.

Harry Greene talked while I looked at one painting after another. I must admit I couldn't help trying to make out the bodies under the paint.

"It all began with his wife," Harry said. "She was a woman from Aruvula. 'Tis an island in the Pacific near the Oluban Archipelago. He used to call in for a cargo of copra and that's how he met her. He only knew her for a few weeks, then he married her and brought her back home with him."

While he was talking, I was figuring out the Captain's method. First, he'd paint the naked body of a woman onto the canvas in a very lifelike way; then he'd paint the lizard on top of her the way he did with real women in the hotel.

"I saw his wife only one time," said Harry. "She was wearing a long dress with long sleeves, and her face was covered with a veil. Under it I could just make out the tattoo. Sure now if you didn't know better you'd have thought 'twas some kind of skin disease. All of the women of Aruvula are tattooed with the lizard."

"Why?" I asked him.

"Well now, I don't know for sure," he said. "But I think 'tis because they believe there's something immortal about the lizard. You can cut off its tail and on it grows again."

He went back to the topic of the Captain's wife.

"Now, a tattooed woman was fine in Aruvula," he said. "But in Scotland, 'twas unthinkable. 'Twas worse than a deformity. 'Twas perverse. So she had to keep herself covered all the time. Not that she had to do it for too long. During her very first winter she caught pneumonia and died."

I was looking at some of the smaller canvases. They were no bigger than a book-cover, but were very exact.

"At the end of each voyage," Harry was saying, "he goes to the Hochmagandie and hires women as models. When he's back at sea, he does the canvases."

He lifted the corner of the cloth draped over the easel and glanced under.

"I'll give you one guess," he said. He held the cloth up so that I could see for myself.

The painting was only partly done. The Captain hadn't even begun to add the lizard. A thin, naked female stared out at me with unflinching eyes. It was the girl I'd seen that final night at the Hochmagandie.

Back up on deck, we stood for a while. The air was barely less stifling than below decks.

I was thinking about the Captain, and how he must have loved the woman a lot to be so obsessed with her memory.

"He must really miss her," I said to Harry Greene.

He shrugged.

"Sure now," he said, "in these matters of love you can never be certain. What if I told you he went back to Aruvula just a year after her death, and tried to find another girl to marry?"

He saw how shocked I was.

"'Tis the truth," he said. "He did just that. The chief and the elders told him to go away from the island and never come back. So that's why I say you can never be sure about love matters. I think maybe he loved that lizard tattoo as much as he loved her. In some of the paintings you can't tell if 'tis a woman who looks like a lizard, or a lizard that looks like a woman."

The whole time we'd been in the studio earlier, I'd been afraid the Captain might walk in on us.

"Does he know you look at his paintings?" I asked Harry.

"Of course," he said. "Indeed, he always asks for my opinion of them."

That just reinforced for me what a strange man the Captain of the *Cumnock* must be. Harry knew what I was thinking.

"Oh now, Andy," he smiled at me. "If you can't find a little bit of madness in a man, you can't trust him."

I didn't know what to make of that.

"Is he a good captain?" I asked.

"God's oars!" he said. "He's the safest captain I ever sailed with, for he avoids bad weather like the plague. He can't paint when the sea's too rough."

Chapter Fourteen

LIKE MOST YOUNG people, it was hard for me to appreciate that adults hadn't always been adults. I wish I'd asked Harry more about his own boyhood: at the age I was in elementary school, he would have been serving his time as a cabin boy on a sailing ship to Patagonia. For education, he'd lived among strange people and visited the remote corners of the world. He'd battled the great storms off Cape Horn.

I know he'd have been only too happy to tell me about his life then, but I didn't ask. I did ask him another thing, though—a very personal question—not long after he'd shown me the Captain's paintings. We were on deck one muggy night, leaning on the rail.

"Are you married, Harry?" I'd been thinking about that, and about what kind of woman his wife might be. I wanted to know if he had children. My curiosity was tainted with a certain amount of jealousy.

He didn't answer right away, and from the fierce way he looked at me from under his eyebrows, I was afraid I'd offended him—maybe crossed some border of intimacy. But he was only thinking, and soon he began to talk quite freely.

"No children. But, indeed, I was married once. 'Twas a long time ago. I'd just come back from a voyage to the Macarenes...."

...he turned twenty-five the day after they docked. He took his usual room in the Sailor's Mission, down by the docks. But then something unusual happened: he became very ill. He couldn't keep down food, and could barely move his arms and legs. The doctor hoped it was only a severe case of dengue fever—"Break Bone Fever," as the sailors called it. Those giant mosquitoes on the Macarenes had surely infected him.

Whatever it was, Harry could tell from the way the doctor looked at him that he was afraid that what he had might be deadly.

A woman who was a part-time nurse at the Mission, and who had a spare room in her house, said she'd take Harry in and look after him. He would either recover or die there.

Her name was Heather.

The house was big and old, with dark wood panels on the walls. It was a gloomy place except for a red-and-yellow parrot called Daisy. Heather's father was a sea captain and he'd brought the bird for her from a voyage to Rio. Its cage was in the kitchen and she'd taught it to say "Hello!" and "Goodbye!"

Heather herself was a small woman, full of energy, with

frizzy ginger hair she tried to contain in a bun. She would sit patiently by Harry's bedside for hours each day, devoting herself to his every need. No one had ever paid such attention to him. Inevitably, in the process of recovering from one fever, he fell helplessly into another. Love.

Soon, he was able to get out of bed and limp around the house. Then he could climb the staircase, and after that, he could walk the length of the street without feeling too tired. All the while, he was falling more and more in love with Heather. She had saved his life and she loved him back. He was sure of that. He could see it in her eyes.

After two months of this convalescence, he told her his feelings. He asked her to marry him, right away. She seemed to hesitate, which he took for modesty. He pestered her, she gave in.

Her reluctance to marry him should have worried him, but he was too thrilled at feeling well again, and maybe at being in love.

The wedding was a small one. Her father was on a voyage at the time, so he wasn't there. The following week, Harry Greene himself was offered a berth on a ship headed for West Africa. Heather didn't object. It was good, she said, for a man to follow his profession. He said he'd take Daisy with him to keep him company and remind him of her. She agreed.

The voyage lasted two months, and all through it, Harry never stopped thinking about Heather. Whenever Daisy said "Hello!" or "Goodbye!" in Heather's voice, he thought his heart would burst with love.

Those were the two longest months of his life. But they passed, and one day in June, the ship sailed into Glasgow heavily laden with mahogany and Harry Greene's love.

The house was empty, with a For Sale sign on the lawn. Harry Greene looked through the windows. All the furniture was gone.

At the Mission, they said she didn't work for them any more. They gave him her new address.

A taxi took him to a district where the City melts into the country, and where, in summer, marauding bands of wild flowers ambush the cultivated lawns of the houses. Harry got out of the taxi at the end of one of the little streets and walked along it.

He saw her before she saw him. She was standing on the lawn of the only old house in the street—the original farmhouse, fieldstone, ivy-covered. He almost called out, but instead, he stood behind a hedge and watched.

She wasn't alone. She was talking to someone who was sitting in an old wooden lawn chair. Harry could see him clearly—a young man in a housecoat, his face lined and grey from illness. She was looking at him with great tenderness.

All at once, she stiffened. She turned towards the hedge where Harry was standing. She looked and looked.

"Harry?" she called.

He came out from behind the hedge, and she walked slowly to meet him. She didn't smile and she made no attempt to touch him.

"I heard your ship was due," she said.

They talked, standing there by the hedge.

Harry wanted to know what had happened, why she had deserted him. She said it was difficult to explain. There was nothing personal in it. She had loved Harry, very much, especially when he was most sick—especially when she thought he might die.

Harry couldn't understand.

Heather said she herself didn't understand. She seemed

only able to love a man, she said, if she could see the grave in his eyes.

Harry pondered that for a while.

"So you don't love me any more?"

"Only if I close my eyes," she said, "and remember how you were when you were sick."

At that point, the young man in the chair called out to her in a feeble voice. Heather's eyes were suddenly full of love and concern, and she went to him. Harry watched them together for a moment, then he slowly walked away.

"Well now, after that," said Harry Greene, leaning on the rail of the *Cumnock*, "I took the first berth I could get and I was gone for a year straight. When I came back from that voyage, I heard that Heather was dead. 'Twas her new lover infected her with whatever he had. I'm sure she didn't mind at all." He shook his grey head. "One of those books in my cabin talks about the cold love of a saint. I can't help thinking Heather was some kind of saint. If I'd pretended to be sick all the time, I'm certain she'd have loved me forever."

The parrot, Daisy, had interested me as much as Heather. I asked him what happened to it.

"Sure now, I took Daisy with me on all my voyages after that. I could still hear Heather's voice saying 'Hello!' and 'Goodbye!' long after she was dead. Then, one time we were sailing off the coast of Brazil and that bird took off, and didn't come back. I'm sure it could smell home." He laughed. "Come to think of it, I missed that bird more than I did Heather."

We'd been at the rail a long time and the night was dark and warm.

"So, Andy," he said, "that was my only attempt at being a married man. Did I tell you that old Johannes Morologus says there's mathematics even in love? According to him, people like Heather and I are the same as two parallel lines—they can run alongside each other, but they can't ever meet." He sighed. "Ah, the love of a woman. 'Tis a great thing...for many reasons you're too young to understand."

It was much darker now, and I was glad the darkness hid my face.

"A woman's love isn't hard to win," he said. "All you have to do is talk to her. So says a French book I read a while back. The author claims words are the brain's love juice. He says when you talk to a woman, it doesn't matter much what you say, you're making love to her." He laughed, then was serious. "I've never married again. I wouldn't think of giving up my voyages and my books. How could any woman put up with that?"

After he said that, his hand thumped down on the railing.

"God's rope!" he said. "Do you know, Andy my boy, this is the first time I've ever told anyone about my marriage? Sure now, you have a way of getting me to talk."

As though he really needed much encouragement, I thought.

He reached out and squeezed my shoulder in the dark.

"Now, I'll let you in on something else. We have more in common than you know. The house in Stroven—the one you talked about—the house you were born in. Do you know who had it built? 'Twas Heather's father. He lived there when he retired from the sea after her death." He was speaking now in a quiet voice he used when he was confiding in me. "And I went there once to visit him. Yes, Andy. I've actually been in the house you were born and brought up in."

He said this as though it were incredible. Adults find

coincidences strange. But for me, at that time, the world seemed full of every kind of possibility. I only wished there was some way of making sure they didn't turn out to be unpleasant.

Chapter Fifteen

WE WERE NEAR THE equator now and still heading south. The air was heavy, and the frequent rains were warm. One evening just before nightfall, I was standing at the rails when I heard footsteps and turned, expecting Harry Greene.

It was Captain Stillar. He leaned on the rail beside me. He hadn't spoken to me since the voyage began. I'd passed him often, but he never seemed to notice me. So I felt uncomfortable as we stood together looking out at the invisible line between sea and evening sky.

"See how the greyness permeates everything," he said.

I remembered his deep voice from the Hochmagandie.

He gestured with stubby paint-stained fingers towards the grey dusk. "This must be the way a colour-blind man sees the world." His eyes, which were blue, and which usually seemed distant and dreamy to me, now were alert.

He was silent for a while, and when he spoke again, he moved his mouth closer to my ear.

"A word of warning," he said. "Don't rely too much on what sailors tell you. Life on shore keeps its secrets from them by standing still."

I didn't understand exactly what he meant but I assumed he was talking about Harry.

"A sailor's mark on the earth," he said, "is as light as the imprint of a bird on sand." He walked his stained fingers along the rail to illustrate. Then, still speaking quietly, he said: "Have you seen my paintings?"

"Yes," I said.

"That's good," he said. He looked back towards the horizon. He sighed. "When she was dying," he said, "nobody could tell, because the colours of the lizard on her body were still so bright."

He turned and looked at me.

"She once told me an old saying from her island: A broken heart mended is stronger than ever before. I'd like to believe that."

Then he walked away without another word and entered the nearby companionway.

Why he felt the need to talk to me on that occasion, I'd no idea. For the rest of the voyage, though I met him many times, he looked past me as he always had, and he never spoke to me again.

That same night, in the middle of the night, I was awakened by the bell ringing for the change of watches, and I had trouble getting back to sleep. When I did, I thought I was back in the high moorland country, though I didn't know exactly where. It was dusk and I was lying in the hollow on top of a rock that stuck out above the surrounding countryside. I could see the ocean only a short distance away, and I could hear the waves, so I knew I wasn't anywhere near Stroven.

Looking over the rim of the hollow, I saw them coming—a procession of black-robed beings winding down a rocky path that ran past my hiding place. I could hear a great droning sound coming from them, an incantation, or a lament.

The procession soon reached my perch, and began

dividing round it, passing on either side, then reuniting. Now I could see the marchers clearly. Their faces were half-covered by their hoods, but the black robes revealed the tilt of their breasts. Their arms were at their sides, and their nails were painted scarlet. At the back of the procession, one marcher stood out from the others. She was tall, and walked proudly, holding in front of her a long wooden staff with a silk flag on it.

My heart began to pound, half in fear, half in excitement.

"Mother! Mother!" I shouted as she passed underneath. I stood up on the edge of the rock and stretched out my arms towards her. She didn't look up. Her footsteps rang like iron on the rocky path.

I couldn't bear that she should be so near and not at least know that I could see her.

"Mother! Mother!" I shouted again. I made up my mind. I was going to leap down from the rock. I'd gathered myself to jump when she looked up at me. Her black hood slipped back from her face. It was the blue face of a lizard, with fringed lizard eyes. And the tiny pupils inside the multiple eyelids were glittering and cold. At the same time, a bitter wind began to blow and the flag she carried billowed out so that for a moment I could read the words that shimmered on it: THE MONSTROUS REGIMENT OF WOMEN.

The days passed, warm and sullen, and I hoped this voyage would never end. But one morning as I was eating breakfast alone in the mess hall, Harry slid open the door and stuck his head in.

"Andy," he said. "Land's been sighted. Sure now, you'll be in your new home by nightfall." His eyebrows were bristling, but he said this in a cheerful enough voice.

I got up and went out onto the deck. The sky was grey. Harry was looking to the south-west.

"Over there." He pointed out over the starboard bow. "'Tis over there."

At first I couldn't see anything unusual. But after a while I could make out, away on the horizon, a smudge that was slightly greyer than the grey of the ocean and the sky.

As the morning wore on, that smudge took on more substance and became a black stain which became, in time, an island. My destination—the Island of St Jude.

Part Three

St Jude

For in every one of us a mad rabbit
thrashes and a wolf pack howls, so
that we are afraid it will be heard
by others.
Czeslaw Milosz

Chapter Sixteen

"THE ISLAND OF ST JUDE is an uninviting place with a small town whose original purpose was to be a women's penal colony; later it became a garrison during times of war. The harbour is adequate but unprotected. The volcanic surface makes growing difficult. Hence the island's indigenous vegetation is scanty, consisting of a few plants and trees of the tropical variety, brought there by tides and migrating birds. Mosquitoes and stinging insects are found year round. Even though the island now serves only a nominal strategic purpose, it still retains a Commissioner, a troop of soldiers, minimal justiciary, medical, educational facilities and a small agricultural laboratory. There are no motorized vehicles. The permanent colonists, many of them former soldiers and their descendants, make a living by fishing and subsistence gardening."

That was the description I read in the mildewed edition of *Letson's Islands and Navigable Waters*, fished out by Harry Greene from under a pile of books beneath the porthole of his cabin early in the voyage.

"Some islands are perfect for burying treasure," he'd said when he gave me the book. "Then there are islands like St Jude that are perfect for burying things nobody wants."

I think he'd no sooner said that than he regretted it and changed the subject quickly, hoping I hadn't understood.

Now I could see with my own eyes the words from Letson's book translated into this heap of rock the *Cumnock* was slowly approaching. The sun, for one of the first times in the entire voyage, broke through. The dazzling blue of the sky and the sea made the lava of the island blacker than black. From the deck of the ship, the island might have been the lid of a huge pot, with Mount St Jude jutting out like a black handle. The island was really the tip of a volcanic eruption millions of years ago, on the ocean floor miles beneath.

We sailed into a wide bay on the east coast where the only town was located—the harbour and garrison town, also called St Jude; here the *Cumnock* was to dock for two hours before continuing on its voyage. From well off shore, I could see the semicircle of battlements protecting the town from attack on its inland flank. The landscape looked as though it had been layered by a giant trowel.

Shortly after four, the *Cumnock* slowly made its way into the harbour till its bows nibbled at the pier. A crowd of islanders, perhaps a hundred, were watching our arrival, waving to the ship. Lines were cast ashore, hawsers were looped over rusted bollards, the engine was cut, the gangway clattered down.

The crew began unloading mail bags and small boxes onto large wooden wheelbarrows on the pier. Heavier crates were hoisted out of the hold by the cranes.

I stood on the deck with my suitcase, waiting for someone to tell me what to do.

There was no wind. The air was suffocating. The *Cumnock*'s engines, which had been the bass accompaniment to every minute of my day for the past few weeks, were silent. All other sounds came to the fore—the shouts of the crewmen, the squawking of gulls, the hull squealing against the rubber fenders, the slap of the waves. And the buzz of insects. These insects were swarming around me and I waved them away. I realized that this was what the islanders on the dock were doing—not waving to us, but swatting at the mosquitoes.

I kept waiting for instructions, but none came. I couldn't see Captain Stillar anywhere. Harry Greene was busy helping the crew with the unloading. He glanced my way several times, but I knew I'd get no help from him. He'd come to my cabin just before we docked and given me a brief handshake. "Sailors aren't good at goodbyes," he'd said. His voice sounded hearty but he wouldn't look me in the eye. "I hope we meet again, Andy Halfnight." Then he'd left without looking backward.

Now I stood on the deck, feeling quite helpless and utterly lonely. Mosquitoes stung me with their soft stings. At last, I lifted my suitcase and walked to the gangway and started down. The assembled islanders stared up at me. Men, women and children, they were dressed in much the same way. The women and the girls wore black dresses and black headscarves. The men and boys, their hair cut close to the skull, wore white, collarless shirts, and black trousers held up by black suspenders. I looked around, hoping for any sign of welcome. A sour smell—the smell of land—pervaded everything.

I reached the bottom of the gangway, and still no one approached or said anything. I stepped onto the pier. It was crumbled at the edges like a stale cake. When I took my hand off the railing, I staggered and almost fell. After so many weeks rolling to and fro, the immobility of the earth was unnatural. I grabbed the railing and steadied myself.

"Andrew!"

A woman came from the crowd of onlookers towards

me. She had a stocky build, and a face that seemed too long for her body, like a reflection in a trick mirror.

But I knew the face—it was so like my mother's. And the green eyes were the same dark green.

"Andrew Halfnight!" She stood in front of me, looking me up and down. Her face was damp with sweat; a layer of mosquitoes covered the black headscarf over her brown hair. Her broad, freckled hand reached out and touched my shoulder.

"I'm Lizzie Beck. Your aunt." Even her voice was deep, like my mother's.

I should have felt comforted. I should have felt secure. But I wasn't. I shrank away from her hand. The sudden awareness of how remote this island was from everything I'd ever known brought on a kind of terror. I looked back at the ship, hoping Harry Greene might be watching and might call to me to come back aboard. I would gladly have turned my back on my aunt and run up the gangway to hide myself forever in the dark recesses of the *Cumnock*. But there was no sign of Harry. The ship herself, from here on the dock, was a forbidding sight with her rust and her dented plates.

My aunt may have known what I was thinking, so she let me look at the ship. Then, after a few moments, she spoke.

"Now, come with me, Andrew," she said. She turned and scuttled away. I didn't know what to do except to pick up my suitcase and follow her past the crowd on the dock and onto the land, and along the street that started where the dock stopped, and seemed to run along the ocean front. That much I noticed, but not much else. The worn cobblestones of the street were reaching up and tripping my feet. The stable surface was like a trap, so unused was I to walking on something that wasn't constantly in motion. I had to concentrate on how I placed my feet or I would have fallen several times.

After a while I got the hang of the land's stability and was able to look around. The street at this end consisted mostly of shabby wooden bungalows shaded by ramshackle verandahs and low, dusty palm trees. There were a number of narrow cul-de-sacs lined with similar wooden bungalows. Everything ended against the battlements that encircled the town on the landward side.

My aunt and I, escorted by millions of mosquitoes, soon reached a part of this main street where there were two buildings of a more impressive sort. They were solid, built with white polished stone I took to be marble, glistening cool, under the late-afternoon sun. The first of these buildings was an elegant mansion with pillars. On the brown apron of lawn was a sign: COMMISSIONER'S RESIDENCE. The other building of similar white stone, two storeys high, stood next to it. The word ADMINISTRATION was sculpted above its entranceway.

As we passed in front of these buildings, I saw they weren't exactly what they seemed. The face of the marble was peeling at the corners—it wasn't stone at all, but plywood with wallpaper glued to it.

Further along the street, I saw this again. The building with the sign POST OFFICE on it appeared to be made of red brick. But the brick was only paper, and was peeling off in places, revealing the plywood base. Then we passed the St Jude Inn. It reminded me of the pub in Stroven with its walls of grey granite and the smell of beer seeping out into the day. Except that the granite was only textured paper, and bulged in places; tacks had been used to stop it from peeling off at the corners. Many of the other buildings along the main street showed the same symptoms.

The walk was uncomfortable for me. The sun was low

and dusk was falling quickly, and I'd never experienced such heat. Also, mosquito bites were quite new to me. They seemed harmless at first, but now they were beginning to itch maddeningly. Brown flies were biting me, and other, smaller flies were sticking needles into my neck. My suitcase was heavier and heavier. I kept hoping we'd soon come to my aunt's house. But we walked past all the cul-de-sacs and the cobblestones ended. We were now at a huge gateway in the battlements. A heavy wooden gate with brass studs all over it was half open.

My aunt went through the gateway and I followed.

We began walking on a dusty track across the lava plain, which rose very slightly towards the mountain. Ahead, I could see how this track narrowed in the distance till it seemed nothing more than a pencil scrawl. My aunt pressed on ahead, saying nothing.

We walked and walked, and all the time, the dusk became thicker, so that the black mountain was gradually dissolving. I was sticky and hot. The whining assaults of the mosquitoes seemed more vicious and personal. My shoes were leaden. The suitcase in my hand was a dead weight leeching the strength out of me. I began to feel sick. I began to feel I would soon vomit. My aunt, shuffling along ahead of me, made no offer to help, only stopped when I stopped to scratch my face and arms, or to shift the suitcase to my other hand. I hated her. I could think of nothing except the weight, the itch, the nausea, the hatred. I'd almost made up my mind to lie down on the track and sleep.

Then, all at once, we reached our destination.

The track had led us past a huge lava outcrop near the foot of the mountain. We passed a sign still faintly visible in the dusk—AGRICULTURAL STATION. Nearby was a stone cottage with a verandah, and a little front yard with an iron gate. My aunt opened it and held it for me to go through.

I was feverish. The very moment I walked through the gate, the dusk became pure blackness and swallowed in one gulp the black mountain and the cottage. This monster darkness terrified me, and I stood holding onto my suitcase in my left hand, as though it were an anchor. I felt a hand take my arm.

"This way, Andrew." My aunt led me a few short steps. I heard her fumble with a doorknob, and the door squealed open. We stepped into a large room dimly lit by an oil lamp hanging from ceiling beams. I put my suitcase down.

"Norman! We're here!" my aunt called out. "We're here!"

She let go my arm and stood behind me, putting her hands on my shoulders. I might have been an offering, or a shield.

I could make out someone sitting in an armchair at the rear of that gloomy room.

"This is my nephew," my aunt said. "This is Andrew Halfnight."

A man's voice, a very deep voice, replied.

"Good. Now we can all have supper."

Chapter Seventeen

So I made my first acquaintance with the Island of St Jude and with my new family. During the early days my Aunt Lizzie asked a few brief questions about my mother's final illness. Otherwise she didn't say much, though she constantly watched me and would smile when our eyes met. I had a feeling she would have liked to be more friendly, but that something was keeping her back. Still, she didn't seem unhappy I was there.

As for my uncle, Norman Beck: he didn't pay much attention to me. When I'd heard his deep voice the night I arrived, I'd expected him to be a big man. But though he was tall, he was very thin, with greying hair, lined cheeks and a slight hump. No matter how hot it was, he wore a black wool sweater that was always frosted with dandruff at the shoulders. He rarely spoke to Lizzie or to me, and never called us by name. There was a kind of chill about him: I noticed that even the mosquitoes in flight veered away from him. If he had any warmth, it was absorbed by his work: the vegetable garden at the back of the cottage; and by his hobby: astronomy.

The vegetable gardening was professional. He was a botanist and had been posted here to look after the government project. He was trying to find which northern vegetables could be developed in this climate. The official garden was at the back of the cottage. It was about the same dimensions as the cottage itself and was enclosed by lava rocks loosely piled on each other to make walls. Tons of northern soil had been shipped in over the years. He was experimenting with types of lettuce and potatoes and carrots and turnips. He tended them with great devotion; but apparently, in spite of his care, and no matter how promisingly they began, they'd rot in the ground.

Lizzie sent me out into the garden the day after I arrived to tell him lunch was ready. He was crouched over, halfway along a row of potato plants, looking at something. He motioned to me to come and stand by him. He pointed to an insect that seemed to be constructed from oversized matchsticks, sitting under the leaves of a potato stalk. The insect looked a little like him, bent over with its forelimbs joined together like a frail monk.

"A praying mantis," he said in a hushed voice. "It's a female. After mating, it eats its mate."

That was the first statement Uncle Norman had made directly to me. When I went back inside, I told Lizzie he'd shown me a praying mantis. She looked at me with a small smile.

"Now there's an insect we can learn from," she said.

When he finished his garden work in the afternoons, he'd sit and read one of his astronomy books till dinner. The tropical daylight would disappear as quickly as though a lamp had been switched off. After dinner, he'd go out into the garden again, this time to his telescope. It was on a tripod at the back, covered during the day by a tarpaulin. He'd sit for hours peering at the crowded skies.

Some evenings, during those first weeks at the cottage, Lizzie sent me out to stand beside him. I think she hoped he might allow me to use the telescope. He never looked at me or said anything, though he must have known I was standing there beside him in the dark, tormented by mosquitoes. He seemed to be looking for something particular in the night skies, and sometimes he'd stop moving the telescope and would hold his breath and gaze intently at some spot for ages, as though he'd found it.

He didn't let me use the telescope, but he did show me something else. I was in the living-room one morning reading a novel when he came in from the garden. He was holding a jar containing a scorpion he'd trapped. It was a brownish colour, the size of my hand.

"Come with me," he said.

He gave me a can of kerosene to carry and we went out to a bare area in the garden. He poked his finger into the soil and made a little circular ditch about nine inches in diameter and an inch deep. He filled the ditch with kerosene and lit it, making a ring of fire.

"Now watch this," he said.

He took the lid off the jar and dropped the scorpion into the middle of the ring. It immediately tried to scuttle away. The flames stopped it. It tried again, and again, and again. No matter where it went, the flames drove it back.

The scorpion stopped and crouched for a while in the middle of the ring. Then it raised its sting and slowly lowered it onto its own back. It gently felt around for a crevice in its scales, inserted the sting, paused and jabbed itself.

It went into a trembling frenzy, then it shuddered once or twice more, then it died. The flames still blazed around it.

"See?" said Uncle Norman. "A scorpion would rather sting itself than die with its sting unused. I read that in a book."

Lizzie bought me the normal island clothing for a boy—a white shirt and black pants with suspenders. That made me feel more at home. Sometimes, I'd see a look on her face that puzzled me. Her green eyes would turn to ice, and her lips would twist the way my mother's did, but in a more bitter way. When she became aware I was watching her, she'd immediately brighten up. I had a feeling that, unlike my mother, she would have liked to show her affection for me. In fact, she was becoming more and more talkative—as though she'd had the words pent up in her and now they'd found a way out and were enjoying their freedom.

Chapter Eighteen

One morning Lizzie was putting some lotion on my bites—the mosquitoes and the little needle-flies were still a torment to me. There was no escape from them, even in the house. The windows had no screens, and the bead curtains over the doors weren't very effective. The net over my bed kept the insects off during the night, but it also kept out whatever air there was, and I'd throw it off in my sleep.

"You'll get used to them, my dear," Lizzie said as she rubbed the lotion on my arms and neck.

She slipped my suspenders off my shoulders, and made me take off my shirt. She let out a little gasp when she saw the purple stain. She touched it. "Ah, yes. Well, well," she said softly and gave me a quick hug. Then she spread the lotion over my chest and back and told me to put my shirt on again.

"Now, my poor Andrew," she said. "Come and sit by the window."

I sat in one of the big rattan chairs by the back window and she sat opposite me. Her short legs dangled an inch or two above the floor. We could see Uncle Norman at work in the garden, metal chinking against lava. She began talking.

"It all happened six months before you were born. It was January, and the snow was falling heavily. He was driving too fast, the way he always did, and the car went out of control and hit a tree."

"Who? Uncle Norman?" I said.

"No, no. Your father—Thomas Halfnight," she said. "Who else would I mean but your dear, dead father?"

She said this quietly, with tears in her eyes. It was odd to see tears in eyes so like my mother's who disapproved of shows of emotion.

"Did Sarah not tell you about that?"

I told her I didn't know anything about it. And so, for the first time, I began to find out the truth about my father and about the incidents at the time of my birth.

"The poor man was pinned behind the wheel for hours before they found him," she said. "His right arm was so badly frostbitten, they had no choice but to amputate it. Can you imagine anything so awful?

"He was in hospital for weeks. When the wound was all healed, they fitted him with one of those arms carved out of wood with wooden fingers. It was either that or a hook, and that would have been unbearable.

"After that, when he woke up in the mornings he couldn't believe his own arm was gone. He said he could feel his fingers, as though they were still attached. The poor, dear man. He wore black leather gloves all the time. I remember the way they used to glisten."

Now, sitting here in this cottage on a remote island, I learned from my Aunt Lizzie about my premature birth and the fact that I'd once had a twin sister, Johanna; about the terrific heat that spring long ago in Stroven; about the naming ceremony, about the party in the garden of the big house. And about my sister's death.

"He asked to hold his babies. Well, that was only natural, wasn't it? Your eyes were wide open, but Sarah gave him your sister to hold, even though she was asleep." Tears were in her eyes again. "He had her in his arms, showing her off, and the blanket began slipping. He tried to hold on to her, to stop her from falling. What kind of father wouldn't have done that? But with that arm, he accidentally killed her. And afterwards, when I tried to comfort him, he wouldn't be consoled. He was out of his mind. He said he believed something in him actually wanted to do it. He said the arm was only doing what he really wanted."

She wiped her eyes with her apron. "The poor man. What an awful burden for a man to bear."

Now she told me about my father's death at the Roman bridge, and how, afterwards, the rumours began to spread.

"No one in Stroven knew about the arm. Even Doctor Giffen didn't know that. So there were a lot of rumours. Some thought maybe your father had cut it off himself. There was a rumour some of the men had cut it off and then thrown him from the bridge while he was still alive."

The chink of the shovel stopped. My uncle was standing upright behind the potato drills, as though he were listening. But she had talked so softly he couldn't possibly have heard a word she'd been saying. After a moment, he stooped over his potatoes again, and began weeding once more. Aunt Lizzie looked out towards him, and her eyes were hard. Then she smiled at me again.

"So your mother never told you any of this?"

"No," I said.

"She never got over what happened," she said. "And who could blame her? Before the little girl was killed, she was a different woman. I'm telling you all this, because you ought to know. Your father was a good man. Even though before he met Sarah, he'd been with a lot of other women. He really fell for her. He'd have done anything for her, he loved her so much. She would have told you: I'm sure she meant to, some time. But just remember this: they loved each other."

Tears began streaming down my Aunt Lizzie's cheeks at this point. She brought the apron up and buried her face in it for the longest time. I didn't know what to do, I felt so embarrassed. After a while she looked up at me.

"They loved each other. Remember that. Love makes up for everything," she said.

That was the first and the only time I learned some of the details about my birth. Lizzie had seen my sister's death, she'd seen my father's corpse laid out on the kitchen table. She also knew many other things about my parents I'd only heard vaguely mentioned by my mother. For example, that my father wasn't very wealthy but had enough of an annuity from his family's distillery in the North to live in a place like Stroven; that his parents didn't approve of my mother any more than of his previous women, so the wedding was nothing more than a visit to the Registry Office.

Lizzie told me she and my mother were the only children of a railway stationmaster in the City, who'd done all he could for them by giving them a good education. She seemed surprised my mother had told me nothing about any of these things.

The idea that I actually had grandparents excited me.

"Do you think I'll be able to see them some time, Aunt Lizzie?" I said.

She shook her head and looked ready to weep again.

"You poor boy," she said. "No, they're all dead, long ago. Otherwise I'm sure your mother would never have sent you here. No. They're all dead. There's only me, more's the pity."

She didn't mention Uncle Norman.

The rest of that morning I spent in my own room. I thought about everything my aunt had told me. But mainly I lay on my bed and wondered what would become of me on this island. I watched a little black lizard that lived and hunted among the ceiling beams of my room, devouring any mosquito that flew too near its long tongue. I'd noticed that if I came into my room suddenly and frightened it, it would puff itself up into a ball and try to frighten me too. But at this moment, neither of us was afraid of the other. It was looking back down at me with its beady eye, maybe wondering if I was puffed up, too, and might somehow shrink and become small enough to swallow.

At one point, I got up and looked outside. Under my window was a garden pond covered in a green slime. Tiny lizards darted round the rocky edges in pursuit of things no human eye could see; in mid-stride, they would slowly come to a stop, and stay frozen in position like wind-up toys run down. Further back in the garden, motionless, my Uncle Norman was bent over his plants. Behind him, looming over everything, was the impenetrable black wall of the mountain.

Chapter Nineteen

OCCASIONALLY, I'D CATCH that hard look on Aunt Lizzie's face that should have frightened me; but I tried not to think what might be the cause of it. As for Uncle Norman's quirks—after a while I took them for granted as the foibles of an adult. Children don't expect the world to be a rational place.

In other words, I began to believe everything was go-ing to turn out all right for me, in spite of my mother's death.

I couldn't have been more wrong. Aunt Lizzie was about to do something awful.

On my third Monday morning on St Jude (I was to begin school the following week), all three of us, Lizzie, my Uncle Norman and I, were at breakfast in the kitchen. The morning was a typical St Jude morning—hot, windless, with insects buzzing. My uncle was reading *The Potato in Southern Climes*, propped against the china teapot on the table in front of him. We ate silently ("No talking at table when I'm reading" was one of his rules). Lizzie sipped her tea, her face blank. I was picking at my food ("Everything on the plate must be eaten," he always said). Fried bacon had always smelt so good on cold Stroven mornings; here, in the heat of St Jude, the smell seemed to coat my tongue with grease. The Darjeeling tea made my shirt stick clammily to my skin.

After a while, Uncle Norman closed his book and rose from the table. He put the book back in its place with the others on the mantel. They were safe enough there; the fireplace was an ornament: the weather was never cold enough to need a fire. He went to the back door, slipped his feet into his old work boots, jammed on his old coolie hat, then went outside to begin his garden rituals of the morning: the plucking of weeds, the removal of insects.

Lizzie watched him leave. She lowered her teacup slowly into its saucer. She turned to me.

"Go to your room. Immediately." She hissed the words in a way I'd never heard her speak before. I got up right away and made to take my plate over to the sink.

"Leave it. Just go." Her eyes were so cold they might have belonged to a snake.

The change in her was so awful, I was almost afraid to breathe for fear of sobbing. I went quickly into my room and shut the door. Through the window, I could see my uncle at work on his potatoes near the back of the garden.

As I watched, Lizzie appeared, still in her apron, walking slowly towards him. He was bent over, jabbing at the ground with a hand fork. He'd no doubt found one of those tough weeds that conspired during the night to strangle his plants.

Lizzie had arrived behind him now. She looked down at him for a while, then she turned and looked straight at the window. She saw me and gave me a smile—a great friendly smile. She kissed her hand and blew it towards me.

A great weight was lifted from me. I was able to breathe again. I smiled back at her and waved. I could have shouted with delight.

She turned back towards my uncle as though she were going to say something to him. But she didn't. Instead, she stooped and picked up one of the jagged lumps of lava that bordered the pathway. She used both hands to lift it, for the rock was the size of the teapot.

My first thought was that I'd never seen Lizzie working in the back garden before.

She held the rock against her body with her left hand, and with her right, she brushed off the soil that clung to it. Then she stepped towards him and raised the rock over his bent head.

I knew then what she was going to do. I could have shouted a warning to my Uncle Norman, but I didn't. He must have caught a glimpse of her white apron out of the corner of his eye, for he turned towards her, still on his knees. Too late. The rock clumped against the side of his head. It was quite a loud sound in the stillness of the morning. His coolie hat toppled off, but he stayed upright on his knees for a moment, then he fell forward across his potato drills, slowly, carefully, as though he wanted to damage them as little as possible. His fall scattered some flies that were among the plants. They quickly overcame their panic and organized themselves again, this time around his body.

Lizzie stood over him. He didn't move and she dropped the rock to one side. She smoothed her apron, the palms of her hands caressing her upper thighs. She must have known I was still standing at the window.

“Andrew,” she called.

I didn’t answer.

“Andrew,” she called again.

“Yes?” I croaked out the word.

“Go for the Doctor.” She wasn’t looking at me, but I could have sworn her voice sounded cheerful. “Go down to the town and bring him back with you. Tell him your uncle’s had an accident.” She called this out in the same tone she used to let us know that dinner was ready.

So it was that I saw the assault on my uncle, and might have warned him, but didn’t. Now, I obeyed Lizzie. I began running down the long, hot path to the town. I ran fast, for I was in a neck-and-neck race with the image of what I’d just seen in the garden. At times I’d get ahead of it, at other times it would nose in front and terrify me. I tried not to contemplate its implications: that the only person on this black, remote island who seemed to care for me was a monster. I had a sickening feeling that once again my life was about to be shattered.

Chapter Twenty

When I reached the town, prostrate in the heat, I ran through the battlements gate. The main street was empty and there was no sound except for the occasional jangle of the rigging of some of the low-masted fishing boats beached along the shore.

I went straight to Doctor Hebblethwaite’s house at the end of a cul-de-sac. The house was actually a stubby tower called The Motte, for it had once been attached to the garrison, and was only a few steps from the battlements. I knocked at the heavy wooden door. A thin, fair-haired girl my own age opened it, letting out a medicinal smell into the morning air. She went back to fetch the Doctor. He appeared a moment later holding a piece of toast in one hand and a cigarette in the other.

"Yes?" He was a slight man with brown skin wrinkled by the sun, and blue eyes that seemed too young for his face.

"My Aunt Lizzie would like you to come up to the cottage. My uncle's had an accident." I used Lizzie's exact words.

He asked no questions, but went back inside, leaving me standing at the open door. The fair-haired girl watched me curiously from the lobby. He soon came back, wearing a white linen coat and carrying a doctor's bag.

"Lead on," he said.

At that moment, a tall thin woman with wire-rimmed glasses appeared in the lobby behind him.

She spoke to the doctor, ignoring me completely.

"Don't spend all day up there. Lunch will be at twelve, prompt."

"Yes, dear," he said.

"And you, Maria," she said to the girl. "Go and clear the table."

We went along the main street, through the gate and began the long walk up the path to the cottage. Doctor Hebblethwaite was a leisurely walker, smoking constantly, wheezing or coughing outright from time to time.

I was afraid he'd ask for details about the accident, and was trying to think of something to say that wouldn't incriminate Lizzie. But he didn't ask any questions; he just wheezed along behind me. Now and then, he'd stop for a breather. The first time, we'd only gone about a quarter of a mile. He looked back down towards the town.

"Well, young chap. How do you like the island?" He had a high-pitched voice with a musical lilt to it.

"Fine," I said.

"I come this way so infrequently," Doctor Hebblethwaite said. "What an enchanting view." His language seemed very refined.

He sat down on a rock, lit another cigarette and began to talk about the island. I was in no hurry to get back to the scene of the crime, so I was the perfect listener, nodding politely, not rushing him in any way.

"St Jude was formerly a women's penal colony," he said. "The doctor's main function in that era was to preside over punishments and executions. To ensure that they were performed humanely, if such a word may be used in such a context. A number of my predecessors left notebooks in which they talk about their responsibilities. It appears punishments were doled out for any kind of minor misbehaviour. Executions were reserved solely for the leaders of riots.

"When an official punishment was to be inflicted, all of the prisoners were assembled below the battlements and the guilty parties were brought out. About nine in the morning: just about this time of day." He looked around. The sky was a killing blue, gulls were wheeling distantly over the harbour in the slight wind, and the insects were busily going about their tasks.

"Punishments were mainly by the lash. The women were stripped of their clothing and spread-eagled on an iron frame in the sun. After the lashing, the sufferers were left on the frame all day.

"In the case of executions, the heads of the guilty women were cut off with an axe. Sometimes more than one blow was required. The heads were impaled on poles, and displayed on the battlements as a warning to the others." He threw away his half-smoked cigarette. "Reading between the lines of these notebooks," he said, "one has a distinct impression that the lashings could be minimized, or the executions made more efficient if the condemned women were willing to do certain... favours for their jailors." He may have glanced at me as he said this, but I made sure I was watching the smoke rising from the cigarette thrown among the rocks.

We began walking again. Doctor Hebblethwaite wheezed along behind me for another quarter-mile or so, till we came to another smooth boulder.

"Let's stop here for a while," he said. He sat on the rock, lit up another cigarette, and continued his history lesson.

"Those were dreadfully uncivilized times, of course," he said. "The idea of penal colonies for women went out of style. It would make an interesting topic for a monograph, don't you think?"

I didn't know what a monograph was. He flicked the ash off his cigarette against the black lava, and the red sparks scattered.

"The island was eventually converted to a garrison and naval base," he said. "The doctors were barber surgeons, and they had quite a task. In naval battles at that time, it was considered quite unsporting for ships to dodge each other. So the main tactic was simply to line up alongside your enemy in a gentlemanly way and fire broadsides. They'd blast away at each other from close range with cannonballs till the wooden hulls were smashed to pieces. Naturally, flying splinters of wood were the major cause of wounds, and gangrene was the result. Amputation was the only hope in most cases. Operations were performed without anaesthetic or disinfectant. The surgeons did what they could, but it must have been quite ghastly. The patient might gain a few more painful hours of life in exchange for a limb or two. Not much of a bargain."

He drew deeply on his cigarette as though he were taking his last breath. He pointed down towards the town. I could see he had more to tell me, and I looked at him encouragingly—anything to keep him from asking what had happened at the cottage.

"Those battlements aren't quite as flimsy as you might think," he said. "Rather large lava rocks have been piled up under the plywood structure. I believe they'd be quite effective against guns. I used to wonder why they'd been built on the inland side. I discovered it was out of fear the enemy might land further down the coast and come at the town from behind." He tapped the ash from his cigarette. "Of course, there is no enemy any longer, but the gate's still barred every night. An island tradition. There's a superstition that someone from outside the walls might still bring some kind of disaster to the island. Foolish, of course. The islanders know it; but they still like to have the gate shut at night." He stubbed out the cigarette and looked at me. "Whatever it is they're afraid of, walls and gates won't keep it out."

I nodded and tried to look wise.

Doctor Hebblethwaite got up from the rock and we began walking the last stretch to the cottage. As we walked, he told me a little about himself. He was a career Medical Officer and had been trained in the best medical schools. He'd been posted to St Jude twelve years ago, just before the birth of his daughter. In the course of time, he expected—and, by the way he said it, his wife hoped—to be sent elsewhere. He'd thought his work on the island would be more demanding, but it had turned out to be quite dull.

"Occasionally there's a birth, or someone's attacked by a shark, or poisoned by a stonefish or a snake. But generally speaking, the islanders are very healthy and there's not much for me to do," he said.

I thought for sure he was going to ask me now about my uncle's accident. But he didn't. He just wheezed along behind me.

Chapter Twenty-one

LIZZIE WAS STANDING at the front gate with a little smile on her face. She greeted the Doctor then led us through the house and out the back door into the garden.

Uncle Norman still lay face down, where he had fallen across the potato drills. A blue-striped dish towel covered his head. Blowflies were in a feeding frenzy in the areas where blood had seeped through the cloth. A lizard had crawled onto the heel of his right work boot and was contemplating the flies.

"Well, well," said Doctor Hebblethwaite. The sight of the body had made him very alert. He carefully rolled up his shirtsleeves and bent over my uncle's body. He tried to lift the dish towel away, but the blood had congealed. He ripped it off quickly and tossed it aside, where it attracted its quota of flies. Then he brought my uncle's arms in by his body and rolled him over.

Now I could see Uncle Norman's face clearly. It was very grey. The bloody right side of his head was stuccoed with garden soil.

"We'll take him inside," said the Doctor.

The flies buzzed around us angrily as we organized ourselves to take their food away from them. The Doctor and

Lizzie lifted an arm each, and I helped by taking my uncle's spidery ankles. I didn't like the feel of the fine leg hair on my fingers. We dragged him along and up the steps to the back door, like a sack of potatoes bumping on the ground.

Inside the cottage, the wooden floor, polished every week with the Abbot's Wax, made it easy to slide the body along into the living-room. Many of the flies had run the gauntlet of the bead curtain at the door; they still buzzed around the body. In the beams above us, one of the house lizards took up position.

Lizzie sat down on a rattan chair, and I stood opposite, with the body between us. Each time our eyes met, she smiled.

Doctor Hebblethwaite took off his white coat. He probed the wound delicately with his fingers. He spoke without looking up.

"A fall, I suppose." It might have been a question. Lizzie looked at me, but said nothing.

The Doctor probed some more.

"These short falls can cause such dreadful wounds." I could hear no mockery in his voice. Now he opened his bag and filled a syringe from a phial. He spoke to Lizzie.

"Well, you'll be delighted to know your husband isn't dead."

She didn't seem very delighted.

"Though he most certainly should be," Doctor Hebblethwaite said. "His skull's cracked rather badly. But he's alive." Lizzie's face was closed like a fist. "Some people," the Doctor muttered, "need practice before they learn to die properly." He pushed up my uncle's sleeve and injected him in the upper arm.

He wiped the spot with a swab then spoke to me.

"Young chappie. I'm afraid I have to ask you to run down to the town again," he said. "Go to the infirmary and tell the nurse I have a patient requiring transportation. You might also call in at my surgery. Tell my wife I may be delayed." He looked at Lizzie again. "I think it would be wiser if I stayed with the patient."

Almost an hour later, I came back to the cottage along with soldiers in red jackets who pushed a four-wheeled barrow. They laid Uncle Norman on a little palliasse and placed him on the barrow. Then they rolled it down the bumpy path, going very slowly. They didn't want to kill the patient; though one of them had told me on the way up that the wheelbarrow also served as a hearse at island funerals.

For three days after that, my Aunt Lizzie and I stayed alone in the cottage. Even though I'd seen what she'd done, I felt safe with her. She would often hug me now, and I got to like that. She never mentioned Uncle Norman, nor did we go to visit him. She acted as though he didn't exist.

At noon on the fourth day, one of the soldiers who'd helped with the cart knocked at the cottage door and said that Doctor Hebblethwaite wanted to talk to me alone. Aunt Lizzie nodded consent.

So I went down to the town. The infirmary was set into the battlements near The Motte. Doctor Hebblethwaite met me in the little office at the entrance.

"Your uncle came out of his coma this morning," he said. "He rather wants to go back up to the cottage without delay." He was watching me closely. "He hasn't the faintest idea how he came to be injured."

I felt very awkward the way he looked at me.

"Will it be safe to send him home?" he asked.

"I don't know," I said.

"I can't detain him here forever." He sighed. "Come in and see him."

He showed me into the infirmary, which was really just one room with three beds. It was gloomy and hot, with little windows high in the wall, and smelt of floor-polish and disinfectant.

My uncle was the only patient. He was lying on one of the beds with his head in bandages. I was shocked at the change in him. Not that he looked awful after his injury, as I'd expected, but that he looked twenty years younger.

"Andrew!" he said when he saw me. That was the first time he'd called me by name. "Where's Lizzie? Is she with you?"

His face wasn't emaciated any more, and even though his lips were a little twisted, they were twisted in what was meant to be a smile. I'd never seen him smile before.

Doctor Hebblethwaite, standing behind me, answered his question.

"No. Lizzie's not here. She's preparing the cottage for your return," he said. "But I'm wondering: wouldn't you rather spend a few more days in the infirmary? Just till you've recovered properly."

My uncle shook his head.

"No, no," he said. He seemed very upset that my aunt wasn't with me. "Lizzie'll look after me, won't she, Andrew?" His voice was animated in a way I'd never heard it before, and higher pitched, like a younger man's. "And I've got lots of work to do. I can only imagine the state of the garden. Three days! That means I've missed three full nights at the telescope." He said this, as though whatever he searched the night skies for might have come and gone during his absence, and he looked anxious. I'd never have believed his face could be so expressive.

Doctor Hebblethwaite told the infirmary nurse to start

preparing Uncle Norman for the journey. He signalled to me to follow him. Outside the door of the infirmary, he lit a cigarette.

"Now, young man. I haven't subjected you to any direct questions, and I don't intend to," he said. "I understand only too well these husband-wife problems. But I hope your Aunt Lizzie knows that if there's a recurrence of this type of thing, I simply will not be able to ignore it. The Commissioner will have to be informed." He took a long draw on his cigarette, his blue eyes narrowing to counter the acrid smoke that drifted past. "It's most regrettable this had to happen after you arrived on the scene. Don't worry though. Maybe everything'll turn out all right yet," he said.

In the mid-afternoon heat, Doctor Hebblethwaite and I headed back up to the cottage along with the cart, pushed by two soldiers. My uncle lay on the cart humming cheerfully, slightly off key. The sun shone brilliantly on his bandaged head, on Doctor Hebblethwaite's white medical coat, on the scarlet tunics of the soldiers, on the flies that hung around us like glittering smoke. Real smoke came from the cigarette of the Doctor, who gradually fell off the pace and straggled along behind us.

From a long way off, I could see Lizzie standing at the gate. Nearer the cottage, my uncle raised his head and was able to see her too. He lifted his arm and waved. Perhaps she thought he was only waving the flies away, for it was a while before she waved back.

When we arrived at the gate, he called out.

"Lizzie! Lizzie!" and he stretched his hand out to her. She hesitated before she gave her hand to him. He drew it to his lips.

"Oh, Lizzie! It's so good to be home," he said. Her eyes widened.

The two soldiers began manoeuvring the cart up to the front door. While we stood watching, Doctor Hebblethwaite arrived, a little breathless.

"He hasn't any sensation in his legs yet," he told Lizzie. "It should return in a few days. He can't remember what happened. His mind's a *tabula rasa*. The whole incident's been wiped clean. How long that will last is a matter of speculation. But probably he'll soon remember some of it. Or all of it. That's generally the way with amnesia."

Lizzie nodded her head slowly.

The soldiers carried my uncle in and laid him on the bed. Doctor Hebblethwaite did a last check on him while Lizzie fussed around, adjusting the pillows. Uncle Norman kept looking at her and smiling. She smiled back cautiously.

I watched all of this carefully. I understood what a strange situation had developed.

Chapter Twenty-two

So it was that my Uncle Norman came smiling home to his murderer.

For the next week, I might almost have believed Lizzie's attempt to kill him had been a misunderstanding, she was now so kind to him, so loving. She would cut red and yellow flowers from her own flower patch and arrange them round his bed, to his delight. She fed him like a baby, spooning the soup into his mouth, cutting up his meat into little pieces. Three times a day she sponged his entire body with rose-water. She shut the bedroom door behind her when she did this. Through the slats of the door I could hear the whimpers of pleasure that accompanied this ritual.

In the afternoons, Lizzie and I would spend an hour weeding his garden. We brought his telescope into the house and set it up by the bed so that he could examine the night skies through the window. He thanked us, but he didn't seem as obsessed with either of these activities as before.

In fact, Uncle Norman was a new man. The ice in his light blue eyes had completely melted. His lips had become used to smiling, so that it started to seem natural. When he spoke, he'd use the kind of homely sayings you'd never have expected from him. Once when I came inside, I'd a rip in my pants from a thorn bush, and he said: "Ask Lizzie to fix that right away. A stitch in time saves nine." One morning when I was sitting at the window looking down towards the ocean, he said: "Look at that view, Andrew. Money can't buy a view like that."

Nor could he conceal his affection for Lizzie. "My old girl," he'd call her, and he'd reach out and touch her whenever she was near the bed. When she talked to him, he'd look into her eyes with rapt attention.

He seemed to enjoy my company.

"Come and sit on the bed, Andrew," he'd say, and he'd ask questions about Stroven and about my adventures on the way to St Jude—things he'd never shown the slightest interest in before. He asked about my mother, too.

"She was a very fine woman," he said. "She and Lizzie were great friends. Their mother died young, and they brought each other up—they went to school together and did everything together. I felt bad about taking Lizzie so far away." He smiled. "But it's so nice you could come and live with us, Andrew. We're going to make sure you're happy here."

He'd ask Lizzie about other islanders they'd known—years ago, before he'd cut himself off from them all. He seemed puzzled that he'd allowed himself to become such a recluse. "I just don't know what must have got into me. As soon as I'm well enough, I'm going to start taking walks down to the town with you whenever you go shopping."

She smiled at him encouragingly.

One night after dark—it was Friday—Lizzie and I were sitting by his bed and he was telling me about his hobby.

"Do you know what I look for at night, Andrew? Meteors. The skies here are so clear it's possible to see meteors no one else in the world has ever seen. The only time we're aware of them is when they flare up and disintegrate in the earth's atmosphere."

He looked at Aunt Lizzie.

"I wonder what I found so attractive in them, Lizzie. They seem such cold, lonely things." His eyes were full of affection for her. "Bring my book, Andrew," he said. "The one called *Heavenly Debris*."

I brought it from the mantelpiece and gave it to him. He opened it at a photograph of a meteor.

"See," he said. "It looks just like one of those rocks in the back garden."

At this naming of the rocks, his eyes suddenly narrowed. He was silent for a while, his eyes looking inward. The word had triggered something off.

"Are you all right?" Lizzie asked.

"I was just trying to think how I hit my head," he said. "I remember going into the garden. Then I remember pulling weeds from among the potatoes. Then everything's a blank."

That mention of the rocks was how it started. From then on, during the time I was with him on Friday night, and all through the day on Saturday, I could see he was preoccupied, racking his brain.

On Saturday afternoon I was sitting with him. Lizzie was making dinner. He'd been silent for a while, then he looked at her and smiled.

"Sorry, Lizzie. I'm not very good company for you and Andrew. I just wish I could remember. It's like something being just on the tip of your tongue. You know how annoying that is."

I wished I knew how to counsel him that it would be better not to remember. Lizzie's attempted murder had transformed him into a human being, and the three of us into the happy family I'd dreamed of.

His memory returned, completely, just after midnight on Saturday night. The sound of his voice awakened me from a deep sleep. I slipped out of bed and looked through the circulation vent in the door.

In the moonlight that illuminated the cottage, Uncle Norman, quite naked, was dragging his scarecrow body and his useless legs across the floor. Lizzie, also naked, stood watching. Her face was stone.

"Let me go," he was saying. His voice was the deep voice of the old Norman. "Let me out of here!"

He scrabbled his way to the front door and got it open. He crawled out into the yard and she followed. I waited then went out into the living-room and over to the open door. From there, I watched.

Above them, in a sky of a billion cold stars, the moon was massive, its mountain ranges quite visible. My uncle had pulled himself along the pathway as far as the gate, twisted and gnarled in the moonlight. As he fumbled with the catch, Lizzie looked around for what she wanted. She took her time. She picked up one of the jagged lumps of lava that adorned the flower-bed.

My uncle kept scrabbling desperately at the latch till the rock crashed onto his head. He fell flat with his arms over his head in a useless effort to protect himself. The rock thudded down again and again, two different types of thudding sound, sometimes against his arms, sometimes against his head. A dozen thuds; then he lay absolutely still. One more thud, and this last time, the rock seemed to stick to his head like a magnet.

My sense of horror was made even worse by the knowledge that Lizzie's blows were doing irreparable damage to my own life too.

She stood for a while looking down at him. Then she turned towards the cottage.

I tiptoed quickly back to my room, closed the door quietly and climbed into bed. I adjusted the mosquito net and lay with my back to the bedroom door. Lizzie's bare feet slapped on the floor of the living-room, my door opened and she approached the bed.

"Andrew." She said my name quietly as though not wishing to frighten me. "Andrew."

I turned and lifted the net. She was standing with a dreamy look in her eyes. Blood and some other substance dripped from her breasts and drooled down her belly. As she talked, her hands smeared the bloody mess over her face, as though she were washing herself.

"Go down to the town," she said through the awful liquid mask. "Go to Doctor Hebblethwaite. Tell him this time Norman Beck's dead."

Chapter Twenty-three

AFTER AUNT LIZZIE was arrested, I was left on my own in the cottage for the three days before her trial.

The first night, I had a nightmare. And each of the last nights I stayed in the cottage, it came back. I'd never experienced anything so awful as that nightmare before. Being already asleep, there was nowhere to escape to. In the nightmare, the earth would begin to subside, and everything would start sliding slowly downwards into a bottomless pit. I was near the edge, trying to scramble away to safety, but the ground was crumbling under me faster than I could run. I'd grab hold of a bush, but it would slowly come away in my hand. Just as I was about to plunge down, down—I'd wake up, bathed in sweat, my heart pounding.

The first day, I didn't go back to sleep. I just sat in a chair, terrified. As soon as it was light, I made some breakfast and went down to see Doctor Hebblethwaite. I waited outside The Motte till he was ready, then we walked together to the graveyard to meet the sexton. That gave him an excuse to tell me the history of the graveyard.

"One of the sextons in the nineteenth century was a weird bird by the name of Wellesley," he said. "Part of his job was making coffins. At that time the cemetery was even smaller than it is now. So to economize on space, Wellesley dissected the bodies to make them more compact and fitted them into boxes no bigger than tea-chests. The various parts hung from hooks in the lid. He made little windows on each side so the mourners could look at the deceased from various perspectives. One of my predecessors says in his notes that Wellesley's dissections were masterly. Says he got the idea from having to deal with bits and pieces of bodies after those sea battles I told you about."

He was puffing on a cigarette as we walked.

"Wellesley's wife was the only artist St Jude ever produced. She composed operas that were performed in the military chapel. From what I can gather in one of my predecessors' notes, the music was quite brilliant. Her heroines were all madwomen who wandered around the lava plain, or jumped off the mountain, singing arias. One night, Wellesley's wife woke up the whole town. She was up on the battlements, half-naked, howling at the moon." He threw half of the cigarette away and lit another. "St Jude does have the potential of driving susceptible souls mad." He said this, I'm sure, to make me feel better about Aunt Lizzie.

The graveyard was just outside the battlements. It consisted of a trench the size of a football field dynamited out of the lava and filled with imported soil. Little stone markers protruded everywhere. The dimensions of the graves were very small, but they were ten feet deep, for the coffins were lowered into them upright, to save space. Doctor Hebblethwaite said it was always a challenge to inter a body without disturbing the remains of those already buried there over the past two hundred years.

The sexton, Mr Rigg, a small, black-haired man with a nut head, came to meet us with his wife.

"Will there be any problem finding a spot?" Doctor Hebblethwaite asked.

"Martha always finds a spot," Mr Rigg said confidently, nodding to his wife, who smiled complacently. She was a curious-looking woman. Uncle Norman, during that period when he'd been restored, had told me about her. He said she was the nearest thing to a successful potato on the island. And here she was: a big, lumpy woman. Even her face had the warty look of a potato: a potato with clear blue eyes.

From the cemetery gate, Mr Rigg and Doctor Hebblethwaite and I watched her perform her craft. She walked to the oldest part of the graveyard where the convict graves were unmarked. She held in front of her a V-shaped apparatus consisting of two human arm bones, tied together at one end with a string. As she walked, she hummed in a monotone we could hear distinctly in the morning air. Whenever the bones dipped, she would stop humming, and stand as though she were listening intently. She did this several times, the last time at a corner nearest the battlements. She stood as though she were listening. I could hear only the buzzing of flies.

Then Martha Rigg looked towards us and nodded her big head.

"She's found a spot," Mr Rigg said proudly. "She always does. Now we can make arrangements."

The burial took place the next day. There was a blustery wind, not refreshing, but hot and salty and irritating to the skin.

We walked from the infirmary, where the body had been kept, to the graveyard. We were a small funeral party: Doctor Hebblethwaite, who'd brought his skinny daughter along; Rigg, the sexton, and Martha Rigg; Commissioner Bonnar, who smelt of rum; and two soldiers who pushed the infirmary wheelbarrow, draped with black velvet cloth for the occasion. I was at the back. I might also include the thousands of blowflies that followed us. They were bad-tempered at being deprived of the meal they could plainly smell through the plywood coffin. So they harassed the funeral party instead.

At the graveyard, no ritual was performed. The soldiers

lowered the plain coffin, feet first, into the narrow, deep grave. We could hear the body slide as they tilted the coffin. It slipped into the hole snugly. They quickly shovelled dirt into the space that was left on top.

I noticed the Hebblethwaite girl watching me throughout. Perhaps she thought I'd cry. But I didn't, though I was sad. I was wondering what was to become of my life now.

Chapter Twenty-four

THE TRIAL TOOK PLACE the next morning. It was held in a hall that jutted out from the battlements and had once served as the military chapel. It looked like the banquet hall of a castle and would have been pleasantly cool if the walls had been what they seemed from the outside—three-foot-thick stone. But they were only plywood, and did little to keep out the heat. Doctor Hebblethwaite sat beside me in one of the heavy wooden pews at the front, his clothes smelling of stale cigarette smoke. The air generally smelt of sweat, for the hall was packed. Small windows in the shape of crosses near the ceiling diluted the gloom slightly.

"Justice and religion," Doctor Hebblethwaite murmured to me. "Neither one of them can stand too much light."

Some of the islanders had brought their children along to see the trial. Doctor Hebblethwaite's own daughter was in the pew behind us. Aside from islanders, there were a few sailors sitting at the back: the SS *Patna* had docked the night before to pick up mail, and here was some unexpected entertainment for the crew.

At nine o'clock exactly, a soldier in a white dress uniform entered the courtroom from a door at the front and stood to attention. Commissioner Bonnar shuffled along behind him. He wore a black robe rimmed with scarlet, and a tightly curled white wig that highlighted the protruding wisps of his own red hair. He was a big-bellied man, and tall; when he sat down on the wooden chair that had been placed on a dais, his knees came up so high, his head seemed attached directly to them.

A moment later, Aunt Lizzie came through the door escorted by a soldier. She sat down on a three-legged wooden stool near the dais. She was wearing her usual black dress, but no headscarf. Her brown hair was brushed back from her forehead and coiled at the back in a tight bun.

Sitting there, so calm, she reminded me of my mother. When her eyes became used to the gloom, she saw me and smiled.

I quickly looked at the floor.

The trial was almost as brief as my uncle's funeral.

The Commissioner called the audience to order. His throaty voice echoed round the hall, hitting the corners and rushing back at him. He seemed to know how to outwit the echo; he broke up what he had to say into short phrases.

"Lizzie Beck. Please stand." His words were a bit slurred.

She stood and faced him.

"You are charged...with the murder of...your husband...Norman Beck. How do you plead?...Guilty...or Not Guilty."

The hall was completely silent; not even the boards creaked. Through those openings high in the walls, we could hear the squawk of gulls in the harbour and even the dull crash of the waves breaking on the shoal a quarter of a mile out to sea.

"Guilty." Her voice was firm.

"Do you have ... anything to say ... before I ... pass sentence?"

Lizzie waited till the last echo faded, then replied.

"Nothing."

He spoke to all of us assembled in the hall.

"In my opinion ... this was ... an act ... conceived ... by a mind ... clearly unsound...."

Then he faced Lizzie directly.

"It is the ... sentence of ... this court ... that you ... Lizzie Beck ... shall be ... transported ... at the first opportunity ... to an institution ... for the criminally ... insane ... where you shall ... be incarcerated ... for the rest of ... your natural life."

I couldn't bear to look. Around me, I heard much sighing. I just kept staring at the wooden planks on the floor beneath me. After a while, Doctor Hebblethwaite touched my arm.

"It's over," he said.

I looked up. The chair at the front was empty; so was the stool. The Commissioner was gone and Lizzie must have been taken back to her cell.

At seven o'clock the next morning, a warm, windy morning, Aunt Lizzie, bareheaded, was escorted by two soldiers in scarlet uniforms to the dock. The *Patna*, a rusty freighter, was ready to sail. I stood among a large number of islanders watching. Crew members of the *Patna* leaned on the rails watching, too. Some of the women near me in the crowd had tears in their eyes caused, perhaps, by the salt wind.

As Lizzie walked along, her face was not calm, the way it was at the trial. She was looking around frantically. The soldiers escorted her up the gangway. She kept turning and looking back. From the top, she spotted me among some of the adults. Her face lit up and her lips moved as though she were trying to say something. I couldn't make it out above the deep grumble of the engines. One of the soldiers took her by the arm and began leading her away. She wrenched her arm away and screamed so that I could hear the words above all the noise.

"Love! Andrew! Love!"

Then she was gone. After a few minutes, the soldiers re-emerged from the recesses of the ship and came down the gangway, which was then hoisted aboard. The *Patna* cast off her lines and steamed slowly away. When she reached the deep ocean, she turned northwards and was soon out of sight around the northern horn of the bay.

Chapter Twenty-five

I WALKED BACK UP the path to the cottage. About halfway, I looked back out over the ocean and I could see the *Patna* disappearing into the heat haze on the horizon. It looked like a black snail at the end of its creamy thread.

When I got to the cottage, I went inside and sat at the kitchen table. I rested my head on my hands and fell asleep from exhaustion.

"Andrew."

The hoarse voice surprised me out of sleep.

Standing at the open door, quite visible through the bead curtain, was Commissioner Bonnar.

I went over to the door.

The Commissioner was holding an old black umbrella that he used as a parasol. With his swollen belly and the fringe of red hair round his bald crown, he looked like one of those pictures of medieval monks. He had changed from his judicial robes and was dressed now in the standard white shirt and black pants.

"I won't come inside," he said. His nose was patterned with broken veins and his words were a little slurred. "Let's sit out here."

We sat together on the curved park bench under the shade of the little verandah—it was only a few yards from where Lizzie had finally killed Uncle Norman. I could smell rum from Commissioner Bonnar's breath; it comforted me, reminding me of those evenings with Harry Greene and his grog.

The smooth wooden spars of the bench bowed and creaked under the Commissioner's weight. He put the umbrella on the ground beside him.

"The reason I'm here is that I promised Lizzie Beck I'd talk to you." He sighed as though it wasn't going to be easy.

"I couldn't do much for her in a legal way. *Prima facie*, she was guilty. In fact, she was guilty twice over. But as to the *mens rea*..."

He saw I didn't understand.

"Legal jargon," he said. "I mean there was no doubt she did it. But what about her state of mind? I went to see her the night before the trial and she admitted she'd been planning to kill him for years. She said the only thing that kept her from going insane was the prospect of killing him."

He was sweating a lot and the flies were attracted to him, zooming in on his bald head. Perhaps it was the sweet smell of the rum drew them.

"Yes," he said, thinking back to the night he'd interviewed her. "That's exactly what she said—that the prospect of killing him was what kept her sane! Of course, when she said that, I knew she was crazy."

The Commissioner had gone to visit her in her cell, hoping he might find out something that would mitigate her crime. He'd stopped in at the pub and had two stiff glasses of rum beforehand.

Her cell in the old guardhouse was stifling in spite of the barred window high in the wall. She seemed glad he'd come, this small woman with the intelligent face whom he'd seen often in the town. His own wife had frequently said she was a pleasant woman, though perhaps her marriage was not a happy one. He usually took his wife's word in domestic matters.

Lizzie began to talk as soon as he sat down. She talked almost without taking a breath, as though the crime had unplugged something in her. He didn't interrupt.

"At first when I knew Andrew was coming to stay with us, I was delighted. What could be better than to have a witness—someone from my own family—to see me do it. I was thrilled at the idea.

"But then Andrew arrived, and he was such a sweet boy, and he'd been through so much. He thought he'd found a home. Even in a few days, I was beginning to weaken. The poor dear's presence was beginning to undermine me.

"I knew if I waited even a little while longer I'd never do it. So I made up my mind it had to be done right away.

"You've no idea the pleasure it gave me when I smashed the rock on Norman Beck's head the first time. It was worth all the waiting just to have that satisfaction.

"Then it turned out he wasn't dead. I hadn't hit him hard enough.

"I thought I'd been thwarted. So you can imagine my feelings when the cart came back up the path with him on it. Then, to find out he'd no memory of what I'd done and wanted to come back to me.

"For Andrew's sake, I actually did consider putting up with that man. I thought maybe I should do it to make a home for the poor boy.

"I might have been able to stand him for the boy's sake if he'd stayed the same mean, cold-hearted Norman Beck. But the blow to the head changed him. He became loving and kind again, the way he was when I first knew him.

"That only made me more furious. The way he acted reminded me of everything he'd deprived me of all those years. I could have killed him at any time, he was so helpless and trusting. But I waited. I hoped Doctor Hebblethwaite was right when he said his memory would come back in due course.

"And it did. On that last night, he was trying to make love to me for the first time in years. It was hard for him because of his paralysis. He managed to climb on top of me. He was just in the middle of telling me how much he loved me when everything came back to him. In the moonlight I could see what a change came over him. His face turned ten years older again. He remembered everything.

"He tumbled off me onto the floor. He tried to crawl away. He knew what a terrible mistake he'd made. That was what I'd been waiting for. I wanted him to know what was happening. Then I killed him properly."

Now, sitting on the verandah, the Commissioner shook his head as he told me all this. Except for the buzz of insects around his head, we sat for a while in complete silence. We might have been the only human inhabitants of this earth. He was silent for such a long time, I spoke.

"Why did she want to kill him?" I asked. I didn't understand that at all.

"Your question was my question," the Commissioner said. He pulled out a red handkerchief and wiped the sweat from his face. "I don't suppose there's anything to drink inside?" he asked. "I don't suppose your uncle kept some rum?"

I told him neither of them ever drank.

"Really," he said. He didn't sound surprised.

The heat in the cell was oppressive, and the rum made him sweat profusely.

"But why? Why did you kill him?" he asked Lizzie Beck.

"I used to love him so much," Lizzie said. "When he was offered the post in this remote place, I agreed. I'd have done anything for him, because I loved him. And he loved me. But then he changed. After we'd been here a while, he became more cold and distant. He cut himself off from me and from all the people in the town. All he was interested in was his garden and his telescope.

"I put up with it for a long time, but I was so unhappy, I couldn't bear it. I thought maybe I'd done something wrong.

"One day I asked him what was the matter. I asked him if he didn't love me any more. 'Love?' he said. 'What a load of codswallop.' And he laughed at me.

"Can you imagine how I felt when he told me that? It shrivelled up my heart, because I knew he meant it. All those years for nothing! The best years of my life for nothing! That's when I made up my mind to kill him. I could think of nothing else. I was obsessed with the idea. I saw him dead in everything I looked at. A kitchen knife wasn't a kitchen knife any more, but a dagger to stab him with. Whenever I saw a tree, it wasn't so much a tree, as a gallows with him hanging from it."

The Commissioner couldn't believe what he was hearing.

"Lizzie, Lizzie. Hold on a minute! You can't be serious," he said. "You can't kill a man for not loving you. That's not a good enough reason for killing anyone. If that were allowed, half the world would be busy killing the other half."

She spoke slowly and precisely.

"And why shouldn't they?" she said. "It's the worst crime of all."

The Commissioner suddenly felt worn out. The heat was suffocating and he badly wanted a drink. He asked his final question.

"Aren't you sorry now for what you did? If you were to show some sign of remorse, I'm sure I might be able to do something in your favour."

"Remorse!" she said, looking at him with astonishment. "None whatsoever. I only wish they could bring him back to life so I could kill him again."

I waved away the flies. The smell of the rum was making me feel a little queasy.

"Well," the Commissioner said. "That's about it. My job is to uphold the law. Your aunt didn't leave me any option. She was like a woman with two heads, the way she went from love to hatred." He eased himself up from the bench, his shirt front swelling out like a ship about to set sail. "She was crying when I left. She said the only thing she was sorry about was that you'd been caught in the middle of it all. She hoped you'd understand she had to do it." He winced up at the sun. "I'd better be on my way." He looked at me. "You can stay here tonight. But tomorrow morning, the cottage has to be destroyed. It's the custom. I'll find another place for you to live, so just have your things ready to go."

He opened his umbrella, shook hands with me and began his slow walk back to the town. For a long time after, my hand smelt of rum.

That night, I packed my suitcase. I searched the cottage for a keepsake, but could find little to remind me of Lizzie.

I realized then how much Uncle Norman had dominated the house. The only adornments on the walls were faded charts of various types of vegetables, and one skyscape complete with stars and cosmic mists.

In the bottom drawer of Lizzie's dresser I found a framed photograph, face down. It was the same as the one in Stroven—of my mother and father standing in the snow. I was going to take it as a souvenir. Then I decided not to. I think I believed it might somehow have been contaminated by the awful thing that happened in this house.

My last sleep in the cottage was not a pleasant one. I tossed and turned. I kept thinking someone was watching me. That scared me so much, I got up and looked around, even outside. But there was nothing. Then, when I did get to sleep, I had an awful nightmare. That column of women was marching towards me, led by my Aunt Lizzie, her face bathed in Uncle Norman's blood, smiling savagely and holding a rock as though I was to be her next victim. I tried to run away, but I must have been in quicksand, for the harder I ran, the more I sank into it, and when I turned she was raising the rock to strike.

I was only too happy to wake up, my heart thumping. I stayed awake till morning came and waited at the front door. At eight o'clock, I saw two figures coming up the path: soldiers, pushing a cart with something on it. Nearer I could see it was a drum of fuel.

They arrived and set about their work without a word. I started on down to the town with my suitcase. About halfway, I looked back. The cottage was ablaze. The flame was a startling red against the black backdrop of the mountain.

As for Aunt Lizzie: neither I nor anyone else from the Island of St Jude ever saw her again. Commissioner Bonnar received a radio message from the *Patna* five days out. A sailor who'd been assigned to bring Lizzie her breakfast unlocked the door and found the cabin empty. No one would have believed a woman her size could squeeze through the narrow porthole; and it must have been difficult, for the metal frame was smeared with blood. The ship reversed course and searched for the entire morning over the deepest ocean trench. At one point, they saw a school of sharks milling around, but no trace of Lizzie. The Captain issued rifles to the crew, and they spent an hour killing as many sharks as they could. Then they continued on their voyage.

Part Four

TEMPEST

And the teachers shall instruct them in silence
Louise Glück

Chapter Twenty-six

"WHEN WE'RE YOUNG we feel we have the freedom to make a million choices." Harry Greene had said this to me one night as we stood at the rails on the SS *Cumnock*. "We're sure we can do anything we want—that we're unique. But when we're older and we look back, our lives don't seem to have worked out all that differently from anyone else's. God's rope! 'Tis as though it's all laid out in advance and predictable. We begin to wonder if we have any real choices at all."

I thought I understood what he meant.

"Is that how you feel, Harry?" I said.

"Sometimes I do," he said. "Yes, sometimes I do."

He sounded sad when he said this. But after what I'd been through, I'd have been happy to believe my life would be predictable and ordinary, like everyone else's.

So when the years following the death of Uncle Norman and Lizzie turned out to be settled and normal, I was thankful. Though on the morning of the burning of the cottage, when I went to the Commissioner's Residence, I was full of anxiety. The Commissioner greeted me at the door and said someone was waiting to see me. We went into the lounge and a man stood up: a lean man with the windburnt face of a fisherman. He had the lightest of light blue eyes.

"This is Mr Chapman," the Commissioner said. "I'll leave you two to talk things over." And he left us alone in the lounge. The strong smell of rum faded a little when he was gone.

Mr Chapman and I stood in silence: I was uncomfortable, and he seemed just as uncomfortable. Eventually, he cleared his throat and spoke.

"So you're all right now, are you?"

I supposed I must be.

"Yes, I think so," I said.

He nodded, and I noticed then how he didn't look at me directly. His eyes would swing towards me, settle on my face for a brief moment, then swing past, like a lighthouse beam. Then back again, and on, and on. But in those instants he looked directly at me, his glance seemed to me very astute.

We stood quietly like this for the longest time. Then he put his hands in his trouser pockets and went awkwardly over to the bay window that looked out across the street to the sea. He began whistling, a tuneless sort of whistle, as if to say: Look, I'm so at ease, I'm whistling. Then he paced back and forth on the long polished floor of the reception lounge. He had a seaman's awkward walk on land.

All at once, he seemed to think of something, and stopped. His eyes were triumphant and I thought he was going to speak. Instead, he reached into his shirt pocket and pulled out an old pipe, knocked out the dross into the fireplace, stuffed some fresh tobacco in, and lit it. Whenever his eyes settled on me now through clouds of smoke, they seemed to be saying: I've done my part, now it's up to you.

I'd never met a grown-up this shy, and I wanted to help out. But I just couldn't think of anything to say. After a while, the room was full of the silence and the stink of his pipe smoke. At last, he shook out his pipe decisively into the empty fireplace and spoke.

"Well, that's enough talking," he said. "We'll go and see Mrs Chapman and the boys." Then his eyes swung faster than ever, and he seemed alarmed at the thought that perhaps he'd gone too far: "I mean, shall we?"

Just then, as though he'd been listening outside the door, the Commissioner came back into the lounge, bringing the smell of fresh rum in with him.

"Everything settled?" he said to Mr Chapman.

Mr Chapman nodded, his eyes sweeping past each of us.

"Good. Well, now you can get on with it," said the Commissioner.

Mr Chapman and I went out together into the stunning midday heat.

We walked north along the main street till we came to the area where the street ended up against the battlements. We stopped at a house I suspected would be the Chapmans': the most odd-looking house of all of them. It looked slightly oval, as though it had been stepped on and slightly squashed. Mr Chapman was more at ease now that he was near home. He said his grandfather had built the house, using the bevelled ribs and clinker boards from the hull of an old sailing ship that had beached in a storm a hundred years ago. On one side of the roof was a widow's walk: a small platform with a railing. From above the front door, the figurehead of the old ship protruded—it was of a carved mermaid, her upper body naked, her eyes blank, all of her badly in need of a coat of paint.

Mr Chapman threw the front door open and beckoned me inside. As I stepped in, a mottled Siamese cat let out a howl and raced away into another room. The house was quite dark, for the windows were small. A flickering hurricane lamp hung from the ceiling, showing the bulge of the walls, which were adorned with nets and hand-harpoons. What with the ribbed walls and the smell of fish, it was like being inside the belly of a sea monster.

A small woman drying her hands on an apron came out of the room where the cat had run. She was on the plump side, and her soft face had an anxious frown on it. She took my hand and looked into my face.

"You poor boy," she said. "Do you think you'll be happy with us?" she said. She saw my confusion.

"Didn't you ask him yet?" she said to Mr Chapman.

His eyes, which had been fairly settled, now began swinging around wildly, avoiding hers and mine. She shook her head in disbelief.

"What a man," she said to me. "He's completely hopeless. No wonder I have headaches." Then she made me sit down on a wooden rocker, and she sat opposite. Mr Chapman stood by the little window.

"Andrew," said Mrs Chapman. "I knew your Aunt Lizzie and I always liked her. Who knows what drives people to do the things they do? Anyway, the point is: how would you like to live with us? At least for now. You can take your time and have a look at us. Then it's up to you if you want to stay."

She seemed so kind and frowned anxiously. In fact, she was always frowning, as though she suffered from a constant, minor pain.

"Yes, I'd like to," I said.

She smiled a big smile and for a moment her frown was gone. Even Mr Chapman was smiling, though when he saw me looking towards him, his eyes began swinging around.

At that moment, in spite of everything that had happened to me, I had a notion I might have found a safe place in a dangerous world. At last.

Later that afternoon, Mr Chapman went to the Commissioner's for my suitcase and Mrs Chapman led me up the erratic staircase to my bedroom. She left me to look around while she went back to the kitchen to get on with making her fish stew for dinner. I had barely checked the room out when heavy feet pounded up the stairs and there was a rapping at my door.

I took a deep breath and opened it to two boys I knew must be the Chapmans. They were older than I, perhaps by three years, and wore the island clothing.

"I'm John," said the bigger boy, "and he's Jim. My mother says you're staying with us." They were ugly boys. John was taller even than his father, and strong looking. He had the same spotty face as his brother, Jim, but bristly black hair sprouted among the pimples.

The two boys looked me over for a moment. Each of them had light blue eyes.

"Come on outside," said John.

The two ran downstairs and I trailed after them, and out through the front door into the hot street. They signalled me to follow and trotted along to a nearby house. John went to the front door.

"Smiley!" he shouted.

A lanky boy about their own age came out.

"This is our new brother," John said.

They gave the boy a few seconds to look me over. Then off they ran with me following to another house where we went through the same ritual. Then to another house, and another. The children, mainly boys, would come out and look me over. Sometimes, I would see girls, or grown-ups peering out the window.

In this way, the Chapman boys introduced me to many of the schoolchildren on St Jude. Along the way, they showed me their favourite places: especially the end of the pier, where they would go fishing for the elegant finger-fish. They pointed out the direction of the cove they used for swimming, just inside the breakers. They warned me never to be enticed outside the breakers into the deep water where hammerhead sharks lurked.

"Sharks never sleep, you know," said John Chapman.

Our final stop on the way back was at The Motte. This time, John didn't shout, but knocked on the door politely. The little girl with the solemn face opened it.

"This is our new brother," John said.

She stared at me. Then tall, thin Mrs Hebblethwaite appeared behind her.

"Go back inside," she said to the girl. She looked angry—maybe even a little afraid.

"What do you want?" she asked John.

"This is our new brother," he said.

"I've seen all I ever want to see of him," she said and slammed the door shut in our faces.

John and Jim Chapman stood for a moment, then they both stuck out their tongues at the wooden door. They were as frightening to look at as a pair of pimply-faced gargoyles. All of a sudden, I liked them.

At dinner that first night at the Chapmans', Mrs Chapman told me the family secret: that her husband should never have been a fisherman.

"He can't bear to eat any of the fish he catches himself," she said. She had to go down to the pier each day when the boats came back and exchange his catch for someone else's.

"No wonder I have headaches," she said.

The boys had obviously heard this before, and they laughed. And even Mr Chapman, though his eyes swung around wildly as she told me about his weakness, didn't seem too upset. I had the impression the two of them were fond of each other and of their boys.

And now of me too, I hoped.

But that Siamese cat I'd seen when I arrived wasn't so soft-hearted. Sophie was her name, and she was always watching me with her cold cat eyes. She never failed to hiss if Mrs Chapman came too close to me, even to dish out my fish stew.

"Bad cat, Sophie!" Mrs Chapman said, but it had no effect. The cat just stood there on the floor near my chair, hissing and looking coldly at me as if she detected something in me the others were too innocent to see.

Chapter Twenty-seven

I BEGAN ATTENDING the one-room school in the battlements and enjoyed it just as much as I did in Stroven. Though, once in a while, something would happen to disturb my contentment.

The annual hiking expedition to the mountain took place after I'd been at school for a month. Twenty of us started out at nine in the morning led by our teacher, Moses Atkinson. He was a stringy man with long white hair and a grey beard that was just as long. His eyes weren't so good, and he wore pebble glasses in wire frames. He'd been the teacher at St Jude for almost forty years.

The morning was warm as usual, and as we marched, the needle-flies accompanied us in brigades to taste the fresh blood of children. We went through the town, past the gate and up the path to the mountain: I hadn't been that way since the burning of the cottage. We'd stop every so often while Moses Atkinson, in his quavering voice, pointed out lava projections, the various cacti and other plants that were able to survive the rigours of the terrain.

I felt more and more uncomfortable as we came near the site of the cottage. Some of the boys were whispering and glancing at me. Then John Chapman came and walked beside me, and after that no one dared to look at me.

Moses Atkinson seemed uncomfortable too, and kept drawing attention to plants and land formations on the seaward side. But I couldn't help looking at the ruins of the cottage. The roof had fallen in, but the walls were still standing, blackened by the fire. Everything wooden—doors, windows, floors—was gone. Already, weeds were sprouting all around the house; the little flower garden at the front was overgrown. At the back, monstrous potato plants with evil green leaves had thrust themselves up out of the imported soil.

We went round the shoulder of the mountain where we could no longer see the cottage. Now we were on the lower slopes and the path rose quite steeply. Moses Atkinson, who always wanted to be in front, was hobbling and wheezing loudly as we climbed.

"Be careful now," he called out. "There are snakes up here."

And sure enough, we could all see a small black snake with gleaming yellow eyes and flicking tongue lying on the path. It quickly slithered away.

"They lie out here in the mornings to soak up the sun," said Moses Atkinson. "They do it instinctively."

"What does instinctively mean?" one of the girls asked. It was Maria Hebblethwaite.

"It means something you're born with," said Moses

Atkinson. "Now take these snakes, for example. They don't have to learn anything from experience. They're born already knowing everything they need to know."

The sun caught his pebble glasses as he said this, and I could have sworn he was looking directly at me.

We kept climbing. The path zigzagged up the mountain and ended at a little plateau near the one-thousand-foot mark. From there, we looked down over the island. All chatter ceased. I suppose the others were thinking what I was thinking: that we were tiny specks on a mountain on an island that was a speck in an ocean in a planet that was nothing but a speck in the universe.

I did all the things the other St Jude children did, including going to the dock each month to welcome incoming freighters. At first, I hoped one day the *Cumnock* might appear. But it never did. I couldn't help hoping for even a letter from Harry Greene. It never came.

The Chapman boys loved swimming. During my first weekend with the family, they took me to meet a group of other boys at the swimming cove they'd shown me. I'd never learnt how to swim: the ponds around Stroven were much too cold. I was excited at the prospect. It was only when, along with the others, I peeled off my trousers and shirt that I remembered the purple stain. All the boys stared at it, some giggling, some looking disgusted. The Chapman boys were surprised too, for they'd never seen the mark before. But John came to my defence.

"What do you think you're staring at?" he said to the others. Naked, he looked like a man, with his muscles, and his body all hairy even though he was only fifteen. I was so embarrassed, I picked up my shirt to put it back on.

"Keep it off, Andrew," said John Chapman. "That mark will scare the sharks away!" He laughed, and the others began to laugh. And that was that. We all ran into the warm water.

In all the rest of my time on St Jude, only one person ever made a comment on the mark on my chest.

Three years passed. John and Jim Chapman both left school and worked on Mr Chapman's boat. I was fourteen, and a stranger would have taken me for a typical island boy: I wore the black pants, the white shirt, the black boots; my face was burnt by the sun. I spoke with the island twang. During those three years, I was happier than I could ever have believed. I had a home, I was part of a real family.

Yet, in spite of everything, I was still visited occasionally by that awful nightmare: I'd be standing at the edge of a great pit and the ground would start to crumble away beneath my feet. No matter how hard I tried to run away, I'd slip backwards. I'd feel myself slipping downwards, downwards, into a chasm so black I couldn't see the bottom. Or sometimes, in the nightmare, I'd be standing at the edge of the pit, quite secure; then I'd hear footsteps running at me from behind and someone would try to push me over the edge. I'd wake up, sweating, and I'd lie there listening to the rigging of the boats on the beach jangling in the night wind. I'd feel such a sense of dread I couldn't get back to sleep, even if I were brave enough to risk the nightmare again.

Near the end of spring in my third year on St Jude, something happened that made that awful feeling seem prophetic.

Chapter Twenty-eight

AT SCHOOL, I WAS becoming very friendly with Maria Hebblethwaite. Our friendship began innocently enough. Like me, she loved school and we'd talk about our homework. She was still a thin, solemn girl with a long face. Her fair hair hung well below her headscarf.

Doctor Hebblethwaite was always kind to me. He had a good collection of books, with encyclopedias and other reference works, in the room he called his library. It was beside his surgery on the ground floor. He encouraged Maria to bring me there to study. The room reminded me a little of Harry Greene's cabin, though it wasn't quite so congested.

Maria's mother disliked me and made no attempt to hide it. If she answered the door when I came to study, she'd let me in without a word. But one night when I knocked on the door, she opened it and smiled—or, at least, tried to smile. That was a surprise.

"Maria's finishing her dinner. She'll be a few minutes yet," she said. "Go on into the library."

I went in and sat at the work table. A book was lying open, face down—a practice Doctor Hebblethwaite warned us against: he said it was bad for books. I was even more surprised when I saw the title: *The Anatomy of Melancholy*. That was the difficult book I'd seen in Harry Greene's cabin all those years ago: the one whose author had hanged himself. I picked it up and looked at the pages where it was lying open. Most of them had been underlined—another practice Doctor Hebblethwaite disapproved of. I looked at the pages and was able to understand them. Either this was a more modern text than the one Harry had, or I was a better reader. At the top of the first page, the heading was: "Symptoms of Love." I began reading.

> Love is blind, as the saying is. Every lover admires his mistress though she be very deformed of her self, ill-favoured, wrinkled, pimpled, pale, red, yellow, tanned, tallow-faced, have a swollen Juggler's platter-face, or a thin, lean, chitty-face, have clouds in her face, be crooked, dry, bald, goggle-eyed, blear-eyed, or with staring eyes, she looks like a squeezed cat, hold her head still awry, heavy, dull, hollow-eyed, black or yellow about the eyes, or squint-eyed, sparrow-mouthed, Persian hook-nosed, have a sharp Pox nose, a red nose, great nose, snub nose, with wide nostrils, a nose like a promontory, gubber-tushed, rotten teeth, black, uneven, brown teeth, beetle-browed, a Witch's beard, her breath stink all over the room, her nose drip winter and summer, with a pouch under her chin, with a long crane's neck, which stands awry too, with hanging breasts, her dugs like two double jugs, or else no dugs, in the other extreme, bloody-fallen fingers, long unpared nails, scabbard hands and wrists, a tanned skin, a rotten carcass, crooked back, she stoops and is lame, splay-footed, as slender in the middle as a Cow in the waist, gouty legs, her ankles hang over her shoes, her feet stink, she breeds lice, a mere changeling, a very monster, or an oaf, imperfect, her whole complexion savours, an harsh voice, vile gait, a vast virago, an ugly tit, a slug, a fat fustilugs, a truss, a long lean rawbone, a skeleton; and to thy judgement looks like a merd in a lantern, whom thou couldst not fancy for a world, but hatest, loathest, and wouldst have spit in her face, or blow thy nose in her bosom, the very antidote of love to another man, a dowdy, a slut, a

> scold, a nasty, rank, rammy, filthy, beastly quean, obscene, base, beggarly, rude, foolish, untaught, peevish, if he love her once, he admires her for all this, he takes no notice of any such error or imperfection of body or mind, he had rather have her than any woman in the world.

There was more of this: page after page—it should have been revolting but it was funny. When Maria came in after her dinner, I showed her the passage, and she seemed to find it funny too.

I wondered if Mrs Hebblethwaite was the one who'd left the book out so that I'd read it; if she thought it might disgust me with women, and especially with her daughter.

If so, it certainly didn't do what it was meant to.

Although, a few nights later I did pay the price for reading it: in a nightmare. I was watching one of those processions of the Stroven women from high above: in a tower, perhaps. As they came nearer, clothed all in black, chanting some kind of dirge, they looked up towards me. The familiar faces—even my mother, even Aunt Lizzie—were now so deformed, they paralysed me with horror. I woke up, sweating. I understood that the words from the book had taken on flesh and blood; at least, the flesh and blood of a nightmare.

But, as I say, if it was Mrs Hebblethwaite who left the book out, and if it was her purpose to disgust me with her daughter, it didn't work. Nauseating though the words were, and frightening though the nightmare was, my body's urges were too strong.

So, at the end of March, my friendship with Maria suddenly found itself on the fringes of a murky, throbbing area—and we became a little self-conscious with each other.

On the last Friday of the month, school stopped early, just after midday. Instead of going straight home as we'd always done, Maria asked me if I'd like to go for a walk with her. I agreed.

We set out together southwards along the shore, close together but not holding hands. Our walk was silent and purposeful though we had to step carefully: the black sands of the beach were infested with millions of tiny crabs that looked like black spiders. After a while we had to take off our socks and shoes to wade across tidal pools and little inlets that separated beach from beach. At last, we reached our destination: a cove a mile south of the town, completely hidden by the headland.

We looked at each other, then rushed together, flattening as much body as was possible against each other, tongues, hands everywhere. We dragged off clothing, startled at the marvellous whiteness of flesh and unexpected hair under the bright sun.

I was painfully conscious of the stain on my chest, but she seemed to take no notice of it.

Lying on our clothes spread over the black sand, we tried to make love. Our first effort was technically not very successful, but it was not a disappointment. We sobbed at the unbearable delight of it. And we were determined learners, with the whole afternoon before us. We tried again, and this time, got the basics right. We began to explore other possibilities. Probing tongues and fingers produced ecstasies we'd never dreamt of.

We lay tangled together, recuperating.

"I love you," I said again and again.

"I love you too," she said. She traced the purple stain on my chest with her fingers. She kissed the stain. "I love you," she said.

That got us started again. By three o'clock, when we

eventually walked back to the town, we'd progressed from being apprentices to fairly skilled practitioners. We were complacent. We were sure that to know another's body so intimately was to know all there is to know.

Who could blame us, after such revelations, for not noticing certain other signs that day: that the afternoon sun had disappeared; that the horizon had a strange, violet tint; that the mountain was like a single table leg holding up the sky?

Chapter Twenty-nine

BUT EVERYONE ELSE on the island had noticed.

That night, the Chapmans talked about it after dinner. Mr Chapman lit up his pipe; so did John and Jim now that they were fishermen, though Jim didn't seem quite as keen on his.

"I've never seen the skies like this," Mr Chapman said. At times, the flickering light of the hurricane lamp made his eyes appear quite steady.

"The fish seem to like it," said John. "We've never caught so many: you'd swear they wanted to be caught." He hadn't changed much since his schooldays. He was big, pimpled, just as friendly as ever, and was soon to be married to Serena Jones who worked in the Post Office. He puffed his pipe and looked at me. "It's a bit of a nuisance for you, eh, Andrew?"

I began to feel uncomfortable. I was glad of the poor lighting for I knew Mrs Chapman was watching me anxiously.

"I hear you've been walking down the beach after school," John said.

"I think I'll go upstairs," I said. "I'm really tired."

"Oh, I wonder why?" John said.

I quickly left the table and went up to my room. As I closed my door, I could hear quiet laughter from downstairs.

I didn't see Maria all of that blustery weekend. But on Monday after school we set out for our cove, as we'd planned. The wind was now steady and strong, making white-capped stairways up the faces of the ocean swells. The beach was so crowded with little black crabs they could barely part in time to allow us past. When we arrived at the cove we threw our clothes on top of them and crushed, I suppose, thousands in the name of love.

Tuesday was more difficult as we headed for the cove again. The wind at our backs was so severe, it pushed us along as though we were running and it whipped up a yellow-grey froth that almost wiped out the distinction between ocean and beach. At our cove, the sand was too wet. So, standing upright, pressed against the lava boulders, Maria and I discovered other varieties of love-making. Walking back to the town, we had to lean into the wind and fight for breath.

I got home just as Mr Chapman was leaving the house.

"Do you want to come with me?" he asked. "The Commissioner's called a meeting about the weather. The boys have already gone."

I hesitated, and his eyes strobed to and fro.

"It's at the Inn," he said. "You can have a pint of beer."

How could I refuse? I'd never been inside the St Jude Inn, and the smell of the beer as I passed it always reminded me of Stroven.

The Inn was crowded, but John shouted to us as we came in: he and Jim had kept space for us to stand, near the bar. The Inn was really just one big room, gloomy because the windows were painted green and the walls were covered in dark brown panelling. Hurricane lamps hung from long wooden beams. The pipe smoke was so thick, it stung my eyes. The elevated bar had above it an imported stag's head that was missing an antler. Two bartenders were pouring pints of beer as fast as they could before the meeting began. We soon had ours.

"Cheers!" John said. The Chapmans all drank deeply, then looked at me as I took my first-ever sip of beer.

I didn't like it. It tasted sour and warm. I couldn't believe anyone could find any pleasure in drinking such awful stuff. But I smiled at them, as though I liked it.

"You should see the look on your face," John said.

Glasses hammered on the tables: The Commissioner had arrived and stood behind the bar so that everyone could see him. The Inn became silent.

"Thank you all for coming," he said. His voice was a little slurred: there was a glass of rum in front of him on the bar. The noise of the wind penetrated the cracks in the Inn, so he had to speak loudly. "I had a radio message this morning that gives me some concern. As is obvious to us all, there's a major storm out there." He pointed vaguely in the direction of the ocean. "Unfortunately, it appears we're right in its path. I don't want to alarm you too much, but I think we ought to start taking some safety measures. I'd be happy to hear any suggestions you might wish to make."

This invitation brought on a general discussion about storms in the past. But only one thing seemed to be agreed upon, and was mentioned several times: that it was always wise to board up windows, so that they wouldn't be smashed by the wind.

Then Jack Harvey, one of the oldest fishermen, spoke.

"My wife wants to know, is it still safe to take the boats out? Or should we stay ashore till it's blown over?" he asked.

That started another discussion, with most of the younger fishermen saying they'd been out in much worse weather than this. Eventually, it was agreed that the weather itself would dictate what to do.

Mr Rigg, the sexton, raised his hand.

"You all know how my Martha can see things others can't," he said. He was so proud of her, no one quibbled. "She's very worried about this storm. She says she senses something evil about it. She thinks it would be best for everyone to move into the battlements. Or maybe even leave the town and head for the mountain. That's what she thinks."

No one spoke against him, but a lot of the men were smiling. And when Moses Atkinson said, in his quavering voice, that he thought everyone should heed Martha Rigg's advice, John Chapman winked at me and there was general winking. Even Mr Chapman's eyes, swinging back and forth, seemed to wink once or twice.

The Commissioner had the last word.

"Thanks to all of you who've contributed to the discussion. Mr Rigg, please give our thanks to Martha. And thanks to you too, Mr Atkinson: we've all valued your advice over the years." That caused general snickering. "I'll keep you all posted as I hear reports on the radio," said the Commissioner. "Now, let's have a drink to close the meeting." He held out his glass to the bartender for another rum.

"Andrew looks like he could use another beer," John said to Mr Chapman, laughing. For my pint was untouched since that first sip.

Next morning, Wednesday, the sea was so rough the boats couldn't go out, even though some of the younger fishermen tried. The wind was much stronger: sheets of plywood were flapping noisily on many of the houses, and looked as though they were ready to tear away. Walking to school was so hard some of the very small children were blown off their feet. In school, we'd barely sat down when the Commissioner came in. He spoke quietly to Moses Atkinson, then turned to us.

"Now girls and boys, I don't want to alarm you. But I've had a radio message that isn't good." The smell of rum was spreading around the room. "So I'd like everyone to go straight home again, and this time, stay inside. School won't open again till the worst of the storm is over."

Maria and I walked home together with the wind in our faces. It was so fierce now, we could barely talk: my lips were flattened against my teeth.

When we got near The Motte, I saw her mother watching us from the window.

"I suppose we won't be able to meet till the storm's over." I had to shout at Maria over the noise of the wind. "But from our house, I can see the top floor of The Motte. If you can come to the window, we can still wave to each other." That sounded very romantic.

"Oh, yes," she said.

"I'll wave to you at three o'clock tomorrow, and every day at three till the storm's over," I said. The door opened, and Mrs Hebblethwaite stood looking at us.

"Come inside," she called to Maria. "You. Just go away!" she said to me. From the way she looked at me, I knew I'd never be able to go far enough away to please her.

Chapter Thirty

WHEN I GOT HOME, Mr Chapman and the boys and I staggered down to the beach where his boat was drawn up. We had to wear coveralls and balaclavas, for the wind was whipping up the sand on the beach so violently, it could scrape the skin off exposed flesh. We unstepped the mast of Mr Chapman's boat, then we helped some of the other fishermen, so that by noon all of the masts had been unstepped and the boats were drawn up high on the beach, like pairs of shoes.

At three o'clock, I climbed up into the attic and went through the door onto the widow's walk. I looked towards The Motte, and there was Maria at the window of the top floor. We waved and waved, and blew kisses till she disappeared. I longed for the storm to end.

On Thursday, the rain began: a fine warm rain that wouldn't have been too unpleasant but for the wind. We boarded up the windows after breakfast, then Mr Chapman went to a special meeting at the Commissioner's Residence. When he came back, he said that according to the most recent radio report the centre of the storm was heading directly for St Jude. Some of the islanders, apparently, didn't trust their houses and were moving into the battlements. One or two families were following Martha Rigg's advice and were leaving the town altogether and heading for the mountain.

"What about the Riggs? Are they taking Martha's advice?" John wanted to know.

"No," said Mr Chapman. "They have to stay and look after the graveyard."

Whether he meant that to be funny or not, we all laughed.

I went up to the widow's walk at three o'clock to wave to Maria; but it was no good. All the windows of The Motte were boarded over. I waved anyway. I kept myself busy reading, or playing card games with the boys. As night came on, the hurricane lamps swayed and the thick wooden beams of the house groaned the way they must have once in stormy seas.

By Friday morning, the wind was a constant howl, joined now by the clatter of the rain, which was no longer fine, but heavy and hard. At breakfast, I noticed how Mr Chapman, who would normally have regarded this sitting ashore watching rough weather as a luxury, looked worried. For at times, the ground beneath us seemed to rumble, as though the island were shifting on its moorings. Mrs Chapman had stayed in bed with one of her headaches. Sophie, the Siamese, became my friend at long last. She tried to sit in my lap, or she wanted to lie in my bed: as though she now felt safer with me than with the others.

At noon, the wind was screeching and the rain hammering the house. Through the spaces between the boards over the windows, we couldn't see much, the rain was so heavy.

Then, at precisely two o'clock, the awful howling of the wind let up. The rain tapered off. I'd been lying on my bed reading, with Sophie beside me, when the wind died. So I got up and climbed the ladder to the attic. I lifted the heavy wooden bar from the door to the widow's walk, pushed it ajar and went outside onto the platform.

I might have been standing in some huge cathedral with black columns all around, and a blue stained-glass dome above.

I looked around the town and was shocked at what the storm had already done. The roofs of every house in sight, including our own, had been partly ripped away. So many panels of plywood siding were missing from the buildings, they looked as though it was a deliberate, patchwork design. What was even more shocking was the way the land had been scoured. There were no trees, no gardens, no lawns, no soil, no outhouses, no garden sheds—only the black lava base. The Motte and the battlements seemed to have held up well. But the main street was a shallow river. The flagstaff of the Commissioner's house was snapped, and his entire house seemed a little tilted to the west. As for the beach, it had been gouged away by the waves. Not a fishing boat was to be seen. The concrete dock was almost entirely crumbled.

I'd only been on the widow's walk a few minutes when I heard a new noise—a dull roar away to the east. At first, I couldn't see anything that might be causing the sound. It seemed to come from the horizon where leaden sea and leaden clouds were welded together. Then I saw that the weld was expanding, becoming thicker. The ocean itself seemed to be swelling with the sound.

Suddenly the blue vault above me was snuffed out and the wind picked up so fiercely I had to grab the taffrail of the widow's walk. That dull roar to the east had become louder and the line at the horizon was already a black ribbon. Soon it was a low, thick wall. The wind seemed to be trying to outrun it, howling with fright.

Now I understood exactly what was coming: that black wall was the hump of an enormous wave rushing upon the Island of St Jude.

I turned to open the door of the attic to warn the Chapmans, but the wind had pinned it shut. I pulled till the doorknob came away in my hand. I thumped on it with my fists, I shouted at the top of my voice. But no one knew I was out there, and I don't believe they could have heard me above the noise of the storm, and the squealing of the house timbers.

The rain was now battering me with numberless fists. I felt a severe pain in my temple, as though my head would burst. There was a popping and snapping from all around. The window boards, the windows themselves, the doors, then the walls were bursting. Behind me, the attic door splintered. I still couldn't go inside, for nails were flying everywhere, popping out of the walls like an ambush. Then I felt the house under me gradually beginning to sink as though it were a balloon with a slow leak.

The whole world was sinking.

I had my back to the taffrail, holding onto it as the house disintegrated, when I was struck from behind, immersed, choking in the green belly of the wave, then bursting through its thick membrane into the screeching and the chaos. My hand still clung to the taffrail and the little platform was still under my feet.

But the platform was no longer attached to the Chapmans' house. That much I knew, though it wasn't easy to see: the time must have been only three o'clock, but it was like night. The widow's walk had become a raft, swept along on top of the wave in the direction of the mountain. I could just barely see its vast outline in the dark. I hoped for a while the platform might be cast up on its slope and me with it. But as we came nearer, the ocean divided around it, and my raft hurtled past the south side. In the dim light I could make out some of the debris whirling along beside me: jagged timber, armchairs, sheets of plywood. I saw bodies, face down, their clothes torn from them. I saw a long wooden box with its lid open, half full of water. It was an empty coffin.

Just before dusk the next day, the bridge lookout of the SS *Nellie*, which had been hove-to during the worst hours, saw a peculiar piece of jetsam through his binoculars: a wooden platform and, his arm tied to a railing by a pair of suspenders, a boy. Me. The storm had outrun me or had worn itself out.

The *Nellie* picked me up and I slept in a dry bunk for twelve hours. When I woke, it was a sunny morning, and Mount St Jude was rising in the distance.

At noon, the ship anchored offshore and a rescue party landed with me as guide.

Where the town of St Jude had been, there was now nothing—it had vanished like the contents of a plate tipped into the ocean. The battlements were gone, even the lava boulders they were built on had been rolled away by the force of the wave. The Chapman house, like the other houses, had disappeared. All that remained of it and its neighbours were the ends of beams protruding like broken toothpicks from holes chiselled in the lava.

I told the officer in charge of the search there might be survivors on the mountain. I hoped, though I knew it was impossible, that we'd find the Chapmans there, safe and sound. We went past the place where the graveyard had been. It had been scooped out, leaving a rectangular hole the size of a football field. Further up, we passed the site of Aunt Lizzie's cottage. There was no trace of it or the garden. The scene of the crime had been wiped clean.

As we reached the mountain itself, we could see debris from the wave, about fifty feet up. Then we heard voices shouting down to us. Out of a thicket, the survivors appeared: half a dozen children and adults. But the Chapmans weren't among them. A moment later, the rest of the survivors stumbled towards us and I could hardly believe my eyes: the first of them was Doctor Hebblethwaite, a cigarette dangling from his mouth. Behind him came his wife. And after her, Maria!

I called out to her, and asked her if she'd seen the Chapmans. She shook her head. I went towards her, but Mrs Hebblethwaite stood between us.

"Keep that boy away from us," she said to the officer. "He's nothing but trouble."

Doctor Hebblethwaite frowned at her.

"I'm afraid we didn't see the Chapmans, Andrew," he said. "I'm so sorry."

The Doctor told the officer from the *Nellie* that there were only ten survivors in all. Two other families who'd been with them on the mountain had decided, during the lull in the storm, to go back to their homes. They'd begun the trek across the lava plain and were almost halfway to the town when they realized the killer wave was coming. They'd turned and started running back towards the mountain. The wave caught them with ease and swallowed them up.

The Hebblethwaites and the others had watched this from high above the water level.

That night, as the *Nellie* began her voyage northwards, I lay on my bunk, trying to sleep. I couldn't at first: my mind was like one of those sharks that never rests. I wondered what would become of me now. I mourned the deaths of the Chapmans. My thoughts turned to the hostility of Mrs Hebblethwaite towards me—I wondered if Maria had told her about our walks to the cove. But her mother had disliked me from the first time she saw me at the door of The Motte. Maybe she believed I was the one who lived outside the walls of the town and would bring ruin. So many awful things had happened wherever I was: the deaths of my sister, my father, my mother, my aunt, my uncle, and now the Chapmans. The obliteration of St Jude. Maybe I was a walking time bomb, a booby trap to be avoided at all costs.

These thoughts exhausted me. Sad and desperate, I once more became a castaway: this time on the wide, dark ocean of sleep.

Chapter Thirty-one

DURING THAT LONG sad voyage north, the Hebblethwaites and the other islanders kept well clear of me: my meals were served to me in my cabin. The Captain of the *Nellie*, a friendly man with a burnt face and hooked nose, made it clear I was under no circumstances to communicate with them. I was frustrated at knowing Maria was so near. But their cabins were on the deck above mine. At the top of the connecting flight of stairs, an iron barrier door, pressure-locked from the other side, was as good as a prison wall separating me from Maria. I could still go out on my own deck and stand at the rail, just as I had three years ago on the voyage south. But now there was no Harry Greene and my watches were lonely: just the vast empty sea.

Occasionally, if there was no one around, I'd slip up the stairs and check the barrier door, hoping it might be open. It never was. Till late one night, in mid-voyage. When I tested the handle, it turned and the door opened with a little squeal. I stepped over the sill and stood in the dimly lit passageway where the Hebblethwaites and the other survivors of the great storm at St Jude were quartered.

But what was I to do now? There were ten cabins along the corridor, and I'd no idea which one might be the Hebblethwaites', or Maria's: or whether she shared a cabin with her parents. I might just as well give up and go back to my own deck before someone caught me.

Someone did.

"Andrew! Is that you?" The words were barely louder than the hum of the ship's motors. I looked back. A small figure in a white gown appeared in the shadows beside the companionway and came into the light of the dim overhead bulb.

It was Maria.

She put her finger to her lips and beckoned me to follow her back along the passage out to the deck. I did, and we found a dark area under a lifeboat hanging from its gallows. We stood, not touching. I felt very nervous.

"What are you doing up here?" she asked. I could smell the soap from her hair.

"I came up to look for you," I said.

She laughed quietly.

"And what about you?" I said. "What are you doing out here?"

"My parents and I are in the same cabin," she said. "Sometimes, if I can stay awake till they fall asleep, I come out and unlock the barrier door. Just for a few minutes: I hoped you might get up here some night."

It was a cloudy night, and we were away from the deck lights, so I couldn't see her face. There were so many things I wanted to ask her. But all at once, I felt her hand on mine in the dark and all questions went out of my mind. We put our arms around each other and just stood there kissing. My heart was pounding so loudly I thought it would waken the whole ship.

And it might as well have. For suddenly we heard a cabin

door thrown open, and a bright light came on in the passageway, Mrs Hebblethwaite appeared at the end of it in a nightgown, adjusting her wire glasses.

"Maria?" she called. She must have seen something, for she was looking towards us in the shadow of the boat. "Maria?"

I stepped forward.

Mrs Hebblethwaite saw me and Maria behind me.

"You!" she shouted at me. "Get out of here! Get away from here and don't you dare come back!" Then to Maria: "Go back to the cabin immediately!"

She shouted this so loudly, it caused a commotion. I heard footsteps running on the deck above, and a sailor shouting over the rail, "Is everything all right down there?"

I hurried past Mrs Hebblethwaite along the passageway and down the stairs. When I was back in my own cabin I sat waiting for the knock at my door. But there was none.

The next morning, the Captain sent for me. He didn't seem at all angry when I came into his cabin.

"I hear you got through the barrier door," he said. "Well, well. I wonder how you managed that." But he didn't ask how. Instead, he said: "Don't go up there again. The little girl's mother's very upset."

Then he changed the subject. "We have to make plans for what's to happen to you after we reach Southaven." He asked if I'd any family: someone who'd look after me at the end of the journey. I told him I'd like to go back to Stroven. I was thinking I'd surely find a home there: perhaps even with Doctor Giffen. The Captain said he'd notify the authorities and arrangements would be made by the time we docked. As I was leaving, he said one last thing.

"By the way, I promised the girl's mother I'd make sure

the door won't be unlocked again." He smiled. "Nothing personal."

And indeed, though I checked the door on many nights afterwards, I never found it open again.

Soon enough, we left the warmer weather behind and the *Nellie* battled her way into grey seas. On a chilly March morning, a pilot boarded us and guided the ship into the dock in Southaven. I stood at my porthole watching as the Hebblethwaites and the other survivors scurried along the pier to waiting taxis. Maria stopped once to look back towards the ship, but her mother pulled her by the arm. The Hebblethwaites got into a taxi and it moved away slowly, dragging its smoky tail through the dock gate and out of sight. I felt awful: I believed that was the last time I'd ever see Maria Hebblethwaite.

An hour later, I was sitting in a draughty office on the dock, being interviewed by a man from the Ministry of Social Services.

"Your request to go back to Stroven's out of the question," he said. "The mine closed down two years ago." He was a brusque, cold man and his words were ice-cold. "In fact, no one lives there any more."

Chapter Thirty-two

ANOTHER BUS JOURNEY. The driver was instructed to let me off near the village of Waltham Close, which we reached after two hours of rolling grassy hills. Another ten minutes and the bus squealed to a stop, let me off and went on its way.

A woman was waiting for me by the side of the road. She wore the black robes of a nun, but they were a little unusual. The front of her stiff, white hood was tubular and stuck out twelve inches in front of her face. Along this tube, I could see her face: a stern face with silver-rimmed glasses. She couldn't see much that wasn't right in front of her—like looking at the world through a porthole. Sewn over the left breast of her robes was an image of a yellow sun giving off snaky flares.

"Mister Andrew Halfnight, I presume," she said. When she put out her hand to me, I noticed a strange lilac scent coming from her robes. "I'm Sister Rose." Her hand was dry and cold. She spoke again and her voice echoed slightly along the tube. "You have no luggage? Follow me. We've a short walk."

We walked a hundred yards along the main road and then up a driveway lined with spruce trees. At the end of it I could see a large, red-brick building; it was as big as some of the factories we'd passed as the bus went through the outskirts of the City. Sister Rose turned and focused her tube on me.

"This will be your new home. I hope you'll be happy here," she said. "But it's not necessary that you should."

This building was called the House of Mercy, and in it I was to spend the next two years of my life—along with four hundred other orphans.

The House was especially designed to keep a large number of orphans under the control of a small number of nuns. It was built in the shape of two wheels connected by a corridor. The wheels were called the Boys' Circle and the Girls' Circle. The hub of each wheel was a tower with walls of darkened glass. The circumferences of the wheels were four storeys high, and divided into little segments, each of which was an orphan's room. The inside wall—the one facing the hub—was made of ordinary glass and had a glass door. The nuns, who worked in pairs, sat invisible in the central towers, and could see into every room just as though they were looking into a doll's house.

Sister Rose explained all of this to me in a brief chat as she checked me in before taking me to my room.

"The inspiration for the architecture came two hundred years ago, to our foundress, Sister Justitia. You've heard of her?"

Sister Rose didn't seem surprised that I hadn't.

"She was a saint," she said. "No lay person can compete with a saint in this kind of thing. She felt privacy leads to vice. So every aspect of our Houses must be public." She touched her hood. "This cylindrical cowl we wear is her invention too. It keeps us from being distracted. We concentrate only on the task ahead of us."

As we were leaving the reception area, she pointed to the insignia on her breast. "The House of Mercy's like this. The sun sees everything, but can't be looked at."

Then she took me to my room. The Boys' Circle was very quiet, the other rooms all being empty: at this time of day the orphans were ouside doing their work. She left me in my room to settle in. It was small but comfortable, with a strong smell of disinfectant. A pair of blue overalls and a blue shirt, the orphans' uniform, lay on the bed for me. As I put them on, I felt a bit exposed because of the glass wall facing the hub. I kept glancing at the dark tower, wondering if one of the sisters was watching me right now.

I settled in quickly at the House of Mercy. The absolute predictability of each day suited me. We ate in silence at exactly the same times in communal dining-rooms. Each morning at nine we went to our segregated classes on grammar and mathematics. In the afternoons, we worked in the gardens for two hours. After that, one hour was allocated for walking, or running round a field enclosed by barbed wire. Then dinner, then study, then bed.

We were constantly monitored to make sure we didn't become too friendly with any of the other orphans. The reason was that Sister Justitia, the founder, believed close friendships were a bad thing; among immature people they inevitably resulted in evil. "You must love everyone," she had said. "It's too easy to restrict yourself to loving just one, or a chosen few."

I often wondered about the girls in their Circle. On very still nights, their giggles or screams would penetrate the corridors that connected their Circle to ours. In the privacy of my room, I milked the memories of those hours on the beach with Maria, and that brief kiss on the *Nellie.*

But that was after lights out. Otherwise, when we were in our rooms, we were as visible as actors on four hundred little stages, with an audience of two. They saw, but were not seen. We were anonymous in our blue overalls, yet for all we knew, any one of us might be the target of our overseers' eyes at any or all times.

I came to not mind being watched. I soon began enjoying life at the House of Mercy, except for an occasional moment when I was overwhelmed with that sense of foreboding that sometimes took all the joy out of my life. Nor did I sleep well after my first week there.

What happened was this: one night, I was having my usual nightmare. I was running desperately away from the edge of a great black chasm, and the ground was crumbling away under me. But this time, I could feel a hand grasp my back foot—someone was pulling me back into the blackness. I was terrified and shouted out. Suddenly, there was a dim light hovering over me, and I thought I'd escaped into another less frightening dream. Then a voice behind the light said: "What's wrong?"

I smelt lilac. Sister Rose was standing by my bed, holding a night light. I couldn't see her face in the shadows of the cowl.

"You were calling out in your sleep," she said. "You were waking up the Boys' Circle with your noise." She spoke quietly, but even at that I was afraid everyone in the Circle would hear her.

"I had a bad dream," I said, as softly as I could.

"A bad dream?" She considered for a moment. "It's the responsibility of rational human beings to control their dreams," she said. "That was one of the primary teachings of Sister Justitia." Her tube was pointed directly at me and I could hear her breathing.

"Was it an evil dream?" she asked quite abruptly.

I didn't know what she meant by that.

"It frightened me," I said.

When she spoke, she sounded a little more sympathetic. "The Ministry of Social Services sent us a dossier on you, Andrew. You've been through a lot. But that's no excuse for relaxing your self-control: especially when you're asleep. Do you understand? Sister Justitia was so insistent on that point. All it takes is a little will-power."

I nodded, though I'd no idea how I was supposed to control my dreams. Sister Rose put out her lilac-smelling hand and touched my cheek. I was surprised, but I didn't flinch, though her fingers were very cold. She leaned over and whispered: "I know you've suffered." And she sighed. "But no more than the rest of us. When it comes to suffering, we all compete with each other." Then she left my room.

From that night on, whenever I found myself in a nightmare, I'd try to force myself awake. My fear of disturbing the Boys' Circle—and of having Sister Rose reproach me in the middle of the night—was stronger than the power the nightmare had over me. Generally, I managed to wake myself when I was in its grip. For the longest time, I felt a great sadness that I couldn't relax even when I was dreaming. But all in all, I preferred that to being the focus of attention.

Chapter Thirty-three

JUST BEFORE BREAKFAST one spring morning, I was ordered to the Sister's Residence. Sister Rose had something for me.

The Residence was a one-storey structure, fifty yards away from the House, along a stone pathway lined with rocks. The door of the Residence was open and I went into the hall. The inside of the building was unusual. All the inner walls were made of glass, so that I could see from one end to the other—even into the washrooms. In some of the bedrooms, I saw nuns lying asleep. In others, nuns were sitting at desks writing, or reading their holy books. Sister Rose was in the kitchen, washing dishes. When I jangled the handbell, she saw me, dried her hands and came to the hall. She lifted an envelope from the table.

"For you," she said. "Read it after breakfast." She said nothing more, but went back towards the kitchen.

This was most unusual: I'd never heard of anyone in the

House receiving mail. As I walked back, I examined the envelope. In the top right-hand corner was a large green triangular stamp with Oriental-looking words on it. The address was written in a tiny cramped hand: quite unlike the big, regular handwriting the Sisters made us use.

I could hardly wait for breakfast to be over. When I got back in my room, I opened the envelope. The letter was from Harry Greene. After all these years, a letter from Harry—a single rice-paper page and very brief.

> Andy:
>
> I trust you are reading and learning as much as you can. I expect to be home in a month or two, and I'll come and visit you. Perhaps I could become your guardian. Think it over. Meantime, stick to your bearings.
>
> Your old shipmate,
> Harry Greene
>
> P.S. I'm still studying that old Johannes Morologus. Do you remember we talked about him? If I wasn't a bit of a cynic, I might think there was more to all this number stuff than meets the eye! I'll tell you about that when I see you.

That the letter was so short was disappointing. But that Harry hadn't forgotten me, that he'd be coming to see me, and—most of all—that he wanted to be my guardian: these things made me feel elated. I read the letter over and over and over again. I kept it under my pillow and read it every day for the next couple of months. I waited in hope. And in due course, one afternoon when I was at work in the garden, Sister Rose appeared.

"A visitor for you," she said.

I went back to the House, and headed for the reception room as fast as I could, without running—that was absolutely forbidden inside the House.

"Are you well, Andrew?"

The voice that greeted me as I entered was familiar all right, but it wasn't Harry Greene's. It was the discreet voice of Doctor Giffen. He was as nattily dressed as ever, though his hair and his beard were a little grey. The pupils of his eyes were like the tips of pins.

I couldn't hide my disappointment from such sharp eyes.

"You were expecting someone else?" he said.

I told him no, but surely he didn't believe me. Not that he seemed upset. I think he was a man who was accustomed to being greeted without enthusiasm; perhaps he even preferred it that way. He looked around the reception room and chose one of the green plastic-covered chairs. He wiped it with his handkerchief, pulled up his neatly creased pants an inch and sat down.

He cleared his throat.

"When I heard you'd come home, I half-expected you might wish to come and live with me," he said.

I was about to say that I did mention his name to the Captain of the *Nellie*. But I kept quiet. I decided I wanted him to believe he wasn't someone I'd especially choose to live with.

Instead I asked him what had happened to Stroven.

In his arid way, he told me the bare facts. There had been a massive cave-in at the mine in the middle of the night and rescue operations couldn't begin till daylight. They found no survivors. One hundred and twenty men and boys were killed. Families lost fathers, sons, cousins. Government inspectors were afraid the whole area around Stroven had become unsafe because of all the mining over the centuries.

"An immediate exodus was advised," Doctor Giffen said. He himself didn't really mind. He'd long been thinking of moving back to the City anyway. And so he did.

He cleared his throat and we sat there, uncomfortable with each other as ever. Eventually, he looked around for his hat: a narrow-brimmed hat with a feather in the band, lying on a nearby chair. He picked up the hat and fingered it. He cleared his throat again.

"I knew your Aunt Lizzie. She lived with your mother for a while around the time you were born. She was a very pleasant woman." He cleared his throat again. "I heard about what happened to her. It was in the newspapers. I'm so sorry about that." He stood up and looked as though he was about to go. Then he spoke again.

"I was very fond of your mother. Very fond. I promised her I'd keep an eye on you if the arrangement with your aunt didn't work out. I've made a decision to go abroad and set up practice. Canada, I'm thinking of. I'll keep in touch with you. When your time is up here, or whenever you wish, if you'd like to come and join me, don't hesitate."

Before he left, he said one last thing.

"By the way, someone wrote to me about you some time ago. A sailor named Harry Greene. He said you met on the voyage to St Jude and he wanted your present address. Of course, I sent it to him."

Then he shook my hand quickly and left without another word.

I stayed in the reception room alone for a moment. I knew Doctor Giffen loved my mother and had my best interests at heart, but I didn't think I'd ever take him up on his offer. In fact, I'd sooner have stayed forever in the House of Mercy, where I had no need to rack my brain for things to say to anyone; where, apart from occasionally being smitten with that awful sense of foreboding, day followed stressless day.

The promised visit from Harry Greene never happened. The weeks passed. The months passed. And it never happened.

At the age of sixteen, my time at the House of Mercy expired. My departure was without any fuss—just as the founder, Sister Justitia, recommended it should be. After breakfast, I packed a cloth bag supplied by the House. It would have been self-indulgent of Sister Rose to see me off, so she sent one of the other sisters to walk me, silently, to the end of the driveway. When the bus arrived, she shook my hand and said, "Good luck!" And that was that. As the bus moved away, I thought of Captain Stillar's remark about how faint was the mark of a sailor on land. My stay at the House seemed like that to me now. I'd lived in it for two years. I suspected that, within two days, the fact I'd ever been there would be completely forgotten.

Chapter Thirty-four

The Ministry of Social Services had arranged a job for me as a ticket clerk in Southaven Central Railway Station, and that was where I worked for the next three years. The clerks were isolated from each other in their individual booths, so I didn't have to associate much with my co-workers. I dealt each day with hundreds of passengers; but my only communication with them was on the subject of fares and timetables. They looked at me as though I were simply part of a ticket-selling machine.

I lived in a cheap room in a boarding-house with many rooms. Mine looked much the same as the others: an old, springy bed; a high-backed chair with broken wicker-work that had an attraction to my wool sweater; a high, blotched ceiling; and walls covered in yellow, blotched wallpaper. The floor was bare except for a small rug, so the room was chilly, even that summer I moved in. All the rooms of the boarding-house were occupied and the house was very noisy, at night, and throughout the night. I ate my meals at a small café not far away and I tried to live a quiet, normal life. My most enjoyable hours were spent in the local library, a small, rarely used place. I loved reading. I read almost everything.

It was in the library, near the end of my third year in Southaven, that I met Catherine Cleaves.

I'd seen her there several times: a tall woman, heavily built, with short black hair. She wore no make-up, but had dark eyes with darker shadows under them. She looked at least ten years older than I. We sometimes sat at opposite ends of the reading-table.

One night we left at just about the same time. With her long legs, she was a quick walker and stayed ahead of me. So I saw where she lived: an old house not far from the café.

After that, I'd nod to her when I saw her in the library, or if we passed on the street. And after a while, she'd nod back. And soon we were exchanging greetings: "Good afternoon" or "Nice day." Though, more often than not, the days were not nice in Southaven, where it rained a lot because of the coastal weather. Nor could the town be called nice, what with its dingy shipyards and polluted sea front.

One night just after dark I was on my way to the library.

As I passed her old house, the door opened and she called out to me.

"Why don't you come inside for a few minutes."

She was standing in the doorway, and I was startled at the way she looked. She was wearing a low-cut blue dress and, for the first time since I'd known her, make-up. Her eyes were mascaraed, her lips were red, and she was smiling. I went to the door.

"My name's Catherine," she said. "What's yours?" And shook my hand warmly.

We went inside.

The hallway was gloomy but the room she led me into was large and impressive. It was one of those old drawing-rooms with heavy mahogany furniture, Tiffany lamps, a brocaded sofa, and armchairs beside a blazing fire. On the walls were paintings of swooning medieval damsels.

What made me feel most at home were the books. One entire wall of this large room was an enormous bookcase from floor to ceiling. Behind glass doors, I could see thousands of books.

"Sit down," Catherine said.

I sat in one of the armchairs by the fire.

"Would you like a glass of wine?" she said. I noticed how she smiled all the time as she talked, so that the sounds of all her words seemed to come through her nose.

I'd never tasted wine: only that beer John Chapman gave me on St Jude not long before the big wave. But I said yes, I'd like some.

She went over to the table and poured two glasses of red wine from a decanter. She brought my glass to me. When she leaned over to hand it to me, her breasts looked as though they might easily escape from the dress.

I sipped the red wine cautiously: it looked so tempting in the glow of the fire. And I liked the taste.

She sat on the chair opposite with her own glass. She sipped, and licked her upper lip.

"My main interest is in love," she said, in that smiling voice. "Or, I should say, in love stories." She told me that since the death of her parents ten years before, she'd devoted herself to the study and collection of love stories. She ran off the names of some of the authors she'd collected, and the titles of their works.

The wine was having a rapid effect on me and it was hard for me to concentrate. But I tried to look interested.

"Have you read any of them?" she asked.

I said I didn't think so.

"Come and look," she said, and we went over to the bookcase. She switched on a light above it. The ceiling was at least fifteen feet high and the shelves filled all the wall, with long glass doors above and smaller doors at waist height. A little movable ladder slid along on rails in front of the shelves.

She opened one of the top doors.

"Go on," she said. "Have a look at them." She was smiling. "This is my collection. This is what I've devoted my life to."

Some of the books were worn looking; most were quite new. I looked at the titles on the spines—I'd never come across any of them: *A Man for the Kissing; Brides of Belladonna; The Gallant Gambler and the Lively Lass; O Passionato!; Star-Spangled Mistress; My Temptress Tongue; Cherished Foe; Savage Embraces; Black Moon Blonde Lady; Amazon Amy; Lovelorn My Love; Apache Woman; True Love and the Parson from Moosejaw; Wife for Rent; Sweet Passion of the Prairie; The Neurosurgeon and the Lost Lover; Whisper Love in My Earnest Ear; Tangled Cupid's Heart; Island of Love's Flame; Lure That Lady; Affaire Immemoriale.* And on, and on, book after book, shelf after shelf of them rising so high I couldn't make out the titles any more. Several were by the same authors: Bicky Becker, Rona Ryan, Heather Hill, Winona Wise; and some of the names were foreign sounding: Darcy D'Amour, Delinda Desprit, Mandive Moncoeur. I couldn't help but be impressed.

"Look," said Catherine. She bent to open one of the lower glass doors, and I thought it was a miracle her breasts didn't spill out. "My journal section."

I looked at the journals to keep my eyes off those breasts. She had whole series of magazines assembled on the shelves, with names such as *Icelandic Love Studies; Romantic Quarterly; Presbyterian Lovefest Annual; Comparative Love Literature*.

My head was dizzied by the books and the wine and the breasts. She was watching me, smiling, expectant.

"This is quite a collection of books," I said. "They don't seem to be in any particular order. How do you know where to find one you want?"

I could see she liked my question.

"These books are my best friends," she said smilingly. "I know where every single one of them is—by instinct."

"Gosh," I said.

We went and sat again by the fire. She told me how she divided most of her days between studying her books at home, and researching others. She said the local library was good at getting the very rarest for her. She'd sample the books there, and if she thought they were of the highest quality, she'd track down a copy for her collection.

She was looking at me quite peculiarly now, I thought. Or perhaps it was the wine that made everything seem fuzzy.

"Right now," she said, "I'm reading a book by Dolores Dolorosa: she's one of my favourite authors. It's a story about an attractive older woman, Rebecca, who falls in love with a young man called Tyler: a man with a mysterious past. I've reached the part where they meet at her house and make love."

She was looking at me smilingly, and I thought, how beautiful she is.

"It's such a marvellous scene," she said. "Let me read you a part." She got up and brought back a book that was lying on the table beside the wine. She sat down again.

"Listen to this: 'As they lay together in a naked embrace on the pink satin sheets, Rebecca spoke secret words into his ear, and her words set his love alight. His rigidity finally broke and the rhythmic motion of his body became frenzied, and she knew it would soon explode in one great shuddering burst of liquescent fire.'" Catherine had read this in her smiling, nasal voice. She closed the book. "Isn't it quite wonderful?" she said.

I felt quite nervous.

"Yes," Catherine said, smiling at me, "he's a very mysterious boy, and she doesn't know anything about him. That's the exciting part of the love-making."

I was very naïve: I was almost nineteen years old, and had no experience of sex except years ago with Maria Hebblethwaite. But I thought I could read the signs: I was sure Catherine Cleaves wanted me. I made up my mind. I put my glass on the table and stood up.

She stood up.

Suddenly I was overwhelmed by the height of her, and those great breasts, and the smell of her perfume and the perpetual smile.

"I have to go now," I said.

Her smile didn't disappear. She looked at me for a while.

"Very well," she said. "Go."

And, in a few seconds, I was standing out on the sidewalk in front of the house, breathing in the cool air. I was disappointed and I was relieved.

That night in bed, I kept thinking about Catherine Cleaves; and I thought about her all next day at work. I made up my mind. After work I put on my best clothes, went straight to her house and knocked on the door. I tried several times; but there was no answer.

I went to the Library. She was sitting in her usual place at the reading-table, with an open book in front of her.

I stood beside her, but she didn't look up.

"Catherine," I said.

"Good evening," she said, without looking up.

"Catherine," I said.

And this time she looked up.

"I was wondering," I said, "if I could drop in and see you tonight. You know, after you finish your reading." I felt like an idiot.

She looked at me.

"No," she said, smiling. "It's too late."

I didn't know what to say.

"It was just that I was so nervous last night," I said. "I'm fine now."

She shook her head.

"Too late. Much too late," she said. "You see, I finished the book last night after you left. Did I tell you it was called *The Handsome Stranger*?" She smiled as she said that; but there was something about the smile now: it seemed to me more like a snarl. "I've started this new one." She held it up for me to see. It was called *Knight of the Velvet Spear*, by Carla Corazon. The cover showed a medieval jousting contest with a lady looking on anxiously from the grandstand. "It's about the Middle Ages, and so delightful," Catherine said. "A knight-at-arms comes to a small town in the forest where the baron has been keeping a young woman captive...."

I tried again.

"So there's no chance?" I said.

"No, it's too late," she said. "Look. Dolores Dolorosa writes four or five books a year, and most of them are about handsome strangers and older women. If I happen to be reading one of them, and if we catch each other at the right time, who knows?"

Her eyes had a strange gleam in them: they seemed sad—or mad.

"Anyway," she said. "It's never as much fun as the book."

I left her there and went home to my room in the boarding-house. And perhaps I might have stayed around and waited for Dolores Dolorosa's next book, and the right set of conditions. But not long after that, I received a letter from Doctor Giffen. He seemed to be doing well in Canada, though he mentioned that his health wasn't what it had once been. Again he invited me to come and join him. I thought about it, and this time I accepted the invitation.

Chapter Thirty-five

I FELT IMMEDIATELY at ease in Ontario. It was like a photographic negative held up to the light: I could see, though not always plainly, familiar outlines. Many of the places had Scottish names and the people tended to mind their own business.

Doctor Giffen lived in Camberloo, a middling-sized city sixty miles south-west of Toronto. The city was big enough that if a man wanted to, he could remain anonymous. He had established a small, financially rewarding practice. He no longer had that smell of ether about him: now he smelt faintly of cologne. He'd always been a small man, but I could see how fragile he'd become: like a brittle puppet. All his energy seemed to be concentrated in his little bright eyes.

His house was one of the big houses in the Woodsides district. The living-room was long, with windows looking out onto the remains of a forest. The focal point was a photograph in a silver frame over the mantel of a stone fireplace. The photograph was familiar: it was the one of my mother and my father. They were standing in the snow in front of a building. An old-fashioned car was parked nearby.

The very first night I arrived in Doctor Giffen's house, he saw me examining the photograph.

"It's from your mother's house," he said. "I took it as a keepsake the day you left Stroven." He pointed at the building in the background. "She told me that was a hotel in Invertay: you were conceived there. It was a little skiing resort in the north. As a matter of fact, there's a town not far from here with the same name. We should drive there some time and see what it's like. Your mother said that was one of the happiest periods in her life."

He persuaded one of his patients who owned the Xanadu Travel Agency to give me a job. To celebrate, we had brandy after dinner.

"For medicinal purposes, of course," he said, holding up his glass. That was one of his rare attempts at humour.

I had more than one glass of brandy, and it loosened my tongue. Before I could stop myself, the question came out.

"Do you remember that hotel you booked me into in Glasgow—where I waited for the ship to St Jude?"

"The Hochmagandie," he said. "I used to stay there

myself when I was in the City. Yes, it wasn't the fanciest hotel, but it was handy." His little eyes were glistening at whatever he was remembering. He was silent then for so long I thought he wasn't going to say any more, so I spoke again.

"The Captain of the ship that took me to St Jude used to visit there when he was in dock," I said. "So did the Steward."

I couldn't tell what he was thinking as he looked at me.

"That's no surprise," he said. "It must have been a good place for sailors." He paused. "Being so near the docks."

A third glass of brandy had me by the tongue now.

"I think it was the women that were the attraction," I said.

His little eyes were bright, but he wasn't taking the bait. So I told him about Captain Stillar, and his custom of hiring bar-women, then painting them. If I thought this would be a revelation to Doctor Giffen, I was wrong.

"So *he* was your Captain," he said. "Well, well. Yes, I heard all about him. One of these bar-women, as you call them, told me. I was ... friendly with her." His eyes gleamed and I actually thought he might be mocking me. "She said he painted her once, and after he'd finished, he looked as though he loved her. But she said that only lasted till the paint was cleaned off." I could see he was enjoying telling me this. "One night when she was with me, the Captain was in the room next door painting another woman. We looked through a crack in the door and saw him doing it." He shook his little head. "So that was your Captain."

I was astounded at the idea of Doctor Giffen and some bar-woman on their knees peeping through the crack in the door just as I'd done! I was astounded at the coincidence! But of course I didn't tell him I'd had the same experience.

"What about the Steward?" I said. "Harry Greene was

his name. He's the one who wanted my address at the House of Mercy. Did you hear anything about him?"

"Well, well. What a small world it is," said Doctor Giffen. "Yes, I remember him. I saw him a few times. He used to sit at the bar and talk with anyone who'd listen. He always had books with him. The women said he talked too much. I heard them say they'd rather be painted by the Captain than lectured by the Steward."

I smiled at that: so much for Harry's theory about words and love-making. What would he have thought if he'd known the women looked on him as a chatterbox?

Doctor Giffen sipped his brandy slowly. I couldn't help noticing how skeletal his little hand had become.

"After I met your mother," he said, "all that kind of thing stopped. It's strange, but after I got to know her, I never had much of an interest in any other woman. Please believe that, Andrew." He said this as though it was important that I remember it. And I have.

On one other occasion after that night, I tried to get him to talk about himself. It wasn't long before his death.

"Believe me, Andrew," he said. "The only interesting thing that ever happened in my life was meeting your mother."

I understood then that she was the love of his life: his ideal. He must have been quite wrong about her, for she was a woman of flesh and blood. But clearly she had never disappointed him, even by dying. Or perhaps her death had ensured he'd never be disappointed in her.

One significant thing happened during my first summer in Camberloo, though I didn't realize it at the time. I used to walk to the Xanadu in the morning: about two miles. It was such a pleasure, everything was still so new to me: the blue jays and the cardinals that flew among the old trees of the suburban houses; the squirrels whose sharp little eyes reminded me of Doctor Giffen's.

I used to take a short cut along a brief avenue to the main road. One morning as I was walking that way, I was admiring one of the more impressive houses: it was white with four pillars in front. I noticed the curtains moving at one of the upstairs windows, as though someone had been watching me and had shut them quickly when I looked up.

For the rest of the summer I walked that way, and several other times the same thing happened as I passed the house. Once or twice, I caught a glimpse of a hand pulling the curtain together. Once, I even thought I saw a face. Perhaps if Doctor Giffen and I had talked more, I might have mentioned what I'd seen. If I had, I might have been spared a great deal of suffering later on.

Chapter Thirty-six

"I HEARD YOU SHOUTING out during the night," Doctor Giffen said.

This was at breakfast one morning after a heavy snowfall. I'd had a bad nightmare and forced myself awake, at about three in the morning. I knew I'd made some noise, and hoped he hadn't heard.

His little eyes were on me, unblinking. He put his hand up and straightened the knot of his tie: he wore his tie and his jacket even at breakfast. The smell of his cologne still hadn't faded much.

"It's not the first time," he said. "You've been living here for more than a year, and I've heard you quite often. I'm a light sleeper."

I fussed with my cornflakes. But he wouldn't let up.

"I suppose it's nightmares?" he asked. "Have you been having nightmares? They must be very frightening."

I prepared myself for the interrogation. Perhaps I would have explained to him that I'd had them under control for years, but that occasionally they were too strong for me. That in my nightmares I was still a boy: not a grown man who might have been able to withstand the terror.

But no interrogation came.

"Don't worry," he said. "I won't ask you to tell me about them. Some of my patients insist on telling their dreams and their nightmares. Quite boring really. I don't place much stock in that sort of thing. Perhaps their fellow dreamers enjoy hearing about them."

He sipped his coffee, and became confessional.

"Do you know, Andrew? I've never had a single dream in all my life. I used to think it was bound to happen, but it never did. I can imagine what it must be like. But I've never actually had a dream myself."

I was surprised at this revelation. "I thought everyone had dreams," I said. "What happens when you fall asleep?"

"Nothing much," he said. "It's quite like an anaesthetic. One minute I'm awake, then the alarm goes off and it's time to be up and doing something. It's refreshing, really, that period of nothingness, whatever it is. I like it."

"But I thought not to dream was unnatural," I said.

He smiled a tight little smile at that word. I tried to apologize.

"No, no." He shook his head. "You're quite right, of course." He sipped again at his coffee and looked past me out the window where snow lay thick on the lawn and the branches of the evergreens. "Your mother once said she felt sorry for me—not to have had dreams. She said it explained a lot about me." He looked back at me. "She said she wouldn't hold it against me."

I thought: How right she was. And perhaps that was why he was so hard to talk to.

"Yes, she felt sorry for me," he said. "But I don't envy people their dreams. I can't conceive what it must be like to live in that kind of anarchy all night long, then wake up and have to deal with the realities of life with any conviction during the day." He finished his coffee and put his cup carefully back in the saucer. "If someone offered to show me how to do it—to dream, I mean—I shouldn't have any hesitation at all in saying: 'No thank you.'"

We lived together four years. He had a professional life that involved meetings with other doctors; and he made occasional trips to medical conferences. He had no social life I knew of, and no women friends. Often I'd catch him standing in front of that photograph over the fireplace, looking as contented as any man in love.

He died quite suddenly after a severe stroke. He'd left instructions for one of his colleagues—a surgeon by the name of Stevenson—to be called to the house within hours of his being pronounced dead. Doctor Stevenson arrived in due course. He was a little round man, nattily dressed like Doctor Giffen. From the way he talked, they must have got along well together.

The body was laid out in Doctor Giffen's bedroom. Stevenson looked it over briefly, then spoke to me.

"Did he tell you why he wanted me to come here?" he said.

I said I'd no idea.

"He wanted his throat to be slit," he said. "Just to make

sure he was really dead. He made me promise to perform the procedure."

He had a medical bag with him which he laid on the bed. He took out a green apron and gloves. I could see the scalpels underneath.

"There shouldn't be any mess. The heart's been stopped for hours and the blood will have congealed. I'll just sever the two carotids." He started to prepare. "Would you like to stay and watch me do it?" he said to me. "It'll only take a few seconds."

"No, thank you," I said. And I left quickly. I must admit I was astonished at Doctor Giffen's bizarre last request. I realized just how superficially I'd known him. Or how little he himself wanted to be known.

The funeral was brief and formal: his body was incinerated, as he requested. He left me everything: the house, a substantial amount of money. And a little box of cyanide pills he'd shown me a year before his death.

"In my profession," he'd said to me, "I see too much unnecessary suffering." He'd intended to take one of the pills if his death was a lingering one. But he died instantly, without the need of them.

I appreciated all he'd done for me, but I didn't miss him very much. After his death, I realized that trying to think of something to say to him during breakfast and dinner had always been a strain. That and the fact that even before he died I was having more than the usual trouble with nightmares, and the sleeplessness that went along with them made solitude seem better to me.

With the money I inherited, I bought the Xanadu Travel Agency. I left the running of it to Lila Trapper, a middle-aged blonde who'd worked there for years. Her two eyes were of different colours—the right one green and the left one blue—so it was always disconcerting to look into them. She was a good worker, and I kept out of her way, spending only an hour or two each day in the office.

The house in Woodsides was too big for me. I sold it. I took some of the furniture and other odds and ends, including the photograph of my parents, and moved into an apartment next to Camberloo Park.

Part Five

THE DEPTHS

We are the half-destroyed instruments
that once held to a course
Adrienne Rich

Chapter Thirty-seven

If I were an observer, writing about Andrew Halfnight, what could I say about the next period of his life? That it appeared humdrum and boring? That at times he gave the impression his physical being was just a burden to be dragged from one unexciting day to the next?

Indeed, it's not at all hard for me to think of those years as though I were somehow disconnected from them: a spectator watching my own life. My nightmares had become so frequent and so terrifying they took a heavy emotional toll: all I wanted in my waking life was dullness. The lack of sleep wore me down, so my relationships with women never amounted to anything. Who would want to spend any time with a man who always seemed apathetic—even though I liked to think I was just exhausted.

I kept going daily to the Xanadu. The office was in the basement of Camberloo Square, and I made myself go in for a couple of hours most weekday mornings, just to keep in touch. Though I didn't really need to, Lila Trapper ran it so efficiently. I'd usually stay in the back office, out of the way. But sometimes, if Lila and her assistants were busy, I'd be obliged to deal with clients, though it was obvious they'd have preferred someone else.

So, it was a relief to Lila when I'd go travelling. And in the early years of my ownership I travelled a good deal, mainly in

Central America. I loved to visit the ancient ruins of Chichen Itza, for example, or Tulum: I'd escape from the guided tours and find a quiet place to sit and think about all the people who once lived there, gone and forgotten. And I loved to wander round the crowded cities where the language and the culture were incomprehensible to me. In a strange way, I felt at home: my sense of alienation was justified.

Then, one February five years after Doctor Giffen's death, I spent a few days on the island of Santo Lobito, checking it out as a possible vacation resort for Xanadu clients: Lila trusted me to do that. The island had only a few hotels at that time and I stayed in one just outside the city: the Hotel Cortez. It was old and luxurious with a private beach and acres of gardens smelling of spices and exotic fruits.

But I didn't spend much time in the hotel. The city attracted me. It was ancient for the New World, with its ornate sixteenth-century cathedral, its crumbling palaces and its teeming alleys. Tourists were discouraged from wandering alone for fear of pickpockets or even kidnappers. Beggars with empty eye-sockets, with limbs deformed, with pocky faces were everywhere.

One afternoon, I was prowling the city looking for something to read. That wasn't easy, for the island hadn't a single bookstore. Often, however, tourists would leave books behind in the hotels, and those books would soon appear on street-vendors' stalls in the city. I came across one of these stalls in my walk, and began examining the books on it. I noticed that the corners of all of them looked as though something had been nibbling at them. Any time I opened the pages, little black specks fell out.

The vendor had been watching me, so I looked at him inquiringly and shook one of the books so that a shower of specks fell from it.

"*Ratas*," he said, shrugging his shoulders.

I didn't need a translator.

Another of the street-vendors told me that the city's indoor market—the Mercado—must surely have a large selection of books, so I went there. It was in the oldest part of the city: a hulking wart of a building at the centre of a maze of narrow streets. The entranceway was at the top of some broad steps strewn with beggars. Guards with machine-guns stood on either side of the doors.

The smell inside the Mercado was bad, but at least the place was relatively quiet after the chaos of the streets. Upstairs was the meat market: I could hear the hum of the air-conditioners at work up there. Down here, there was no air conditioning: only the heat and the smell.

I wandered from stall to stall, accosted on all sides by small, anxious men and women trying to interest me in their merchandise. But I didn't want guitars, statues of the virgin, golden earrings, ponchos, flick-knives or any of the usual artifacts. I wanted books.

I struggled my way round the entire labyrinth, sweating. Every time I passed a stairwell leading upstairs, I could hear the air conditioning from the meat market. I envied those who shopped up there. But I had come to find books. I found none.

At last I was back at the main entranceway. The sound of the air conditioning from upstairs attracted my attention again. I thought perhaps some astute bookseller might have managed to set up his stall in the cool up there. So I went up the stairs.

The humming became louder and louder, and the smell was so thick it caught in my throat. I got to the top landing and looked around. I saw immediately that I'd completely misunderstood about the air-conditioning system. I could see the entire area, windowless and dimly lit—and a hundred stalls all selling meat. There was no air conditioning. The source of the noise was the flies: countless millions of flies. They were everywhere, coating the walls, the ceiling. The meat was under constant attack from swirling hordes of them, buzzing angrily at the vendors who swiped at them with sombreros and rolled-up papers so that buyers could examine the meat.

I saw all of this for only a few seconds before I hurried back downstairs and out into the stifling air. But that awful smell was still inside of me as I barged my way along the streets, trying not to vomit. Eventually I got out of the old city and back to the Cortez. But the humming noise and the bad smell stayed with me all that night, and became part of my nightmares.

That was my last trip south. The tropics had always attracted me, the way the beauty and the corruption existed side by side. I was afraid now I would no longer be able to find the beauty.

In fact, I'd lost my taste for any kind of travelling. From then on, I stayed home in Camberloo. I stopped using my car. My world became the few miles around my apartment. My appearance changed as the years passed. In bodily terms, I matured. My hair thinned, my waist thickened. When I contemplated myself in the mirror after a shower, I used to think how much I looked like the man in the photograph in my bedroom. This plumpish man of average height was the reflection my father used to see.

At other times, when I inadvertently caught a glimpse of myself in a mirror in a store, say, or a restaurant, I looked like a man afraid of something. I began to wonder if that was how others, such as Lila and her clients at the Xanadu, saw me: a plump, frightened man. I worked hard to erase that image. I practised in front of a mirror and tried to stay in control of my appearance at all times. After a while, I believe I succeeded.

If I were to sum up those years, I'd say I began to feel detached and secure. Most of the time, I actually looked on my detachment as a kind of victory over the world. Few things surprised me; nothing much excited me. If it hadn't been for the nightmares and insomnia, I could easily have been convinced I was as happy as anyone had a right to be.

Chapter Thirty-eight

On a late afternoon in mid-December in my tenth year in Camberloo, someone knocked at my apartment door. Outside, there was snow on the ground—the brittle sort—and a bitter north-easter was blowing. I was reading and at first ignored the loud knocking. It got louder. Reluctantly I got up and opened the door.

An elderly, bearded man in a dark blue knitted hat and a pea-jacket stood there. He had unmistakable eyebrows. It was Harry Greene.

"Harry!" I could hardly believe my eyes.

"Andy. How are you, my boy? God's rope!" he said, as fiercely as ever. "What a cold country you live in!" He held out his hand and I took it, and brought him inside while he chattered on.

"I can't believe a lad as smart as I thought you were would want to settle down in such a freezing part of the world." He sat down but wouldn't take off his jacket. "I'm too cold," he said. "I've only half an hour and my taxi's waiting for me outside: I'm on my way to join a vessel on the west coast. I've a few hours between flights so I thought I'd drop in and see how you were doing after all these years." He took off his knitted cap. His grey hair was as wild as ever. He glared at me from beneath his bushy eyebrows. "So, how are you, Andy? Sure now, I wouldn't have recognized you." With my plumpness, my thinning hair, I could easily understand that.

I gave him a glass of rum to warm him up. He himself looked no older than before. Perhaps it was the unruly grey hair and the grey beard that had made him look older on the *Cumnock* than he really was.

"Andy, my boy," he was saying, "I'm sorry I didn't come and visit you when you were in that orphanage. Another berth on a long voyage came up and I couldn't refuse it. 'Tis bad to get a name for turning down berths."

"That's all right, Harry," I said. "It was so long ago I can barely remember it." I changed the subject quickly. "How did you know I was living in Camberloo?"

"Ah, sure now, I made a few inquiries, that's all. A sailor has to be good at navigating the perils ashore. And here I am."

I told him I'd come to Camberloo at Doctor Giffen's invitation and that the Doctor had since died. Then I gave him a brief run-down of my life after that. I told him everything was fine.

He was watching me carefully. He nodded when I'd finished. Then he looked over at my bookshelves.

"So you're reading a lot?"

"Well, I still read," I said.

"Novels?" he said, with one of his ferocious looks. "In spite of my warnings."

"Well, mainly," I said.

"We had a passenger last year who was a novelist," Harry said. "He told me he thought I was right to avoid reading fiction. He said he himself couldn't see people at all for what they were: he was always turning them into characters. He said he couldn't even enjoy a sunset: he was too busy thinking of a way to put it into words." He shook his grey head. "Now, what use is that to anyone, Andy?"

I smiled to keep him happy.

"And now you're on your way to another ship," I said. "I thought you'd be retired by now."

"Retired?" he said. "God's oars! Sure I'm not seventy yet. I think my heart would stop beating if the sea wasn't tossing it up and down, shaking it like an old clock."

"And Captain Stillar? Is he still at sea?"

That stopped him for a moment.

"Ah, sure now you wouldn't know about that," he said, his voice softer. "He's been dead these past ten years. I still have a few of his paintings. I take them with me on voyages. To remind me of him, I suppose."

The news of the Captain's death was more of a blow than I would have thought. He was such an enigma, and I'd always marvelled at the idea of him somewhere on the rough seas of this world, painting his hideous, beautiful women.

"What happened to him?" I said.

"Well, to start with, his eyes went bad. He got to the stage where he was like one of those old captains you read about who have to rely on the First Mate to make landfalls and steer them into tight moorings. But that's only in novels. He failed the annual physical exam and lost his Captain's ticket. The *Cumnock* was sent to the breaker's yard and Captain Stillar was beached in an old sailors' home in Glasgow. I visited him a couple of times, but I couldn't stand it, he was so depressed. He could still see well enough to paint, so I said to him, Why don't you get on with your painting? He said he'd tried, but he couldn't.

He said if he couldn't sail, he couldn't paint, and that was all there was to it. He died not long after. 'Twas just as well, I suppose."

We both sat silent for a while. He finished the rum and I poured him another.

"What about you, Harry?" I said. "How are you doing?"

"No change, Andy. Sure now, there's not a bit of change in me. Old sailors don't change much. But what about you? Come on now, tell me. Do you have a girl?"

I told him I had no girl, but everything was fine. By the way he was looking at me, I was beginning to wonder how long I could keep him at bay. If only I could think of the right questions to distract him.

"Have you been back to St Jude?" I asked.

"We've sailed past, but we don't call in there any more. 'Tis a barren place altogether now. No one lives there." His eyebrows lowered fiercely as he looked at me. "God's rope! That must have been a terrible thing for you to go through," he said.

"And are you still reading as much as ever?" I asked him quickly.

"God's rudder!" he said. "I've read some great things lately." He immediately forgot about everything else. "Do you remember Morologus? I know I told you about him, numerology and that sort of stuff. Ah, if only 'twere true."

I filled his glass again while he talked.

"He has a theory that the path of your footprints all through your life spells out some great message. Now, wouldn't that be a grand thing to see? On the other hand, how could you keep track of every step you've taken? You'd have to have someone following you around when you were a little baby, making notes. And when you got older you'd have to log every day's course just like a ship's captain. In fact, now I come to think of it, a man could plot out his course in advance to spell out a message he liked, eh, Andy? Though I think that would be cheating."

He slapped his thigh and drank his rum in one gulp.

"But then, maybe I don't always understand Morologus. He gets most of his ideas from the ancient Greeks. So I've had to spend a lot of time reading them."

Now he began to tell me about some of the books he'd been studying in his attempts to grasp Morologus. If I hadn't known him all those years before, I might have found it incredible that an ordinary sailor should be such a scholar. The names fell from his tongue with great familiarity: Xenophones of Colophon, Hermes Trismegistus, Megasthenes ("sure now, he wrote about all the strange religions of his day—and some of them were very strange, Andy"); Ptolemy, Zeno, Themistocles ("he was a man who didn't like going to bed at night: he said sleep was a kind of death and dreams were a doorway to the afterlife"), Plato, Heraclitus, Empedocles of Agrigentum, Anaxagoras ("he believed in an infinite number of inhabited worlds: Morologus spoiled the idea a bit with his notion of the Second Self"), Origen, Zarathustra and—most of all—Pythagoras ("'twas he who first figured out that numbers were at the root of all human understanding").

Harry talked and talked about his studies. I remembered how it felt as a boy on the *Cumnock* and I sat back and relaxed. There was no more pressure on me. Every question he raised, he answered himself.

And time rushed by.

"God's oars!" he said eventually, looking at the clock on the wall. "Sure now, Andy: you always knew how to get me talking." He stood up. "I have to be on my way. My plane leaves in two hours."

I tried to coax him to stay longer, knowing he couldn't. On the one hand, I wanted him to stay; on the other, I didn't: if he had time, he would find out too much about me. Walking down to the front door with him, I felt sad: Harry Greene was the last remnant of whatever childhood, whatever innocence, I once had. Yet I wanted him to go.

His taxi was waiting at the entrance with its engine running. The snow was heavier than before. We stood in the lobby for a few moments looking out.

"What an awful place," Harry said. "How can you stand this northern weather? This trip, I'm headed for Aruvula again. You remember it? Where Captain Stillar found his wife all those years ago? I think he'd be very disappointed with it now: all the old customs are gone. You don't see a tattooed woman any more. Except in his paintings."

"What happened to all his paintings?" I said. "I mean, aside from the ones you have?"

"He asked me to burn them all after he died. They were in a storage room, heaped on top of each other. I kept a few aside for myself. Sure now, I don't think he'd have minded. I took the rest down to the shore line, like he asked me, and I made a big bonfire of them. They looked weird, writhing in the flames as though they were alive."

We went outside and he got into the taxi. He told the driver to wait, and he opened the window. His breath tromboned into my face.

"Do you remember, Andy, I said I'd give you the directions to Paradise some day? I haven't found them yet, but I will. I haven't given up. I just have to keep working at my Morologus."

"Don't worry about that, Harry," I said, smiling at the idea of it.

He knew what my smile meant.

"Oh well, you never know. If I do find them, I'll send them to you right away." His fierceness was gone, and he looked sad and old. He reached out and took my hand.

"Sailors are no good at goodbyes, you know that," he said. "But I want to tell you you're the nearest I ever had to a son. I always think of you."

He let go of my hand, raised the window and the taxi pulled away. I went back into the lobby and watched the taxi move out of the driveway and into the white street. The snow was thick and heavy, and the bottoms of the windows of the lobby had little snowdrifts in them, like in an old-fashioned Christmas scene.

The taxi slowly disappeared down the street and with it went my sense of what I once was. As though I'd caught a brief glimpse of myself on the far bank of a river, and the figure was receding into the distance forever. I slowly climbed back up to my apartment, and it, and my life, never seemed emptier.

Chapter Thirty-nine

THE YEAR AFTER Harry Greene's visit, I made a journey to Stroven. I don't know why I did: perhaps some homing instinct. And I don't know what I expected.

I left Camberloo at the end of March. Snow still lay on much of Ontario, but spring was beginning to creep up from the south. The flight was an overnighter, so when the plane banked over London, it was about eight in the morning and the landscape was snowless. The traffic far below glinted in the occasional sun like endless columns of beetles.

I rented a car at Heathrow and set out northwards. The sun had put in its brief appearance for the day. Now rain took over, a steady rain under low grey skies. I was in no rush, so I kept to the slow lane of the motorway. The rain and the steam on the windows made it impossible to see much of the passing countryside. I stopped occasionally at service centres for gas; and for sandwiches that tasted like the wrapping paper they came in.

Around dusk I crossed the Border and started to think about a place to spend the night. I got off the motorway and onto a narrow, winding road into the blunt hills of the Uplands. I stopped at a roadside hotel—the Cutty Sark Inn—a squat building with a whitewashed front, and I took a room, ate supper and went to bed. I dreamed about driving.

I got up the next morning at first light and looked out my window. I should have been able to see the hills, but the fog was so thick it was hard to see beyond the parking lot. I stood for a long time, looking, remembering my childhood. After a while, I dressed and had breakfast. By the time I'd finished, the fog had cleared enough that I checked out of the hotel and headed north-east again.

The next two hours' driving was not easy. I could see fifty yards ahead through the fog but the road was so winding, and with so many ups and downs, I felt quite tense trying to anticipate them. Sometimes a car or a truck would materialize—as though it had just this moment been created—and howl past.

By noon, the world began to take shape and soon I could see clearly in all directions. I was deep among the hills and getting very near to Stroven. I knew the road now: it was the very same road the bus had rumbled along with me as its passenger, that morning long ago.

As I came nearer to Stroven, big yellow road signs appeared: DANGER... ROAD ENDS... NO EXIT. I came to a portable hut with GUARDHOUSE written over it, beside a military escutcheon—"Army Engineers." I could see that beyond the hut the road was unused; weeds were taking over again. I parked. A young soldier, looking a bit startled, opened the door of the hut, adjusting his army beret. Perhaps he'd been having a nap.

"I'd like to go into Stroven," I said.

"You can't do that," he said. "It's a prohibited area."

"Why?"

"All the land around the town's in danger of subsiding. There's a big sink-hole. The engineers won't let anybody past here."

"I've come a long way," I said. "I used to live here."

He saw I was disappointed.

"Really?" he said. "Look, maybe I shouldn't tell you this, but I don't see any harm in it." He pointed down the disused road. "About half a mile away you'll come to an electrified fence. It runs all round the Stroven area. You can walk along the outside, if you want. That's all the engineers do when they're inspecting the place. If you follow the fence, it goes up the Cairn Head and you can look down and see the whole town. Wait a minute." He went into the hut and came back with a pair of binoculars. "You can borrow these."

I thanked him and put them round my neck.

I began walking down the road and soon came to the fence he'd mentioned. It was heavy wire mesh, about ten feet high, with coils of razor wire along the top. Little metal signs in red—DANGER–LIVE—were attached to it at intervals.

I climbed the low stone wall that bordered the disused road on the eastward side, jumped into the moorland and began walking alongside the fence. I wished I'd brought Wellington boots, for the ground was boggy, and my shoes and socks were soon mucky. But at least my coat was warm, and it felt good to be here in the clean air, good to be walking here where I'd walked so long ago.

As I moved across the moorland, I saw clusters of sheep on the hillsides, browsing the spring heather. They looked at me, but weren't afraid. In the grey sky, the peewits wheeled and mewed. The land rose more steeply as the fence climbed along the side of the Cairn Head. I'd climbed it often when I was a boy. The hill hadn't changed, but I had: I was breathing heavily and sweating with the effort. But I knew I was almost there. Just round the last shoulder of the Cairn was a little shelf where I'd be able to look down on Stroven.

And suddenly, there it was, nestled among the bookends of hills.

From where I stood, a thousand feet above the town and half a mile away from it, you would have sworn nothing had changed. Except that it was deserted. At the edge of the town, the mine elevator stood dominant as ever under the grey sky. The granite buildings of the main street—the Town Hall, the Bank, the Church—all looked the same. Everything around the Square—Glenn's Pharmacy, the Stroven Café—looked to me as it always had. The miners' row houses were as neat as ever. And of course, the house where I was born, where my mother died. It looked intact.

The entire scene might have been early morning before anyone was stirring in the streets and houses of Stroven, before the mine elevator began hoisting the men up from tunnels thousands of feet below.

I looked for a long time.

Then I lifted the binoculars. As I adjusted the focus, reality assaulted my eyes: broken cables dangled from the mine elevator; grass and weeds of every sort had sprouted along the main street: the paving was cracked like a jigsaw puzzle. The middle of the Square was in shadow, but the buildings round it were as pathetic as any ghost town: paint had peeled away; windows were shattered; doors drooped from their hinges; roofs were riddled with holes where the slates had fallen.

I swung the binoculars over towards the house where I was born. The roof had collapsed on one side, the windows were broken, the chimney stack had crumbled. In the garden, hay and thistles and nettles were almost as high as the wild hedgerow.

Now I swung further west: towards the graveyard.

That was when I noticed something odd. Most of the monuments over the graves were broken. But what was surprising was this: they looked as though they'd been deliberately pushed over so that they pointed in one direction—towards the town itself.

I swung the binoculars back to Stroven and noticed now, for the first time, the same phenomenon there: every single building had a slight tilt, but not an arbitrary one. They were all leaning towards the Square. I examined the Square again. I had thought the middle part—a fifty-yard patch of greenery with the war memorial and some benches—was in shadow. But what I'd thought was a shadow was in fact a huge sink-hole. Everything round it—buildings, telephone poles, street-lights—was tilted towards that great hole in the earth.

And even while I was watching, I saw everything move, ever so slightly, nearer to that hole: just an inch or two, but a definite movement—the way a glacier must move. Then the fronts of some of the buildings which were nearest the edge—the Library, Darvell's Grocery, MacCallum's Bakery—began to crumble, then slid into the pit in a great cloud of dust. What remained of them stood precariously on the edge, their insides open to the world, like ruined dollhouses.

Just then, something awful happened. I heard a dull rumble, like thunder, but underground. The ledge I was standing on tilted, just a little, towards Stroven. The Cairn Head itself began to move, ever so slightly, in the direction of the great hole.

What with the rumbling and the movement of the hill and the horror that this might be the start of a general, irretrievable sliding of the earth towards that sink-hole, I panicked. I turned and started running.

And someone ran after me.

That was the most frightening thing of all. I was running, and I could hear the footsteps behind me. Out of the corner of my eye, I could see him, or at least his shape. He seemed to be wearing black clothes and he was determined to catch me and bring me back to the crumbling ledge. The terror of him made me run faster than I've ever run. I kept glancing back, hoping, hoping I could stay out of his reach. I was going down the steepest part of the downhill, I was leaping rather than running, when my foot caught in the heather and I tumbled hard down the slope of the Cairn Head and tumbled and tumbled till I came to a stop against a boulder.

I got to my feet, winded, but ready to fight him off and keep running. I couldn't see any sign of him. I looked back towards the Cairn. Nothing. The only living creatures were a pack of sheep grazing nearby, some of them watching me. I could hear nothing and feel no movement of the earth. I touched my face and my hand came away with blood where the edge of the binoculars had cut me.

I took a few deep breaths and made myself walk deliberately the rest of the way back to the road. At the guardhouse I thanked the young soldier for the binoculars.

"Are you all right?" He was looking at the blood on my face, the mud on my clothing and shoes.

"I'm fine," I said. "Did anyone else pass this way after me?"

"No," he said. "The engineers won't be here till tomorrow."

"Did you hear any noises? Did the ground shake?"

"No, nothing at all," he said. "Are you sure you're all right?"

"Yes," I said.

As I walked back towards the car, I realized what I'd been through was so like my recurrent nightmares. I tried to tell myself it was impossible that a nightmare could inject itself into my waking life, nor could a creature out of a nightmare have any substance in the real world.

Common sense should have reassured me. But it didn't.

The rain began again as I drove out of the maze of hill roads and came onto the motorway. My plan for this trip had been vague except for the visit to Stroven. Now that was done and I'd no other reason for being here. No one lived here any more. Perhaps I could have found out where they were and looked them up; but I wasn't sure I wanted to see any of them or that they'd have wanted to see me.

I drove north, towards Glasgow. The day was getting near dusk, and the rain was heavy. By the time I reached the City, it was night. The sidewalks were crowded with people, some holding umbrellas, most with bare heads, their coat collars turned up against the rain. They seemed to me like zombies, their eyes blank: if they were looking anywhere, it was inside.

An overhead sign pointed in the direction of the river, and I followed the cars headed that way. Most of them crossed the bridge, but I took the road along the north bank, towards the docks.

I drove slowly, for I knew the Hochmagandie was near

here. I thought I might take a room, stay the night. I was curious to see if the little man with the nose-cone still worked there and whether he'd remember me. I'd ask him for the same room I'd slept in when I was a boy. I don't really know what I was thinking: that I'd be able to peep through the crack in the door and see some bar-woman with a strange sailor?

But there was no sign of the Hochmagandie. The old tenements and warehouses along the river bank had been demolished. The railway lines had been paved over and the giant cranes and bollards had been taken away. The docks had been replaced with flower gardens where nothing bloomed at this season, except for garbage planted there by the chilly winds. Behind everything, the river still glinted in the city lights.

I found a side street and turned back. I drove south over the river towards the airport and arranged for a flight the next morning. I took a room in the airport hotel and tried to sleep.

But I was tormented by a nightmare: I was once again high on the Cairn Head, watching the town, when I heard a sound, a distant whining. I looked towards the graveyard, and as I did, the graves opened and out climbed the women of Stroven, all dressed in black. They took up their positions and began marching, marching to the sound of pipes and drums, with their pennant flying, heading straight for the Square. And as I watched, all of the buildings in Stroven began to lean even more, then they started to crumble and slide towards the great pit. The column of women reached the main street and marched towards the Square. I shouted to them to stop, I tried to warn them, but they paid no attention: they began to slide, along with everything else, sliding and sliding over the edge, their garments fluttering as they disappeared row by row into the bowels of the earth. Till the last of the women slid to the edge—a tall woman still carrying a pennant with words on it I couldn't read. At the last moment, she found a rock to rest her feet against, and she looked up in my direction. She held out one hand towards me as though appealing for help. "Mother!" I called out. And I was about to risk everything and go to her, when I noticed her eyes: they were burning like a wild beast's and I was afraid that if I went to help her she'd pull me down with her. She stared at me. Then, holding her pennant aloft, she turned and leaped into the pit.

I didn't sleep much after that: my mind was like one of those caged wolves that prowled endlessly back and forth, back and forth at Camberloo Zoo. By seven o'clock, I was on a flight headed home, the drone of the plane's engine like a lament. From the window, the land below looked sterile and harsh and the shore line appeared to be eroding: as though at any moment the whole island might be overwhelmed by the cold, grey-green ocean.

What an unpleasant place, I said to myself: just the place for a disaster. But I couldn't convince myself of that: it was no better and no worse than any other place. When you're unhappy, *every* place is perfect for disaster.

Chapter Forty

THE NEXT FEW MONTHS at Camberloo were difficult for me. I had accumulated some fresh nightmares: I was in a dark tunnel deep underground, closed off at both ends; the air was turning foul and I was slowly suffocating. Or, I was locked in a cell in a long corridor of empty cells, in a place like the House of Mercy. I could smell smoke, and hear the roar of flames. I'd call out for help; but there was no one to hear. There was no hope for me. Or, I was walking in what seemed to be a high, dreary warehouse filled with people; but they had the eyes and beaks of vultures and long talons instead of fingers; at any moment they'd realize I was a human being and tear me to pieces. And on and on, night after night, month after month, the bad dreams repeating and interweaving in terrifying combinations.

I tried sleeping pills. They only brought on worse nightmares and made it harder for me to wake from them. I tried drinking scotch, often till two in the morning, to dose myself into unconsciousness and dreamlessness. Sometimes it worked, sometimes not.

Once or twice I was so weary of it all, I even took out those cyanide pills Doctor Giffen had left me. If I didn't swallow them, I think it was more from the fear they might taste bad, than that they'd kill me.

One evening, I called in at The Prince, a bar near my apartment. The bartender had served me often over the years. He looked at me thoughtfully as he poured my drink.

"You really look as though you need to relax," he said. "You need to unwind a bit." He said he knew of a place where more than one person had found an infallible cure for their worries. Maybe I should give it a try. He wrote down an address.

That was how I first became acquainted with an old mansion with ornamental turrets along Regent Street, not far from the County Courthouse. It opened to me an aspect of Camberloo I hadn't been familiar with. The city was small, but it was big enough to have its seedy side. The old mansions in the tree-lined streets north of City Hall had been deserted by the wealthy long ago. Some had been converted into late-night bars and clubs.

The turreted mansion offered a unique kind of experience. I started going there at least once a week, and for a while at least, I found an escape from my nightmares. The visits seemed somehow to erase the fearful imagery from my mind.

On a particular Wednesday night in late October, I was in that mansion. I was lying waiting on a bare mattress, my favourite mattress, in the dark corner of a long, brown-curtained room lit by candles. It had once been a dining-room. A dozen mattresses had been placed around on the wooden floor, and three or four of them were occupied too. The sweet smell of the smoke was thick in the air.

The owner came and knelt on the floor beside me. I never knew his name. He was a thin man of about fifty; a dirty band round his forehead kept his long hair out of his face. With a knitting needle, he impaled a lump of the sticky brown mixture from a tray and held it over a candle. When it began smouldering, he put it in the bowl of my pipe. I sucked on the long stem and exhaled. He nodded, and got up and left me.

I lay back, drawing slowly on the pipe. Before my eyes stopped focusing on the world outside of me, they happened to settle for a moment on a form stretched out on onc of thc mattresses nearby. A woman.

That was a surprise. I'd never seen a woman here before. She was small and dark, and wore dark clothes. How thin she looked, lying there. When the candles guttered, her face became a death's head, with black hollows for eyes.

Soon, my mind drifted away from her. My eyes closed and I saw nothing but marvels. I lay in that state for at least three hours. When I got up to leave, I noticed that the mattress the woman had occupied was empty. I went home and slept a few refreshing, dreamless hours.

I saw her the following Wednesday night, just after midnight, walking along Weber Lane. She had a stiff walk that somehow seemed right for her, and was headed in the opposite direction from me. She didn't look my way. Later that night I saw her again—at the turreted mansion.

After that, I kept seeing her on my Wednesday prowls. She'd be walking along the street, or sitting alone in the corner of one of those seedy bars, drinking. She was not a woman whose face attracted company. It had a molten look, a sheen, as though it was covered in a quarter-inch of wax. She always wore a headscarf, tied under her chin.

Once, I saw her in a bar just after midnight. When she left, around one o'clock, I left too. She headed, as I'd hoped, for the turreted mansion. I followed her inside and chose the mattress next to hers. When I took off my coat and lay down, I saw she was watching.

"My name's Andrew," I said, and held out my hand.

"Amber Tristesse," she said, not taking my hand. I thought she'd said something in a foreign language.

"Pardon?" I said.

"My name's Amber Tristesse," she said.

What an artificial, stagey name, I thought.

Her voice was as gruff as a man's, surprising in that slight body, and coming from thin, tight lips. It was barely above a whisper—a conspirator's voice. She had taken off her headscarf. Her hair was dark brown, cut very short so I couldn't help noticing her left ear. It consisted only of a hole in her skull surrounded by a ridge of shrivelled flesh under the hairline. Her eyes were almond shaped—I couldn't see the colour in the candlelight.

We didn't talk any more. But every Wednesday night after that, I kept an eye out for her slight form, her awkward, stilted walk. She even began nodding a greeting to me if we passed on the street.

One night, I was already in the mansion when she arrived. Several of the mattresses were vacant. She looked round, saw me and came over and lay down on the mattress next to mine. I was pleased.

The following Wednesday night, the weather was unpleasant: a tired rain, occasionally livened by a gust of wind. I went into a bar just off King Street, and saw her sitting alone in a corner. The bartender said she was drinking mulled wine, so I ordered two and took them over. She gave me a thin smile and I sat down at her table. We sipped in silence for a while. She spoke first.

"I rarely talk to people," she said. "And I never go out in daylight." I could see her eyes now. They were a greenish yellow colour, and the irises were like flowers, the petals opening and closing rhythmically while she talked. I'd never seen such eyes. They seemed to know things most human beings could never know.

I was trying to figure out how old she was. Depending on how the light caught her, that molten appearance made her face as smooth as a baby's. From another angle, it was like an actor's mask. Any emotion had to be expressed through the voice, and the peculiar eyes.

She was the daughter of an architect, she said. "He built our house on a hill overlooking the Grand River." She began to tell me about the house, and I didn't interrupt her, only nodded encouragement when she'd pause for any length of time. She spoke very deliberately, choosing words as though they were gold nuggets. I was finding this willingness of hers to unveil herself to me very flattering.

This house her father had built, she said, wasn't so much a house as a dome—a glass dome. In fact, it was a conservatory with a little tropical forest inside and living-quarters in the middle of a bamboo grove. A steam-heating system allowed him to grow palms and exotic fruits —guava, papaya, mangosteen, rambutan, akee and tamarind—they were available all year long. He stocked his forest with cockatiels and parrots that squawked noisily in the treetops. At the centre of the dome was an aquarium. Coral heads grew in it, little cities for populations of guppies, platies and tetras, sea horses and goldfish, angelfish and Siamese fighting fish.

In this dome, Amber Tristesse was born. She and her mother, her constant companion, rarely went outside.

But it was an odd kind of divided life for her father. He still had to go to work. Winter was especially hard on him. Some mornings in January he had to leave his tropical paradise and face blizzards that heaped ten-foot drifts of snow against the side of the dome.

Amber Tristesse looked at the clock behind the bar. I sensed it was getting near time for the turreted mansion.

"Let's go," she said.

We went outside, but we didn't go to the mansion. She took my hand and we walked through the rain, northwards along unlit alleys, the buildings on either side like bookcases in a darkened library, past railway yards. After twenty minutes, we came to an old warehouse on the corner of Bridgehead Road. She unlocked an iron door and we went inside and along a cement floor. Only a little light came through the high, sooty windows; but still she held my hand and guided me. At the far side of the warehouse, we climbed a staircase. She opened a door and switched on the light. This was where she lived.

The room was long and white with high windows, a few paintings, two chairs, a bed with a black iron frame, a rug on the polished wooden floor. A low partition enclosed a kitchen in one corner, and a toilet in the other with a shower. The only notable colours were in the paintings, which were all scenes of a crowded tropical market-place. And the rug on the floor by the bed was scarlet.

Amber Tristesse gave me a moment to look round the room, then she switched off the light and led me, in the almost pitch-black, towards the bed. We undressed in the dark.

She surprised me with her love-making. Not because of any particular weirdness (though I was ready for anything). But I hadn't expected her to be so energetic. She used her wiry body like a gymnast, extracting as much from me as I was able to give. At the end, she was astride me, no heavier than a bird, kneading my breasts, which were as big as her own, moving violently up and down, crying and shuddering.

She then lay down beside me in the dark and was quiet. After a while, she began again to tell me more about herself.

"My mother died in the winter, when I was seven. After the funeral, my father and I went back to the dome. He took out a rifle and I thought he was going to kill us both, but he started shooting at the roof of the dome, pane after pane, till there was a big hole in the top, and the snow was falling down on us and the parrots and cockatiels were screeching.

"I phoned for help. But by the time the police arrived, a lot of the birds were already dead from the cold, lying around us, and the others were huddled on branches, shivering. The vegetation and the tropical fruits were shrivelling up. The fish in the aquarium were swimming slower and slower as the water cooled. A few birds and the fish were saved by the police. But that was the end of our little paradise."

She and her father moved to a regular house in the city. For the first time she discovered what it was like to live like everyone else. She went to school, she did all the things other young girls did. That lasted till she was seventeen, when her father died.

Since then, she'd lived in her warehouse, seldom going out in daylight.

"Everything's so lurid in the light of day," she said. "Things that are full of mystery at night become tawdry."

I wondered if her aversion to daylight had anything to do with her face, and the way people looked at her.

She'd been lying down as she talked. Now she sat up and began running her fingers over me in the darkness: through what was left of my thin fair hair, down over my face and plump cheeks, circling my nipples, then over the swell of my belly, fondling me as I held my breath.

"I've waited so long," she said, softly.

She got out of bed and I heard her clothing rustle as she dressed herself in the dark. Then she switched on the light, dazzling me for a moment. For the first time she saw the purple stain on my chest, and came over to examine it. Then she leaned over and kissed it. She turned her head to let me have a better look at her shrivelled right ear.

"A man did this to me three years ago," she said. The petals in her eyes were tightly closed. "You're the only one who's been up here since."

I wondered what had happened, how such a mutilation had been done. She looked as though she might tell me more about it, but instead, she said it wasn't too late, and she'd like to go to the turreted mansion. I said that was a good idea.

Chapter Forty-one

THROUGHOUT MY relationship with Amber Tristesse, she never again spoke about her past. I kept waiting to hear more, in vain. Nor did she ever ask about my life, or show any interest in what I did when I wasn't with her. We met only on Wednesdays. Usually we'd go to her warehouse first, and the love-making was raw and loud. But sometimes we'd make love after we'd been to the mansion. Remnants of the smoke would still be in us, and our love-making would be a silent ecstasy.

For the other six days of the week, we lived our own lives. I became dissatisfied with that, and so, one night when Amber Tristesse and I were together, I said I'd like to meet her more often. She said no, that our relationship would sour if we made it an everyday affair. I accepted this, though part of me was a little jealous that she could so easily do without me. I loved those Wednesdays. I loved being with her. When I wasn't with her, the very thought of her strange life excited me.

But everything was not as it should be.

One Friday night I was walking down Weber Lane. I saw Amber Tristesse. She was coming directly towards me. There was no mistaking her emaciated figure and odd shuffling walk.

I stood in the middle of the lane.

"Amber!" I said. "What a surprise."

She didn't even look at me. She walked on past as though I wasn't there.

The following Wednesday night, I met her at the warehouse. We made love strenuously and went to the old mansion later, and carried on as though nothing odd had ever happened.

That should have been a warning to me; but I paid no attention. She was an exotic creature—my wounded Bird of Paradise—and I loved her.

By the end of March, the weather was becoming milder. At dinner-time one Sunday, I strolled down to The Prince for dinner. I ordered a scotch and sat at the bar looking over the menu and, as always, half-thinking about my next meeting with Amber.

"May I have a word with you?" A thin-faced man had sat on the stool next to mine. He was about my own age, with brown hair slicked back, eyebrows like little wings, and a short pointed beard.

I didn't really want to talk. Perhaps some instinct warned me this might not be a pleasant conversation. But there I was, and I could do nothing but listen.

"I understand," he said, "you've been seeing my sister."

He then, in a curt, methodical way, began to tell me about the enigma I loved—Amber Tristesse. Not her real name, of course—that was Gladys Brown. Nor was she born in an exotic dome, the daughter of an architect. Nor was anything else she had told me about herself true. This serious, bearded man was her brother, a lawyer who tried his best to look after her. He paid the rent on the warehouse for her. He only allowed her to spend one night a week there—Wednesday—on condition that for the rest of the week she lived in his house, under his care. I didn't doubt that I was hearing the truth.

"The shrivelled ear?"

"She cut it off herself."

"What happened to her face?"

"Fire. She set a mattress alight in the Smithsville Institute for the Deranged. She spent six years there."

I asked no more questions.

"She broke our parents' hearts," he said. "They both died much younger than they might have. My own wife left me after I insisted on taking her in. She was afraid of Gladys." His face was stern, but he had soft eyes. "I thought you ought to know these things," he said. "I have nothing against you, personally. She's had a string of men over the years and it always ends badly."

I felt awful.

"I'd like to talk to her, one last time," I said. "If you don't mind."

"Not at all," he said. "It might be better that way. She's at home right now. I won't be back for a couple of hours."

He gave me an address in Woodsides.

Outside, it had started to rain and the night was colder—at least it seemed so to me. I took a taxi and was at my destination before I'd time to think of what I'd say.

I rang the bell. No reply. I checked the doorhandle: it turned. I took a deep breath and went inside.

From the hallway, I could see under the arch of the staircase into the living-room. She was sitting on an armchair, facing me, wearing a green dressing-gown. She showed no surprise at seeing me, but didn't speak.

"I wanted to talk to you," I said, feeling uncomfortable before that unreadable face.

"I only see you on Wednesdays," she said. Her voice was cold.

I moved towards her.

"Stay there," she said. "Don't move another step."

I stood, awkward.

"I met your brother," I said.

"You came here to tell me that?" she said. "Fine. Goodbye."

I didn't really know why I'd come, but I kept on.

"I only wish you'd told me the truth," I said.

If a face as incapable of expression as hers could sneer, she was sneering.

"Truth?" she said. "That's a laugh, coming from a man like you. What do you care about truth? I told you things you wanted to hear." Her words were cutting. "Truth?" she said. "Does a lover of truth prowl around the backstreets after midnight and do the things you do?"

I stood there, humiliated; I couldn't think of anything to say.

"Get out of here," she said. The flowers in her eyes seemed to be writhing.

I was only too glad to be dismissed. But as I reached for the front door, she called out.

"You think I don't know you? I know all about you," she said. "I used to watch you from the window in the mornings when you walked past. Didn't the little Doctor tell you I was his patient before he gave up on me?"

I stumbled through the door and outside into the night where it was rainy and cold, and I could breathe again. I hadn't noticed the house when I arrived, I'd been so full of my own thoughts. Now I went out into the roadway and looked back. It was the big white house with four pillars. And I remembered the moving curtains. The face I thought I'd seen there must have been the face of Amber Tristesse.

I went to the turreted mansion the following Wednesday. Amber Tristesse had arrived before me and had already taken a pipe. The flowers in her eyes were in the process of contracting when she saw me and concentrated on me.

"Want to come with me afterwards?" She said this in a wheedling voice I'd never heard before. "Want to come home with me?"

"No," I said.

"Afraid?" she said.

I didn't answer.

"Poor baby," she said, pretending to pout. Then she lay back and her eyes turned inward, searching for the half-opened entranceway to the place that spawned her dreams. I looked for a mattress at the furthest end of the room from her and lay on it. At four in the morning, when I rose to leave the turreted mansion, her mattress was empty.

The rest of that spring was fairly typical. Week after week of rain washed away the dirt left behind by winter. Then the sun shone and the warm days seemed as though they'd never end.

I saw Amber Tristesse—I couldn't think of her as Gladys Brown—one more time.

We were in her warehouse apartment, and we'd made love, in the dark, as usual. Afterwards, she fell asleep lying on her back. I'd never seen her naked, but this time, I felt I needed to. I slipped out of the bed softly and switched on the light. She didn't wake. I lifted the corner of the sheet and pulled it gently away. She might have been as beautiful as I'd always imagined, but all I could see was the stain that marked her from breast to navel—a dark purple stain that was a mirror image of my own. I was staring at it in shock when I became aware that her eyes were open, and the flowers were throbbing, throbbing, like hearts beating.

I awoke, sweating, and was thankful it was only another

nightmare. And yet, it seemed a fitting place to meet her. Yes, the woman I loved had become an inhabitant of my nightmares.

Chapter Forty-two

So my nightmares began again in earnest not long after the end of my affair with Amber Tristesse—and they included her. My weekly visit to the old mansion wasn't helping. So I started going there more often: sometimes three or four nights a week, except Wednesdays. I knew that going so often was unwise; but the more I went, the more I needed to go.

As for women: the relationship with Amber Tristesse seemed to have broken the ice. I quickly became friendly with other women who hung around the seedy bars in the early hours of the morning. Though friendly is hardly the word: it wasn't their friendship I was looking for, and they knew that. Sometimes, in return, they wanted money, sometimes a paid visit to the mansion. From week to week I could barely remember their names.

This state of affairs lasted about six months. Then I stopped. Cold turkey. I woke up one day in a motel room with a woman I didn't know beside me in the bed, and I was filled with self-loathing; I'd had enough of myself. I decided at long last I preferred a clear sense of what was real in this world and what wasn't—even if it meant putting up with the nightmares. Even if it meant death. I stopped going to the old mansion. I made my apartment my prison for eight whole days, and I sweated and suffered: eight awful days till my hand was steady enough to hold a cup of coffee.

Then I took the next step: I began going to the Xanadu, which I'd completely neglected for months. I told Lila Trapper she could expect me for two hours each day. One of her eyes seemed to believe me, the other looked doubtful. I wasn't too sure myself.

One day I was passing a pet store and saw some black-and-white kittens in the window. I remembered Mrs Chapman's cat, Sophie, and thought perhaps it might be good for me to have a distraction. I bought one of the kittens and named it Minnie. At times during the next few months, the need to look after that little cat was all that stopped me from going back to my old ways, or from swallowing one of the pills I'd inherited from Doctor Giffen.

I made one other major decision: to change my birthday. Often, lying on the bed, I'd contemplate the photograph I'd brought from Doctor Giffen's: of my parents at the skiing resort. He had told me I was conceived there. So I considered that day, before all their troubles—and mine—began, as a day worth remembering. I did a quick calculation, taking into account the fact my sister and I were premature, and settled on the last day of October.

Strangely, after I did that, my state of mind began to improve even more. Incredibly, my nightmares disappeared. Without any scotch, or drugs, or unusual effort on my part, they stopped. My dreams were ordinary: an extension of my waking life. I slept soundly. This went on for two years, and I started to think I had once again survived the storm: I might at last be able to live a sane, ordinary life. I was now approaching my thirty-third birthday, according to my new method of calculating.

Then everything went wrong.

I was helping out in the Xanadu one Saturday morning—a sunny day at the beginning of September. Lila Trapper asked me if I'd mind delivering an itinerary to a client in St Janus, a little town a few miles west of Camberloo. I was only too pleased to get out of the office.

The road was busy and I drove carefully: I hadn't trusted myself with a car for a long time. Aside from the usual traffic, there were a number of horse-drawn buggies moving slowly along the gravel shoulder of the road. They belonged to the Hagarites, a severe religious sect for whom the clock had stopped in 1800. Men, women and children, they were all dressed in black. They were on their way back from the St Janus Farmers' Market, where they sold their wares. If I half-closed my eyes, I could easily persuade myself they were the inhabitants of St Jude, cast up here by the big wave, thousands of miles from their island home.

Even the stone farmhouse, with its small verandah and neat garden—I noticed it as I passed the final buggy at the corner of Bergson and North King—looked quite a bit like Aunt Lizzie's cottage. Not far from it, at the edge of a field, was a crude, hand-painted billboard.

CAST THE BEAM OUT OF THINE OWN EYE
AND THEN SHALT THOU SEE CLEARLY TO
PULL OUT THE MOTE THAT IS
IN THY BROTHER'S EYE

I'd seen the billboard before and not paid much attention to it. But this sunny day, in the car, I was struck by the awkward, old-fashioned language. And especially by that peculiar word "mote."

I dropped off the itinerary and was back home around three o'clock. Black-and-white Minnie came to greet me at the apartment door and nuzzled against my legs, purring.

She was happy, and I was relatively contented at having got out of the office and done something useful. Otherwise, I'd nothing particular in mind; in fact, my mind was almost blank—a state I'd found to be very useful during the period of my reformation.

So, there I was, just after closing my apartment door, right in mid-stride on my way to the living-room when I saw it.

A black spot.

It was just in front of my eyes, floating through the room. I reached out and swiped at it with my right hand, as if it were a mosquito. It didn't go away. It wasn't something that landed on a ceiling, or a wall, or a carpet; but it was everywhere I looked. It was just a tiny speck, and sometimes it seemed to be sliding, like a falling star. If it wasn't in the room outside of me, I thought, it must be something in my eye, a speck of dust, though it wasn't at all painful. Blinking didn't help. I couldn't even tell whether it was in my right eye or my left. In fact, it seemed to be in both. I shut my eyes completely. I could still see the spot as clear as clear could be. Then it disappeared.

This first experience only lasted a minute. At the time, I thought I really must have succeeded in blinking it away. And I remember thinking of it as a "mote"—the word I'd seen on the billboard.

In this simple way the horror began.

For the next few weeks, from time to time, the mote would appear: mainly when I was at home; but not always. Once it came when I was on the phone to a client at the agency. I didn't let it bother me too much, but I was very aware of it. Another time, it came when I was driving. I was just making a left turn from Thorndale onto Fisher; I was so distracted by it I almost hit a car coming the other way.

I pulled into the Beechwood parking lot and waited for my eye to clear.

That near-accident convinced me that the problem was becoming more than just a nuisance—so I looked for help.

My own doctor, Doctor Lu, a man whose astute Oriental eyes always made me think he saw more than I wanted him to see, sent me right down to an ophthalmologist with an office in the same building. I knew her, too—a tall, talkative woman who'd booked vacations at my agency. I stared into a device, and she stared back at my eye through a scanner on the other side, all the time talking about her travel plans for her next vacation.

Whiff!—the machine blew a measured puff of air into my eyeball. That startled me and stopped her from talking. She stared through her eyepiece for a long time.

"I thought I saw something," she said. "But I can't find it now." She tried the test again.

Whiff!

"No. I can't see anything," she said. She became talkative again and reassuring. The problem, she said, might be one of those little fragments of protein that drift in the eyeball inside that mini-ocean around the iris. It was probably nothing more than a piece of debris, or flotsam, and in time, with luck, it would float out of range and I'd never see it again.

I was walking back along the corridor to Doctor Lu's office when the mote appeared. He shone a little light into my eyes and spent a long time searching. I could see the mote, but he couldn't.

"To be on the safe side," he said, "I'm sending you down for a brain scan."

The lab was at the other end of the building, and when I got there, the mote was still quite visible to me. Good, I thought. Now I'll find out what you are. But no sooner had the technician attached the electrodes to my skull, than it disappeared. Afterwards, he examined the plate very carefully.

"No," he said. "Nothing to worry about here. Your brain's quite normal."

I did worry, but not too much. The mote's appearances never lasted very long, and, as a matter of fact, something about them was different—they'd become quite pleasant.

I remember the first time that happened. I was sitting in the armchair of my living-room, looking out onto the Park. The trees were beginning to show the first signs of fall. At that moment, the mote appeared, and I felt a kind of euphoria—almost as though I were back on the mattress in the turreted mansion, and had taken that long, first draw on my pipe. There was a friendliness about this appearance of the mote—an intimacy. I realized, it was *my* mote. Like Minnie, who'd hang around my neck purring when we were alone, but would run into the bedroom and hide if a stranger came into the apartment. Yes, whatever the mote was, it was all mine, and was nothing an ophthalmologist or a brain specialist could detect.

Chapter Forty-three

THIS PLEASANT PHASE lasted for about two weeks, in the course of which the trees, deprived of their summer heat, changed colour. During that brief time I had come to the conclusion that I was, in a way, privileged. I'd been singled out for something unique and delightful. Every time the mote appeared, it gave me a jolt of happiness. The fact that it had taken to appearing two or three times a day now didn't bother me.

I even began to convince myself that I was in charge: that I was the one who *willed* the mote's appearance whenever I needed a lift.

But after four weeks, something began to happen that had nothing to do with my wishes.

I first noticed it one evening in the middle of October. I got home from the agency around six. I'd brought some files to go over before heading out for dinner. As I sat down at my desk to look at them, it struck me that I hadn't seen the mote all day.

The thought no sooner crossed my mind than it appeared. And almost right away I noticed the difference. It had always been black, but now it seemed even blacker than before. But no, something else was happening. The more I examined its appearance, the more certain I was that the change wasn't a matter of shade, but of size.

Yes. The mote was getting bigger while I watched.

Nor did I feel any euphoria this time. On the contrary, there was something menacing about it, I didn't know why. Fortunately, it didn't stay long. But it made three more appearances that evening. Each time, it started at its old size, and then became a little bit bigger, then went away.

I tried not to take this development too seriously. I thought of the lizard in the beams of the cottage on St Jude, and how it would puff itself up to frighten me, even though it was harmless. That night in Camberloo I made myself think of the little lizard, and tried not to worry.

Things remained this way for a week. The mote was definitely bigger. And it only appeared at night, in my apartment.

That is, till one Tuesday afternoon.

I was at the agency talking to a client on the telephone, and, suddenly, the mote appeared. I hung up, locked my office door and sat down again.

The mote this time kept growing till it was bigger than I'd ever seen it. From being nothing but a speck, it developed till it was the size of a black eye-patch; then it grew bigger yet, like one of those black manta rays we used to watch rising to the surface from the clear deep water around St Jude. I couldn't believe how big it was, and it still kept growing and growing, round and black. I could see nothing but the mote. I felt like a man trapped in a cave, its entrance blocked off. The centre of my mind had been eclipsed; only an aureole of light, of memory, was left around the edges.

I was gasping for breath. I was suffocating. Then more light began to break through, then a little more light. The boulder was shrinking slowly, but steadily. Till it became a spot again, a tiny black spot. Then it disappeared.

Someone had been knocking at my office door. I got up and opened it. My legs felt weak.

"Are you all right?" Lila Trapper was looking at me anxiously. "I heard noises," she said. "It sounded like a dog yelping." She went to the desk, took a Kleenex out of a box and handed it to me. "You've been drooling," she said.

I left the office that night after everyone had gone. I put a note on Lila's desk saying I was a bit under the weather and needed to take a few days off.

The next day was October thirtieth, the eve of what I had come to consider my birthday—my thirty-third birthday.

The morning and the afternoon passed without any visitation from the mote. That gave me a chance to collect myself. I felt I'd been through enough in my life so far to prepare me for whatever kind of ordeal might be in store for me. I put the little box of cyanide pills in my pocket. They would be my allies if worst came to worst.

By six o'clock, it was already dark outside. I was sitting in the armchair, waiting, when the mote appeared and rapidly began growing, just as it had at the office. Again, it darkened my inner being so much, I felt as though I were walled up alive in a cave. Again I did the only thing I could: I concentrated all my strength on not looking at that dreadful blackness. I squinted at the edges, I tried to hold on to the slivers of light that were left; it was as though a trapdoor had been slammed shut on a dungeon. Only one thin blade of light was left.

After a while, as before, the sliver began to widen: the mote was dwindling, slowly but surely, till it was soon only a spot again. But it didn't go away completely this time. It remained at the fringes of my awareness, a tiny throbbing area. What was most disturbing was the sense I had that it was just waiting, building up its strength for another onslaught.

That was when a new, more frightening thought came to me. All along, I'd assumed that whatever the spot was, it always began as something tiny that was capable of growing bigger. Now I wondered whether it ever had been as small as I'd thought. The more I thought, the more certain I was that it had all been a matter of perspective: the way the moon, because of its distance, appears no bigger than a silver dollar. The mote was actually something massive: it wasn't a case of its growing bigger; in fact, all that happened lately was that it was coming nearer.

Not a very reassuring thought.

It had been a humid day. Now, at seven o'clock, one of those vicious fall storms hit Camberloo. The wind and the rain were awful. Balled lightning ran down the telephone wires in the Park. There was a period of calm. The mote, which had been pulsing in the distance, chose that moment to begin its approach.

I took some breaths and prepared myself.

As the mote came nearer, I heard noises. At first I thought they must be coming from me, I must be whimpering because I was so afraid. But it wasn't me. The noises were unpleasant, snarling sounds, like something a wolf might make. And they were coming from the direction of the mote.

I was terrified, but I concentrated on the surface of the mote as it advanced. Was there a face hidden in its blackness? Was there a mouth? Were there any features? Was the face like a gargoyle's, or some awful creature of the imagination?

It was very close now, shutting me up in my cave. Its snarling was loud and angry. I kept looking desperately at that surface, but all I could see was an impenetrable blackness.

As before, just when I thought there was no hope, the mote stopped and began its steady retreat. Again, it lingered in the distance.

The mind's a curious thing. Even though I was terrified, I kept trying to analyse the object that was doing the terrifying. And I came up with a theory that seemed to me very convincing: the mote itself was an implement, a tool of something else, something behind it—SOMETHING THAT SNARLED—something that pushed it forward, something that had a purpose. It wasn't out to kill me. It wanted to squeeze me out. It wanted to take my place.

Maybe I should have been relieved to think my life

was in no danger. But I wasn't. Quite the contrary. I found the idea of being taken over not only frightening, but disgusting.

I made a resolution, knowing the mote, flickering in the distance, was watching me.

I slowly took the little pillbox out of my pocket and put one of the pills on the table beside me. Then I sat back in the armchair and waited. I felt a strength I'd forgotten I had. If I was to be annihilated, I'd do the job myself. Maybe, for all I knew, in that way I'd wipe out whatever was behind the mote along with myself. One thing was sure: I'd die before I'd allow it to take me over. My pride in my own, independent existence was stronger than my fear of death.

So I sat, waiting.

"Do your worst," I thought. "You can't win."

I didn't have to wait long. The mote came rushing forward at a breathtaking speed. The snarling sound was ferocious.

I didn't flinch, in spite of the blackness and the noise. Soon, only a glimmer of light was left. I was having trouble breathing. But I didn't panic. I held the pill up to my lips.

"Leave me alone!" I shouted. "Leave me alone!"

The noise, the darkness were awful. I couldn't fight them any longer. It was useless. I opened my lips to swallow the pill.

As soon as my hand reached my mouth, the onslaught let up. The mote slowly backed off. The snarling changed to a whimpering sound. I could hear laboured breathing. I was suddenly alert: could that heavy breathing mean that the thing behind the mote had to struggle too? What if it was as hard for that thing to push as it was for me to resist? What if that thing was capable of growing tired?

More and more light shone in. I kept up my new, defiant mood till the mote seemed to be on the run. Even when it was just a faraway, throbbing spot, I didn't give up.

"Leave me alone!" I shouted, over and over again.

Its flickering became more and more irregular. Then it disappeared. I looked for it everywhere. No sign of it. For the first time in weeks, I was alone.

I was happy, but I wasn't complacent. I sat in my armchair, alert, waiting. A half-hour passed. An hour. Still no sign of the mote.

Two hours passed. It was nine o'clock.

I began to allow myself to relax. Like a soldier who's been under fire for a long period, and now the mortars have stopped. Or like an animal that's slipped out of the claws of a predator. I was suddenly starving. I hadn't eaten since lunch, and I'd been through hell. And it was the eve of my birthday.

I went to the kitchen and made some sandwiches. I drank a beer and a large cognac in celebration of myself. Maybe I believed the mote was gone for good. Maybe I just felt confident about how to deal with it from now on. Maybe the combined effects of the beer and the cognac gave me false courage. Whatever.

Not long after, I was undressing for bed when a huge flash of lightning shorted all the electricity in the building and the street outside. I didn't worry. I lit some candles in my bedroom. I put one of them on the dresser in front of the photograph of my mother and father I'd inherited from Doctor Giffen. I put another candle on the bedside table and laid a cyanide pill beside it, within easy reach.

But I wasn't really worried. I thought: The mote never comes when I'm asleep. Even if it comes to torment me again, it won't be while I'm asleep. When I'm asleep, I'm safe. I remember yawning and thinking: It never comes when I'm asleep.

I left the candles to burn themselves out. Minnie lay at the bottom of the bed, purring.

I don't know how long I'd been asleep when the final attack began. What woke me was the sound of Minnie's claws scrabbling on the wooden floor as she leapt from the bed to escape. The candles were burned halfway down.

The mote was blacker than ever and came at me with paralysing speed. My arms were crossed on my chest and I couldn't move them to reach for the pill. With the candles around me I was laid out like a corpse at a wake. The mote's approach was absolutely silent. No snarling, no laboured breathing, no noise of any sort. Just blackness and awful presence. I had no hope, but I was still curious. Why had I been chosen?

Who, or what, was Andrew Halfnight about to become?

Chapter Forty-four

Did you ever feel you could walk away from yourself? That was the way it was with me the next morning, the morning of my birthday. It was as though I were watching someone else awaken; as though I no longer inhabited my body. I was an objective observer, could see what was going on in my mind, but it was no longer under my control. I saw it as though from behind a glass or under water. I watched myself, a plump white man with dull eyes, get out of bed and dress. The little black-and-white cat watched me too.

When I was ready, I pinned a note to the outside of my door for the building superintendent, and went to a car-rental agency that rented out used cars. I chose one of those old monsters, the kind of car people used to drive long ago. Then I drove out of the city, heading north, and I drove and drove for hours, past small and large lakes towards the hills where the season of snow comes early.

Where I was exactly among those snowy hills, I didn't know.

These things I did know: that I'd driven endless miles along an ever-narrowing road gouged out by a snow-plough; and that it was my birthday. No cars passed me; those I overtook were also of the old-fashioned kind, all fins and humps, like this one I was driving.

As for stopping, I stopped only once, at a place called High Point Look-out. I pulled in by the barrier fence and rolled my window down. I breathed in the brisk air and gazed across the frozen waves of hills. The cold tickled the little hairs of my nostrils.

All so familiar, I couldn't help thinking. It's all so familiar.

I arrived at the motel after a few more bends in the road, an old-fashioned motel with a flickering electric sign: The Highlander. By the door was a carved figure of a kilted soldier with a raised claymore. The receptionist didn't look up when I came in, nor when I asked for the room number.

"Thirteen," she said, her needles clacking, clacking, a grey-haired woman intent on her knitting.

I walked along the spongy corridor with its stain-proof, dark brown carpet. It seemed to me I'd walked along so many such corridors.

At number thirteen, I turned the handle and pushed the door open.

The room was like a million other motel rooms, but just a little old-fashioned, with its dark panelled walls. She was standing by the bed, naked and smiling; and something about her made me feel I should know her. For some reason, the sight of her filled me with such sadness I could have wept.

So it has come to this, I kept thinking over and over again; after all these years, it has come to this. She stood there, in the stuffy room, prepared for me. I breathed deeply and shut the door behind me. I leaned against it for a moment, wanting to say something—ask her name perhaps, where we had met before—I needed to do at least that. I tried to speak. But she only smiled, put her finger to her lips and shook her head.

"Say nothing, my dear one," she said. "Come to me now."

So I took off the old plaid coat I'd found in the car (how I came to be wearing it, I couldn't remember—a coat with a musty, familiar smell). And as I stripped off the rest of my clothing, I stripped off my sadness too. I concentrated only on the dull urges of my body, till they obligingly took charge, the way they always did. My chest began to thud so that I feared it might split apart and give birth, at last, to a heart. I wanted to spill myself into her quickly, get it over with quickly, get it done quickly, go back quickly to wherever it was I belonged.

But my mind was no mystery to her.

"No, no," she said. "This time you must not rush."

She pulled back the covers and made me lie on the bed. A bottle of oil stood on the bedside table. She poured some of it into her hands. Then she knelt on the bed and spread the warm ooze of it on me, rubbing it into every part of my body, rubbing, lingering especially on the purple stain on my chest, then on down, stroking me softly, after a while turning me over, humming to herself as she worked.

When the oiling of the body was over, she sighed—contentedly, I thought—and then she herself lay down.

"Now," she said. "Let us begin."

I climbed onto her, propped myself up on my arms for a moment and looked into her eyes: I felt I must see into her, discover who she was. I would even have kissed her on the mouth—something I rarely did. But she avoided my lips and kissed my cheek, fondled my thinning hair, ran her hands over my plump body (every day in the mirror, I noticed how plump I had become, plump and white: a plump, white man). She caressed me for a while, then she moved my head down to her breasts, and held me while I sucked. I felt her nipple rise to my tongue and I closed my eyes, buried my nose in her softness, thought I could even smell milk just a quarter of an inch beneath the flesh.

"Enough," she whispered. "Enough, my dear."

And now she pushed my head gently down, past the convergence of her ribcage, and down past the sweet mandala of her navel. Down I slid on her arching body; I slid over her belly to the junction of her legs and the soft cluster of hair, the sweet, sweet smell of her. I tried to enter her with my tongue.

"No," she gasped. "No."

And now she began to revolve under me, turning smoothly with the oil, till she had inverted herself a hundred and eighty degrees, and I could feel her head between my knees.

Ah, I thought. Ah.

I urged my penis towards her face, waiting to feel the soft wetness of her lips.

But "No," she said. "No, my sweet."

And she continued slithering upwards till only our legs were still entangled, she lying face up at the bottom of the bed, I face down in the pillows.

What did she want of me? I wondered. Why was she delaying?

Then I felt her hands stroking my right foot, felt her lift it and place it between her thighs, felt her fingers grasp my toes and gently begin to insert them into herself. Immediately I was all attention; attentive to her soft wet warmth, attentive to her gasps as she spread herself, gradually, gradually, till each of my toes was inside.

She paused a moment, then her hands went to work again, drawing in my oily forefoot, then the bony arch, then the rough heel. Till, miraculously, even my ankle was inside her, my entire right foot, and she gasping and grunting with the effort, the pain of it.

I forced myself to be silent (I had been whimpering with excitement), and she was silent now for a moment, too.

Then I felt her hands again, this time on my left foot; and she began the process again. As before, she tucked my toes into herself first, one at a time. Her breath rasped. Slowly and surely, she went about her work. She inserted the forefoot, the bridge, the heel, the ankle, till the whole of my left foot was in, oil sliding against oil, snugly alongside the right.

I was afraid some involuntary spasm of mine might injure her, so I lay there, quite still, my feet bound together in the wet, warm, flexible tube. It was so long since I had felt such excitement, yet I could not stop myself from sobbing quietly.

"Hush," she said. "Hush, my dearest."

I knew I must stop this sobbing, and I did, and lay quiet, expectant. This was, after all, only a lull. Soon, the muscles of her abdomen took up the work. They began sucking my legs in, impossibly sucking my legs into her. Inch by inch, I felt my calves, then my knees, slowly being drawn in.

I twisted my head around to look at her. But from over my shoulder I could see only her distended genitalia, a fringe of hair, and otherwise nothing but my own thighs, my plump thighs, gradually disappearing into her. I turned my head back and lay still. When she reached the oily bulge of my buttocks, her panting and gasping increased, punctuated now with howls of pain as she stretched to enclose me.

If she felt pain, I myself was in no pain whatever. All of my flesh had taken on a purplish hue; my whole body was engorged, it longed to slide into her.

She gave a loud cry as she enveloped my buttocks, but still her muscles did not rest. They kept sucking till I was in her past my waist and still sliding. Some instinct urged me to press my arms to my sides to facilitate entry, and so I did, for I was sliding faster now. I could have believed a rope was attached to me, I was being pulled inside so inexorably, an ecstatic spelunker in this smooth, timeless tunnel. Even my well-oiled chest and shoulders somehow contracted themselves enough to accommodate passage.

I wondered now, I wondered for the first time, might I die? Might a man die of so much pleasure? Might this be how a rabbit feels, caught in the slim, loving jaws of a python?

Such thoughts were in my mind when the sucking, all at once, stopped.

I listened, alert as never before. I noticed that the quality of her groans had changed: despair was now mixed with pain. And I knew what was wrong. My head, my balding, plump, oily head, was too massive for her.

As her will slackened, the grip of her muscles eased, and I felt myself sliding back out of her—so many hard-won inches surrendered. I howled with frustration. To be thwarted, with the prize so near. I knew I would be unable to bear it.

Then she spoke. Her voice was so urgent, so kind.

"Help me, my honey. Please help me, my sweet darling."

Yes, yes, I tried to tell her. She must believe, yes, she must believe how much I wanted to help.

I tensed my body and I wished and wished and wished. She shuddered, and miraculously, her muscles took hold again, the sucking resumed. My shoulders re-entered her, then my neck. I tucked in my chin and took a last breath. A wall of slow, sweet flesh covered my lips, flattened my nose. As I closed my eyes, I heard her utter one last great shriek of effort, or triumph, or love.

Then, darkness.

I felt myself shoot along a brief tunnel and spill out into a balloon of pink light and opaque waters. A great throbbing surrounded me, my body vibrated with the beat of it. I tried to say the word for this, my rapture. But no word came, only a gurgle, and I cast myself off from all words....

Chapter Forty-five

...WORDS...WORDS...WORDS reached me from a distance, rousing me from sleep.

My nose and mouth were covered but I was breathing the purest of air. I opened my eyes. I was lying on a bed in a white room full of sunlight. My whole body felt stiff and sore. I could see tubes coming from a gallows, leading towards my left arm. At the side of the bed was a machine with a pulsing graph.

A man in a white coat, with a long face, was at the foot of the bed, talking. His voice sounded like a tire on gravel. He had a stethoscope round his neck. With him was a woman in a nurse's uniform.

I tried to speak.

The nurse came forward and unfastened the oxygen mask.

"So you're awake," she said.

I tried to move, but my left arm was heavily bandaged and fixed to the bed by a strap.

"Where am I?"

"Invertay Hospital," she said.

A familiar name, though I didn't know why.

The man came over.

"I'm Doctor Burns," he said. "You've been in an accident. I'll just check a few things, then the nurse can take over."

He examined my eyes with a little flashlight, and as he did so, I remembered the mote. I looked around for it, but could see no sign of it lurking in corners, waiting to attack.

The Doctor probed around my chest.

"Interesting birthmark," he said, running his fingers over the purple stain. He went to the bottom of the bed and scribbled on the clipboard for a while. Then he put it away. "I'll call in tomorrow," he said, more to the nurse than to me, and he left.

She'd been businesslike while the Doctor was in the room, but now she smiled and relaxed. She was a solidly built woman with short grey hair and glasses. "You've been here for two days," she said, and told me what she knew. Apparently I'd been discovered by the driver of a snow-plough clearing the mountain roads twenty miles from Invertay. My car had gone off the road into a tree. I was suffering from hypothermia and had severed tendons in my right arm. I was lucky not to have lost it.

"You talked a lot before you came to," she said. "We lifted the mask a couple of times to listen. But you weren't making any sense."

Now she asked some questions: who was I? where did I live? and so on. She especially wanted to know about the accident, but I could remember nothing, no matter how hard I tried. As she asked her questions, I became more and more aware of the pain in my arm. She noticed, gave me a shot of morphine, and left me alone.

The next day I felt better, though my arm still throbbed. It was unstrapped and I was able to get up and walk around. A policeman came to ask for some details about the accident—but I still couldn't help. I could only wonder how it might have happened, the way Uncle Norman must have wondered, long ago on St Jude.

After my morning dose of morphine, I was feeling quite genial. That was when another visitor arrived. He was a big man shaped like a barrel: a barrel in an expensive suit.

"Mr Halfnight. Good morning. Cacktail's my name—Doctor Gordon Cacktail. Please call me Gordon. I'm a psychologist," he said, smiling. We sat on two chairs by the window of my room. It had snowed the day before, and now the sun shone brilliantly on the hills around.

"Burns thought it might be a good idea if I saw you," my visitor said. "In cases like yours we often find there's a lingering trauma. It's good for the patient to talk."

He was big, but not in any way threatening. As though all his physical strength was used in concentrating his mind on helping me. He gave the impression of being someone to be trusted.

"You don't seem to have any head injuries," he said. "But I gather you can't remember anything at all about your accident. That may be a sign there are other things at the root."

I felt very comfortable with him, but I didn't say anything yet. He clasped his big hands together.

"I understand," he said gently, "that you talked quite a bit before you recovered consciousness. Burns thinks you may have been under some kind of severe stress before you got in the car. This is a good opportunity to talk about your earlier state of mind. That may make you remember what happened in the car."

The morphine made me feel so good, and Gordon Cacktail was so kind, and it was so long since I'd talked to anyone, I just opened up. The words were like hot coals I couldn't spit out fast enough. I just talked and talked. I went right back to the beginning and talked about my birth and the death of my sister; my father's death, my mother's final illness; I told him about my voyage on the *Cumnock* and my friendship with Harry Greene; I told him about St Jude and Aunt Lizzie's murder of Uncle Norman; I told him about my stay at the House of Mercy and how I came to live in Canada; I told him about my years of tranquillity, then the nightmares that led to my trips to the turreted mansion, and my affair with Amber Tristesse; I told him about my struggle with the mote, and about my journey to the motel in the hills; I told him about my experience with the woman there: I said that was the most wonderful thing that had ever happened to me.

But when it came to the circumstances of the accident, I said I just couldn't remember anything. But I did tell him I thought it was curious I should be lying here, in a place called Invertay, the same name as the place where my parents conceived me. And I told him I remembered something else—a dream I'd had my first night in the hospital: how I was at an upstairs window in a house among hills, watching a procession of women dressed in black. How they were paused in mid-stride, like a movie stopped at a single frame. How the leaves falling from nearby trees were suspended in mid-air, as though time and the wind had ceased. How a tall woman, poised for her next step, was carrying a banner. How the banner itself was stretched out rigid, and the words on it were quite legible: THE MONSTROUS REGIMENT OF WOMEN. How I looked across at the house opposite and saw, standing at the upstairs window, another watcher all dressed in black, and he was watching me with cold, fearful eyes.

Gordon Cacktail was a good listener. He nodded frequently while I talked, encouraging me. When I was finished, he said he had a few things to ask me.

The funny thing was, as soon as I'd stopped talking, I suddenly began to regret that I'd talked at all. I suppose the euphoria of the morphine had worn off while I'd been telling him my life story and I'd been too interested in talking to be aware of what I was saying. Now, I just couldn't believe I'd done it. I couldn't believe I'd betrayed myself. Resentment filled me. How could this man have taken advantage of me when my will was so weakened? I was angry. I completely lost control of myself.

"You should be ashamed," I shouted at him even though he was only a yard away, "prying into a man's private life when he's full of dope. It's psychological rape. You're nothing better than a rapist!" The fact I was capable of that outburst showed there was still some of the morphine left in me.

Gordon Cacktail smiled and was as pleasant as ever.

"Good, good. It's quite normal to have these feelings," he said, "after what you've been through. All I want to do is ask you a few simple questions. If you help me, I'll be able to help you."

My eyes blurred, and when I rubbed them, I discovered I was weeping. I felt utterly humiliated.

"You quack, you parasite! Leave me alone!" I shouted. "Leave me alone!"

"Good," he said, getting out of his chair without any hurry. "Don't hold it in. I'll come back again some time when you feel better."

The next afternoon, a grey-haired police officer drove me to the scene of the accident. We travelled in silence along monotonous, snow-covered roads.

"The snow's come so early this year," he said after a while. "Is this area at all familiar?"

These roads all looked the same to me, like bookshelves in a massive library. How was anyone to tell the difference between one and another?

"We're almost there," he said.

The road divided just ahead, and he took the left fork. It was actually a short driveway through the evergreens, and ended in an open area the size of a football field. The policeman parked and pointed towards the trees.

"That's where they found the car," he said. "You must have thought you were still driving on the highway. When you came to the end of this clearing, you braked and slid over the embankment into a tree."

Through the windshield, we could see a tree with broken branches and a fresh gash on its trunk.

"Does any of this ring a bell?" he asked.

I said no, I couldn't remember anything. At least, that's what I told him. But there was something familiar about the place, even though I could have sworn I'd never been there in my life.

"I used to patrol this area years ago," he said. "A motel was located here. It was demolished a long time ago."

I wouldn't even have thought of asking him the name of the motel. But he told me anyway.

"It was called The Highlander," he said.

Chapter Forty-six

SATURDAY WAS MY last day at the hospital. I was completely rested, and felt physically well, except for my arm. Doctor Burns said with any luck I might regain the use of it in due course.

I had an hour to wait for the taxi that was to take me back to Camberloo. I was standing behind some potted ferns at Reception when Gordon Cacktail and Doctor Burns came by. They were carrying cups of coffee and stopped to chat only a few yards away, quite unaware of me. I suspected they might be talking about me, and I was right.

"...a classic case," Gordon Cacktail was saying. "A pity he's leaving. He has all the signs of a chronic oedipal condition: in fact, he believes he made a journey back into the womb. And he has massive survivor guilt. He says his twin sister was killed as a baby, and since then he's lived in places where large numbers of the population have been wiped out. He went through a broken romance, and a few years of heavy substance abuse that brought on various delusions. He has a definite touch of paranoid schizophrenia, too: he believes that not long ago he was possessed by an alien being." He shook his head. "Really, Burns. It's the kind of case I don't often come across."

Just then, Doctor Burns saw me, and cleared his throat. Gordon Cacktail turned and saw me too.

"Ah, Mr Halfnight," he said. "I was just talking about you."

He was completely unashamed of being overheard. What a frightening man he seemed to me—a man with no secrets, who'd never say anything in private he wouldn't want the world to hear. Doctor Burns looked a little less comfortable and excused himself.

"Mr Halfnight," said Gordon Cacktail, "if only I could convince you to see me again." He had put on his most persuasive voice. "Now, look. I go down to the Camberloo Mental Health Centre once a month. I'd be only too happy to set up a schedule of sessions."

I said I wasn't interested and he saw I meant it.

"Well," he said, "if that's the way you feel. But if you do change your mind, you know where to get in touch with me. Believe me, putting experiences like yours into words is very therapeutic. Even if you don't want to talk to me, or anyone else, for that matter. You really should consider writing them down. That can be such a healthy exercise."

I was walking away in disgust when Gordon Cacktail said something that made me stop just a moment more.

"You mentioned 'The Monstrous Regiment of Women' when we spoke. I just thought you might like to know it's part of the title of an old book. The full title was *First Blast of the Trumpet Against the Monstrous Regiment of Women.* Maybe you already knew that? I looked it up in the encyclopedia. It has nothing to do with an army of ugly women, though. 'Regiment' used to mean rule by a king. The book was opposed to women being rulers. So that's all it means—'a warning against the dreadful government by women'—or something like that. Though it seems the author wasn't too fond of women generally. He probably wouldn't have objected to your notion of a regiment of them marching around, terrorizing the world."

I was back in Camberloo that evening. The superintendent of my apartment block welcomed me. He'd seen the note pinned to my door and said he'd taken good care of Minnie while I was gone.

I thanked him. I didn't take the elevator, but climbed the stairs to my apartment with a certain dread. Perhaps I was afraid the mote might still be there, waiting for me. I opened the door cautiously and a black shape came rushing at me. I flinched—but it was only Minnie, her tail in the air, her purr louder than I remembered.

I closed the door behind me and made a quick check of the apartment. Everything in the living-room seemed normal. In the bedroom, the candles I'd arrayed round the bed were now wax blobs. The black pill still lay on the bedside table. I put it back in the bathroom.

I poured myself a scotch and sat in the armchair with Minnie on my knee. I stroked her, and for the first time in such a long time, I prepared to let myself relax.

But not yet. I moved Minnie aside and brought the photograph from the bedroom. I laid it on the living-room table and examined it with a magnifying glass: my mother and father were standing in a snowy parking lot with a building behind them and a car parked nearby. The car was one of those old-fashioned cars that don't exist any more, all humps and fins.

The sight of that car made my heart beat faster. I turned

the photograph over, loosened the little holders with a penknife, took off the backing and lifted the photograph out. I turned it over. About an inch along the top had been covered by the matt. I could make out, faintly, an old-fashioned neon sign above the door of the building.

My hand, holding the magnifying glass, trembled as I held it over the sign and tried to read it. I squinted, I tried every way to decipher it. Did it say The Highlander? The photograph was very old and the focus wasn't that good. The entire picture dissolved into dots the closer I examined it. The more I looked, the more I realized I'd never be certain—and the steadier my hand became. At last, I gave up. I went back to the armchair, Minnie settled again on my knee, I settled again with my scotch. And this time I did relax.

Part Six

The Comet

...The face that arrives is never
the face that left us

Jane Mead

Chapter Forty-seven

TWO YEARS PASSED. At least once a day, every day, I tried to remember that accident in the car. I just couldn't.

As for my left hand, I would squeeze a tennis ball in it every day for a few minutes, but the muscles and flesh of the arm began to atrophy. My hand took on the appearance of a large claw. Some nights I'd wake, terrified, feeling something crawl over my body. It was the hand, which seemed to have a mind of its own. It was a nuisance in another way too: I'd got myself into a work routine again, and went to the agency for a few hours each day. I couldn't help noticing that clients were a little put off by the sight of the hand.

I took to wearing a leather glove on it.

I was now living a very disciplined life and sleeping well. If there was any benefit from the accident, it was that since then my nightmares had completely vanished. So far as those other pleasures were concerned: I didn't miss them at all. In fact, I took a perverse sensual pleasure in my self-denial. I came to enjoy my abstinence as much as I'd enjoyed my over-indulgence. I was so sure of myself, I'd flushed the cyanide pills down the toilet.

In June of that second year, two items in *The Camberloo Record* caught my attention. The first was the death of

Amber Tristesse—or, as the report called her, Gladys Brown. The warehouse she lived in had burned down, and her body and the body of an unknown man were found inside. The fire seemed to have been deliberately set in her upstairs apartment, and investigators suspected arson, though it might possibly have been suicide.

The other item was the approach of the Comet Zabrinski. The papers were full of it. It had been spotted first by an amateur astronomer, and experts forecast it would be a great spectacle as it passed close to the earth.

I first read about the comet one Tuesday, at lunch-time. I'd taken the newspaper to the Park to eat my sandwich and was sitting on a bench under a big maple. There was no wind, flowers were in bloom everywhere, the trees were heavy with growth, children were playing, wading through shallow lakes of white butterflies. As I read about the comet, I was remembering Uncle Norman, and his hopes of spotting a meteor from his garden on St Jude.

Just then, I became aware of a woman sitting on the next bench along the path. She was wearing a headscarf that partly covered her face. She had taken out a thick paper-back, and was reading. As I looked, she glanced up. I put on my sunglasses, and pretended to carry on with the *Record*; now I was able to examine her without her being aware of it.

She was of medium build, and seemed to be in her mid-thirties. She wore a white blouse and a red skirt. Her skirt was knee length, and on her bare feet she wore leather sandals with intricate bindings.

I had a feeling I ought to know her. Did she live in my apartment block? Was she one of those women I'd been involved with during my drug stupors? That possibility always made me apprehensive.

After a while, I gave up speculating and went back to the

Record. When I'd finished reading, I folded it and got to my feet.

As I was passing her bench, she looked up at me and the sun shone directly on her face. It was bracketed by wisps of longish fair hair that protruded from under the scarf. The features were very regular, with high cheek-bones. The dark eyes were darkened even more with mascara, and the corners of them were little sad birds. All in all, it was an interesting face. But the skin was pitted with pock-marks.

She kept looking at me, so I spoke.

"Isn't this a lovely summer's..."

I didn't finish the sentence. For all at once, I recognized her.

"Maria!" I said. "Maria!" This grown woman was, astoundingly, Maria Hebblethwaite!

"Andrew Halfnight!" She was on her feet now too. "I thought I knew your face. How extraordinary!"

We didn't hug; we didn't even shake hands. We just stood, speechless with surprise. When we'd enough presence of mind to sit down again, we exchanged awkward platitudes. But when we relaxed and really began to talk, I asked her about her life since I'd last seen her, all those years before, scurrying into a taxi at the dock in Southaven.

"How long ago was that?" she said.

"Almost twenty years," I said.

"I remember it so well," she said. "I was so sad. I'd have given anything for you to have come with us that day, Andrew. My father wouldn't have minded. But my mother said she'd sooner bring a viper along with us. After the storm, I think she was never quite the same." Maria spoke softly with no trace of the St Jude lilt. She wore some kind of lemony perfume that smelt good.

"Ah well," I said. "It was all so long ago." As Maria talked on I tried my best not to look like a viper.

The Hebblethwaites had gone to live with relatives in the village of Abbot's Chase, where many of the houses had been built in the Middle Ages. For Maria, born on St Jude, it was a novel experience to live in a landlocked, stable place where the walls were not made of plywood, where old things really were old.

But stability consists of more than geography and architecture. After only a few weeks in Abbot's Chase, just as she was about to enter the local school, Maria developed a high fever and collapsed. It was the smallpox, which she'd never been exposed to on St Jude. She recovered quickly enough, and was able to go to school; but she discovered that her newly pock-marked face and her Island accent were enough to keep her from making friends.

Fortunately (from Maria's standpoint, if not her mother's), the family didn't stay long at Abbot's Chase. The Doctor was appointed to various short-term positions as interim Medical Officer in remote and dangerous parts of the world. For a time, they had to live on a coral atoll that barely held its head above the ocean: that was in the Kuvalu Archipelago; for another period, they were on the main island of the Birikati group; there, the daily rumbling of the volcanic Mount Tula would shake the Medical Residence, and pictures, books, even pots on the stove, could become dangerous to anyone near.

Maria was eighteen when her father was posted to one of the oil emirates. There she met an attaché at the Embassy, a man who was ten years older. He took her on as his research assistant, and was kind to her. When he received an appointment at the Embassy in Ottawa, he asked her to come with him as his wife and she accepted. She was twenty. They lived together happily; they had no children. Then, just three years ago, returning from government business in the High Arctic, his plane went down in a blizzard. There were no survivors.

Since then Maria had been on her own. She had given up her job in the government archives and was free to go anywhere. She liked Canada as much as anything for the absence of the bullying nationalism and flag-waving she'd seen too much of in other countries. She decided this was where she would stay.

As I listened to Maria talk, I realized how I'd always tended to assume, whenever I thought of her, that she was somewhere in the world, pining for me, when in fact she was getting on with her life quite nicely. As she talked, I paid as much attention to her face as to what she said. I kept seeing glimpses of the old Maria: the little curl of the lips, the delicate ears, the serious eyes. I kept remembering our adventures together on the beach and wondered if she remembered them too.

"But why are you here? Why are you in Camberloo?" I asked. "Are you visiting someone?"

"I live here," she said. "I had a house built here last year." She told me her husband had always wanted to retire here. He loved this area of the province with its farmlands, and settledness, and more moderate climate.

"And what about your parents? How are they?" I didn't really care much about Mrs Hebblethwaite, but I was interested in the Doctor, who'd always been kind to me.

"They're both dead, eight years now," she said. "They were posted to the Lesser Malukus. My father was really getting too old for those tropical postings. They both picked up an intestinal parasite and died very quickly."

"I'm sorry," I said.

"But what about you, Andrew?" She'd glanced several times at my gloved left hand. "What have you been doing all these years? How do you come to be in Camberloo?"

If her account of her own life had been short, I gave her an even more brief, more selective summary of my own. And when I'd finished, we just sat there together in the shady, tangled world beneath the trees, not wanting to part and go out into the bright sun.

Chapter Forty-eight

Maria and I parted reluctantly after that first meeting in the Park. We arranged to meet at the Wagner for dinner that night, and I was early arriving. It was a Tuesday and the restaurant was quiet. I sipped a glass of wine while I waited for her.

When she appeared, she was wearing a black dress with some pearls and looked marvellous. She seemed happy to see me, too. We held hands across the table and sipped wine for a while, filling out some more of the details of our lives.

"Why did your mother dislike me so much?" I asked her.

"During the big storm, when we were confined to The Motte, she saw me trying to wave to you." She was smiling, or at least her eyes were smiling. "You remember we said we'd wave at three o'clock? She asked me what we'd been up to those days previously on the beach."

"And you told her?"

"I didn't want to, but I did," she said. "No one ever taught me how to tell lies."

I believed her. I believed her absolutely.

"But in addition to that, my mother was always superstitious. She said there was a legend on the Island about somebody from outside the town bringing disaster. She thought maybe it was you." She smiled as she said this, and I was relieved.

"What about your father?" I asked. "Was he angry too?"

"No, I don't think so. He laughed at her superstitions. He always seemed to like you," she said. "I think he would have taken you with us if she'd let him."

I asked her about the relationship between her parents. Her mother, I said, seemed to be the one in charge.

"That was just her way," Maria said. "She didn't want anyone, especially my father, to know how much she loved him and depended on him. But she followed him from one awful place to another all her life, so he knew all right."

I may have looked sceptical.

"Love comes in many forms, Andrew," she said. "But it's still very rare. You must take it as and where you find it." She glanced, perhaps unconsciously, at my gloved hand. So I said I had something to tell her, and I did tell her how the hand had been injured in an accident that I couldn't remember anything about.

After dinner, we took a taxi to Pinewood, a hilly area near the university. Her house had been built on the model of one of those Olde Worlde cottages, like Aunt Lizzie's cottage on St Jude.

As for the inside: everything was simple and elegant; the reproductions that adorned the walls were, I presumed, the essence of good taste.

She showed me up to her bedroom and I took her in my arms and kissed her. It seemed quite natural, the years stripped away, for us to undress and go to bed together. Her body was now the body of a mature woman, and that was a delight to me. But I was afraid she might be repelled by me: I'd lost my plumpness, but there was still the arm, the hand, the purple stain.

She put her hand out and touched my withered arm and the claw at the end of it, to show she was not disgusted. Then she touched the stain on my chest as she had all those years ago on the beach. The stain seemed to me less innocent, less forgivable now, on a grown man. But she smiled, as she ran her fingers over it, as though it was the assurance she needed that I really was the boy she'd once known.

When we made love, it was nothing like the frenzy in the cove on St Jude. Then, we'd thrown our whole being into it. Now we were both quite restrained, even at the height. She closed her eyes and breathed hard but made no other sound. I was conscious of trying not to sweat. The love-making was satisfying, but the rawness was gone, as though time had dulled some vital nerve in each of us.

We lay silently in each other's arms for a while, then we put on our clothes again, went downstairs to the living-room and drank a cup of coffee.

So Maria Hebblethwhaite was back in my life. We didn't overdo things: we went out for dinner, or to a movie, once or twice a week. We stayed overnight at her place, or my place, but not too often.

After the first week, we didn't talk so much about our shared past. It was like a book we'd both read long ago; we'd read too many others since. We were reading one now. I was so happy and enjoyed being with her so much I told her I loved her—I felt it was the least I could do. And she told me she loved me, perhaps for the same reason.

I used to watch her and wonder what was going on in her mind; sometimes I'd catch her looking at me, no doubt wondering the same thing. She never said very much about her late husband. Maybe she meant one day to talk about him more. Maybe she thought I didn't want to hear about him. She was right about that. I didn't want to know too much about her life—the fact that there would always be great gaps in my knowledge of her was part of the attraction.

She didn't seem to share that feeling. I suppose I wasn't as forthcoming as she would have liked.

"I don't believe love can survive too many secrets," she said one night. We were lying in bed in my apartment at the time. That was when she asked me outright about the accident.

"I don't know," I said. "As I told you before, I didn't remember then, and I still don't."

"I wonder why you don't remember," she said. Her eyes were trying to look inside me, but I was on my guard.

"I don't know," I said again. "I just don't know. I don't even think about it any more." That wasn't true.

The photograph of my parents was on the dresser, and she reached for it and studied it closely for a while.

"Where did you say this was taken?"

"Outside a motel," I told her. "Doctor Giffen said that was where I was conceived."

"Really?" she said. "I wonder who took the photo. Was it another guest? Was it someone they knew—a third person?"

"I don't know and I don't care," I said. That wasn't true either.

I asked her to marry me six months after our meeting in the Park.

The day of the marriage was late November, a cold day with a driving rain that was at times sleety. The ritual—

really just a bureaucratic act by a Justice of the Peace—was quickly performed in a bare office in the City Hall. The two witnesses were strangers who were impatient to be gone on their own business. I wouldn't have recognized them if I saw them in the street five minutes later.

That was almost a year ago. Maria wanted to do something, so she found a job as archivist for the local government: it needed only three days a week. And we settled down.

Life together at first wasn't easy. We'd each married someone who'd ceased to exist twenty years before. At times, when I kissed the roundness of her mouth, it would seem like a kind of zero. At times when I looked at her face, I didn't see the beauty, but the pock-marks. At times, when she smiled at me, it seemed to me less a smile than an involuntary raising of the upper lip—the way Minnie did when she was using her extra cat's sense to examine the scent of something unpleasant.

When I felt like this, Maria seemed to know, and she'd find an occasion to stare deliberately at my withered left arm and my claw. Can you imagine, she seemed to be saying, how it feels to have that thing roaming over warm, living flesh?

Nor can I forget how once, in the middle of the night, I woke up, terrified. I'd been dreaming that my dead hand was at her throat, and I could do nothing to stop it. The dream was so realistic, I even switched on the light and looked at Maria's neck for bruises. She woke up.

"What is it?" she said.

"Only a dream," I said. But after that, I was afraid to go back to sleep.

Chapter Forty-nine

THE COMET ZABRINSKI came and went. It was a disappointment to astronomers. It didn't seem to want anything to do with our world, and remained invisible to the naked eye as it sped past this planet and back into the darkness.

My nightmares had come back, bad as they'd ever been. When I woke up, I'd be afraid to go back to sleep. I spent many nights on the couch, reading till dawn. Maria—the little sad birds were in the corners of her eyes again—wanted me to see Doctor Lu. I refused.

One night in bed—it was after midnight—I switched on the lamp and woke Maria.

"What is it?" she said.

"Listen to this," I said. "A man's standing with his back to a forest. He's wearing an old coat. He's looking down into a box-camera. He's taking a photograph of a man and woman standing in front of a motel. There's an old-fashioned car parked near them. He says, 'Smile,' and he snaps the shutter."

Maria was wide awake. The photograph of my parents was on the dresser near the bed. She looked at it, then back at me.

"Who's holding the camera?" she asked. "Who's taking the photograph?"

"I am," I said.

Her face was hard to read.

"Dreams," she said. "They can be so strange."

"It didn't seem like a dream," I said.

"What do you mean?" she said.

"It seemed more like a memory than a dream," I said. "Could it be a memory?"

We were lying on our sides, facing each other. She put her hand on my shoulder.

"Andrew, Andrew. Don't even think such things. The photograph was taken before you were even born. How could you possibly have been there? Just ask yourself that. Anyone could have taken it. Lots of people ask strangers to take photographs for them."

"I suppose you're right," I said. "I wish I could be sure."

When I said that, she looked alarmed.

A few days later, I was drinking my breakfast coffee when Maria, across the table, said: "Amber Tristesse."

I almost choked. I'd never ever mentioned that name to her. She was looking at me.

"Tell me about Amber Tristesse."

"How do you know about her?" I asked.

Maria's eyelids flickered the way they did sometimes when she was uncomfortable.

"You called out her name in your sleep," she said.

I didn't believe her. For the first time since she'd come back into my life, I didn't believe her. In that instant, the idea came into my head that Maria Hebblethwaite wasn't to be trusted. I wondered if she'd heard gossip. I even wondered if she'd somehow got in touch with Gordon Cacktail. That led me to start doubting everything about her. Maybe she only pretended not to see my faults, my withered hand, so that she could lure my secrets out of me. Maybe, like Amber Tristesse, she already knew much more about me than she'd claimed to, right from the start. Maybe it wasn't a coincidence she'd been in the Park the day I'd met her. Maybe she'd been searching for me all those years!

I knew my face was turning pale, but I tried not to

let her see how shocked I was at what was going through my head.

"I don't want to talk about Amber Tristesse," I said.

She had a puzzled and hurt look.

So, the nightmares were back and I'd lost faith in Maria. Those things were bad enough. But now, I began to fear something even worse: the mote. Yes, after all this time I was certain it had come back and was stalking me again. Not that I'd seen it; but I *felt* it was near, waiting to strike. And that was not a good feeling.

On a wet Saturday in October, Maria and I were sitting on our balcony watching the Harvest Parade. We hadn't been doing much talking lately, and we were quiet now, wrapped in blankets, drinking hot cider. Sparse crowds lined the parade route. It was hard not to feel sorry for the marching bands and the baton twirlers, turned into stiff puppets by the cold rain.

While we were sitting there, I saw it coming: there, in the distance, a black shape, snarling and shimmering. I clutched the railing of the balcony and braced myself.

"What's wrong?" Maria said. She looked along the street where I was looking. "What's the matter? What is it you see?" She was looking at exactly the place. "I can't see anything," she said, "except the tail-end of the parade."

I looked harder—and of course she was right. It wasn't the mote. It was only a group of marchers, their black coats glistening in the rain. The snarl came from trumpets that were accompanied by the clatter of drums.

Then I saw who the marchers were.

They were dressed much the same as that day long ago in Stroven when they marched to the graveyard. They wore long black cloaks, but this time their heads were bare to the wind and rain. They marched in platoons four abreast. They played kettle drums and snare drums; some played trumpets. Their march was ragged and the music was like the noisy breathing of some great beast.

Even at fifty yards away, I was sure I recognized some of the Stroven wives though I hadn't seen them in many years: Mrs MacCallum of the bakery, Mrs Glenn of the pharmacy, Mrs Darvell of the grocery. All three with trumpets to their lips.

The procession came nearer and I saw something that took me by surprise: the Stroven men. They were wearing the black cloaks and they were beating drums: the Principal of Stroven School was there, and Provost Hawse, and Jamie Sprung, and Constable MacTaggart—and even Doctor Giffen, wearing a black hat with a black feather. The next drummer was the little clerk from the Hochmagandie, with his black nose-cone; then, fingering their trumpets, a group of bar-women. Now came a large platoon of men: the crew of the *Cumnock*—among them was Captain Stillar, with a wooden box under his arm; then Harry Greene reading a book opened on the top of his drum. At the back of that group, blowing her trumpet, marched the old widow who'd growled at me. Now came the islanders of St Jude. I knew them all: the entire Chapman family, with Sophie, the cat, perched on Mrs Chapman's shoulder; Moses Atkinson, with his beard hanging over his drum; the gaunt figure of Uncle Norman; Doctor Hebblethwaite, smoking a cigarette; Mrs Hebblethwaite, my enemy, blowing sternly; Mr Rigg, the sexton, and Martha, his wife—she was holding the trumpet to her mouth with a contraption made of bones; then Commissioner Bonnar, staggering a little as he marched.

Most remarkably, none of the marchers had aged: they looked just the way they did when I knew them long ago.

Now came a squadron of nuns, trumpets protruding

from their tubular hoods—one of them, I was sure, had the walk of Sister Rose of the House of Mercy. After them, blowing loudly, marched Catherine Cleaves and shuffling Amber Tristesse. Then came an old woman with a trumpet held to her lips by a wire device so that her hands were free to knit as she marched—the desk clerk from the motel among the snowy hills; the nurse from the Invertay Hospital walked alongside her; they were followed by Doctor Burns with a kettle drum; and the hulking Gordon Cacktail, beating on a drum the size of a barrel.

The noise was at its height now, as a final trio of marchers came near. One of them was a plump, balding man who beat on a snare drum with one gloved hand. Two women walked beside him: a short one blowing a trumpet, and a tall one carrying a banner.

Were these the three I'd been waiting for? I strained to see their faces. But the chill wind had bleared my eyes and I couldn't be sure. Then I saw another behind them: he was dressed all in black and he seemed so menacing, I was sure he would destroy them. In a few seconds it would be too late, so I screamed as loudly as I could above the awful noise of the instruments.

"Mother! Aunt Lizzie! Father!"

The awful discord of the trumpets stopped, and the drums were silent. The procession halted. The faces which all this time had been directed ahead, now turned slowly up towards me. As they did so, my eyes cleared and I saw hundreds of molten faces with eyes writhing as though they were full of little snakes. Then they looked away from me again. The drums began to beat, the trumpets screeched, and the procession advanced along the parade route, black coats shimmering in the rain, then disappearing round the long bend into Empire Street.

I was standing up.

"What is it, Andrew? Are you all right?" Maria was saying, watching me anxiously. "You look as though you've seen a ghost."

"An army of ghosts," I said.

"You're crying," she said.

"No, I'm not." I was having difficulty saying anything. "It's the cold wind."

She put her hand out to me, and I took it.

"Poor Andrew," she said.

I leaned on her and we went into the apartment. She helped me to the armchair and poured me a scotch. She dragged the footstool over and sat facing me.

"Andrew. You must trust me. You must talk to me. Please tell me everything," she said. "This can't go on. I love you. I need to know everything."

I looked at her, and I knew she meant it, and I wanted to tell her everything. But where, where was I to begin? There was so much—so many strands to disentangle—and how would I ever find the words? I needed time.

"Maria," I said. "Will you let me write it all down? And then will you read it and tell me what you think?"

"Of course," she said.

So I drank one more scotch to steel myself for the task then I went to my desk and got out a thick notebook with lined pages. And I began writing.

Chapter Fifty

WELL, IT TOOK MUCH longer than I'd ever have imagined. Three days, in fact. Who would have thought so many things in a life need to be told? For three days, on and off, I kept writing. Maria supplied me with coffee and meals and made me sleep when I was exhausted. I slept serene, nightmare-less sleeps.

At times, when I was writing down some familiar experience, it would suddenly seem quite different to me, as if a stone had burst out into song. Other times, the writing was an ordeal. Contrary to Gordon Cacktail's theory, putting certain things into words didn't dispel them, but just gave them another kind of terrifying concreteness. The mote, for instance. While I was writing about that, and even when I looked back on what I'd written, it was like living the horror all over again.

On the other hand, I must admit that writing about other matters—for example, that meeting with the woman in the motel among the snowy hills—made me feel wonderful.

One curious thing happened late on the Sunday night after Maria had gone to bed. I was sitting in the armchair drinking a scotch and giving Minnie her nightly session of petting. While I stroked her, I was going over in my mind those things I still had to write about: especially the car accident that injured my arm. I was wondering for the millionth time why I could remember nothing about it.

When suddenly—I remembered. It was as though someone had switched on a series of lights in a dark tunnel. I remembered everything: the way Uncle Norman must have regained his memory, all at once, that night on St Jude.

I remembered I'd been driving for hours, all the way from Camberloo. I was in an old-fashioned car I'd rented, all fins and humps, and I was wearing an old jacket. I recognized it now: it was one of Doctor Giffen's I'd kept when I sold his house.

So there I was, driving among hills, and the night was snowy. The headlights were reflecting back on the thick snow. Trees and the darkness were leaning in on me menacingly, and I had to crouch forward and peer down the road. I was tired after driving so long—hypnotised by the narrowing road and the snow. I didn't know where I was; all I wanted was to find some place to stop, somewhere I could stay the night. I must have dozed for just long enough to step on the gas pedal. When I opened my eyes, I was going too fast. I braked hard but the heavy car skidded and lurched over the embankment. For a split second, in the headlights, I saw the thick branches of a spruce, laden with snow. There was a splintering noise, I was catapulted forward, then—nothing.

When I came to, I was in Invertay hospital.

Now, sitting in my apartment, with Minnie on my knee, I could have let out a cheer. My mind, which had been split in two by that gap in my memory, was joined together again. If I was sad about anything, it was because I saw now that my ecstasy with the woman in the motel, which had seemed so real and so necessary, had never happened. It was the delusion of a man who'd struck his head on the dashboard and whose brain was unravelling as his life slowly ebbed away into the freezing night.

I petted Minnie.

"You see," I said to her. "There's always a rational explanation—not as exciting, but real, just the same."

Minnie yawned.

I finished my drink, sat at my desk and completed my account. Then I went to bed.

After breakfast the next morning, I gave Maria the notebook. She settled on the couch and began reading.

I was very nervous. I tried to pet Minnie, but she wasn't in the mood and sidled away with her tail slashing the air. I tidied the bookshelves. I walked from room to room. I stood for ages, just looking out the window at the trees in the Park, their leaves slowly suffocating under the grey sky.

Sometimes Maria would sigh and look up, thinking about something in the notebook. An hour passed. Once, when she was near the middle, she smiled at me, and I guessed she was reading about our days on the beach at St Jude. I brought her a cup of coffee, which she reached for without saying a word. Two hours passed. She was into the final pages now, and reading intently. I think she had come to the part about her reappearance in my life.

At last, she finished. I was standing by the bookshelves again. She got up from the couch and came and put her arms around me.

"Thank you, Andrew," she said. "Thank you for trusting me."

I felt very awkward.

"Well, now you know all my secrets," I said. "Not that they're really worth much."

She pressed against me.

"Not worth much?" she said quietly. "How can you say that when you've paid such a price for them."

I loved her for that.

Then she was all business. We sat on the couch and she began asking me questions, so many questions. About the nightmares, for instance: what could cause a man to be so tormented?

The fact was, I felt very uncomfortable talking about these things. Writing had been fine: a solitary exercise, a communication with the silent paper. The written words were out there at arm's length, divorced from me. Even the "I" who wrote them was only a stroke of the pen, a character in a story, not the real me, Andrew Halfnight.

But talking was something else. The mouth that spoke was my mouth, the words were formed by my vocal cords, my spittle, my tongue; the spoken words were alive and part of me.

Nevertheless, I had come this far. So I forced myself to talk to Maria. I tried to answer all her questions. About the turreted mansion and Amber Tristesse: What made me crave those kinds of experiences? About the mote—she said that part frightened her: Was it just an awful nightmare, an accumulation of the unpleasant things I'd been through, all gathered together against me? About the woman in the motel room—she said that section moved her: Didn't I think the experience was very positive? Hadn't it something to do with rebirth, and a second chance?

Maria's questions were astute, and I tried my best to deal with them. I must admit, after a while, the talking was easier. So much so, I wanted to ask her some questions. For example, I wanted to know about her life with her dead husband. So I asked her.

She looked happy and surprised.

"I've been hoping and hoping you'd ask," she said. "I've been longing to tell you about him. He doesn't deserve to be forgotten. He was a good, kind man and I think of him every day."

She began talking about him fondly as we sat there together on the couch, and I was surprised to find how much I enjoyed hearing about their life together. While she talked, the weather brightened up, so that the carpet was striped with sunlight through the venetian blinds. After a while, she leaned against me and was quiet, and I thought it was over. I began to relax, to enjoy the silence. But she wasn't finished.

"Andrew," she said. "What about that photograph of your parents? Why did you wake me in the middle of the night to talk about it? Why did you keep mentioning it in your notebook? What worries you so much about it? I didn't quite understand that."

Her question made me very uneasy again.

"It was just a silly delusion," I said.

"Well, explain it to me."

I wasn't sure I could explain, and I told her so.

"Please try," Maria said.

So I tried. I talked about the number of coincidences in my life—including the fact that she herself had turned up in Camberloo, of all places. And surely it was odd that my arm had been injured, just like my father's, near a place called Invertay.

"As I was writing, I noticed so many things like that," I said. "I suppose everybody can expect a few coincidences in their lives, but isn't there a limit?"

Then I told her how I'd always been disturbed by the fact that people, and even places—like Stroven, then St Jude—had been annihilated after their contact with me. I told her how frightening it was to see that huge sink-hole in Stroven: as though my nightmares had been prophetic. And how terrifying it was to be pursued by someone I could never see, who didn't mean me any good.

"I think Harry Greene has to take a lot of the blame for that," I said. "When we were on the *Cumnock* he talked about the Eternal Cycle and how dangerous the Second

Self might be to me. It must have made more of an impression on me than I thought: I half-believed everything when I was a boy."

I told Maria that when I was writing these notes, twenty years later, it dawned on me that I must have identified the mote with the Second Self, and thought it had caught me at last. It had been chasing me throughout my nightmares. In fact, all through my life.

"I believed it must have been watching from the moment I was conceived, cancelling out all my chances to be happy," I said to Maria. "I made it responsible for my sister's death, then my father's, then my mother's. It was the cause of my nightmares, of every awful thing that happened to me."

Maria was listening attentively.

"As for the photograph," I said, "I often lay there in bed, looking at it and thinking about it. I was in such a state, I believed there were two Andrew Halfnights: and the other one was there the very day I was conceived, and took that picture." It sounded so silly. "It's embarrassing to talk about it. But it all made sense to me, Maria. Everything fitted. It was logical. Like the logic of a nightmare."

Maria was quiet for a while. Then she said she still had a lot of other questions she wanted to ask, but she'd spare me them for now.

"Thank you for that," I said.

"Harry Greene was a good friend to you," she said. "I know that. But if you hadn't seen that *Monstrous Regiment of Women* book in his cabin, you might have been spared a lot of your nightmares. And why did he mention all that Morologus nonsense to a young boy?"

"He didn't mean any harm," I said. "He just loved the idea that there was some mystery behind everything. Not like Gordon Cacktail's view of the world."

"Cacktail!" she said, as though she'd smelt something unpleasant. "That awful man!"

We were both agreed on that.

"But when you come to think of it," she said, "there isn't that much difference between Cacktail and Morologus. Their theories about the world are nightmares too, but nightmares they want to force on the rest of us. Sister Justitia wasn't much better: her idea about love, for example. If you ask me, it's much harder to love one single person than it is to love everyone in the world."

"I suppose it is," I said.

"Believe me," she said, and those little birds in the corners of her eyes seemed very lively, "I know that. From experience."

I thought I understood what she meant.

Chapter Fifty-one

NOW, I SWEAR, THIS is when the strangest thing happened. Another coincidence—perhaps the biggest: something you expect to find in a book, but not in real life. And Maria was there to witness it.

We were sitting on the couch, having just finished talking about Harry, when there was a knock at the apartment door.

I don't know why, but it made the hair stand up on the back of my neck. I got up and went to the door. I opened it as cautiously as if I expected some monster to be there. The monster turned out to be a man from the courier service with an envelope for me. I signed his form and he gave me an official-looking manila envelope, addressed to me. On the left top corner, it said COUPAR STEAMSHIP LINES, and it was stamped London, England.

The courier left and I came back into the apartment, closed the door quietly behind me and tore the envelope open. It contained two things: a letter and another, smaller airmail envelope. The letter had the COUPAR STEAMSHIP LINES heading.

Dear Mr Halfnight:

The enclosed envelope was given, last December, to our agent in Aruvula to be sent to you.

I regret to inform you that the sender, Seaman Henry Greene, who'd served with our line satisfactorily on two previous voyages, is deceased. He was one of the crew of the vessel SS *Magus*, which struck the Aruvula reef during a storm, while exiting the lagoon. All hands perished.

It has taken us this long to forward the enclosure to you, owing to delays caused by the usual official inquiries.

Thank you.

Yours, etc.
J.S. Dale, Solicitor
Coupar Steamship Lines

I stood there at the door, stunned. Harry Greene dead! I imagined him now, at the bottom of a warm sea, his books shifting with the eddying currents, the wavering pages browsed by parrotfish that swam in and out of his skull. And Captain Stillar's last paintings, down there too! They would have become waterlogged, the lizard tattoos would have peeled away from his models, the models themselves in time peeled away, the canvases scoured clean by the salt water, the whole process of painting reversed.

"What is it, Andrew?" Maria called from the sofa. For I was still standing by the door. I went over and gave her the letter. She read it quickly.

"Oh, Andrew," she said. "I'm very sorry."

She got up and put her arms around me.

"It's hard to believe," I said.

"You were so fond of him," she said.

"I was," I said. "Yes. I was."

We sat down on the sofa. I was still holding the other envelope. It was one of those thin, rice-paper envelopes with the air-mail edges. I recognized Harry's handwriting on the outside—it always looked as though he was stabbing at the paper, trying to pin the words to it. I carefully tore the envelope open. The letter inside was a single page.

Dear Andy:

We're anchored in the Aruvula lagoon. It's a hot place with enough mosquitoes and needle-flies to keep us on our toes. The harbour master says a ship headed north will be here in a few days and he'll give them this letter to mail when they reach port.

Aruvula's changed so much. Did I tell you the young women don't get the lizard tattoo any more? They all go to school now, and read books. I suppose that's better for them, if not for us.

I enjoyed visiting you. Is it five years ago now? I hope you've met a good woman. You need one in that cold place. I'll check her out when I come back to see you. This time I'll come in the summer.

But the reason for this letter is to keep a promise. Do you remember I said I'd let you know the location of Paradise if I ever came across it? I must say, when I saw you, you looked like a man who could use the information! Well, I've been working extra hard this voyage at my Morologus and I do believe I've figured out his system at last. So, according to my calculations, here are the exact co-ordinates of Paradise: Latitude 44.168° North, Longitude 80.448° West. Look them up for yourself!

See you in a few months.

Happy sailing.

Your old shipmate
Harry

I gave the letter to Maria, and she read it too.

"I wish I'd met him," she said. "He must have seen how unhappy you were when he visited you."

"I guess he wasn't easy to fool," I said.

"He was old for a sailor, wasn't he?"

"He must have been around seventy. I doubt if he ever intended to stop. He and Captain Stillar were alike: they both had to keep making yoyages to do the thing they loved most."

"Well, let's do as he asked," Maria said.

"What?"

"Look up the co-ordinates," she said. "If he spent so many years trying to find them, we should at least check them out." And she went to the bookcase and came back with an atlas. She studied it for a while.

"There it is!" she said. She pointed to the map. "See?" She was smiling.

I looked: the co-ordinates were right over Camberloo.

"Not a very likely spot," I said.

"Perhaps, and perhaps not," Maria said. "Do you remember the sign on Harry's cabin door? Do you remember the words?"

I'd seen it almost every day of the voyage to St Jude. I could see it before me again:

The mind is its own place, and in itself
Can make a Heaven of Hell, a Hell of Heaven

I recited it for her.

"It seems so true," she said. "What if Paradise is where you are, only it's hard to realize it? What if you can't find it till you love and trust somebody enough, and then wherever you are is Paradise?"

I said it sounded like a good idea.

"My mother used to complain about some of the places my father was sent to," Maria said, "and he used to tell her they weren't so bad. He'd say, 'A rose can grow even on a dunghill.' Not that Camberloo's anything like a dunghill. But I'm sure it doesn't look the way people expect Paradise to be."

That got her thinking about Harry again. "Do you remember he told you a good book can be a talisman," she said, "even if you never actually got round to reading it? Maybe the same thing applies to words. Why shouldn't a word be a talisman, too? Even if you're not sure exactly what it means? Why shouldn't 'love' be a talisman? And 'trust'?"

I wanted to please her.

"Maybe you're right," I said.

"Remember what Moses Atkinson said when we were on the mountain—that snakes never learn anything by experience?"

"Yes," I said.

"Well," she said, "he may have been right about snakes, but not about us. Human beings can learn how to love."

We were sitting on the sofa with the atlas still between us. She sat upright suddenly.

"Andrew, I have an idea. Will you add all this to your notebook? After all the nightmares and the horrors, will you go back to your desk, right now, and write this down?"

I was reluctant. I felt foolish.

"Please," she said. "If you won't do it for yourself, will you do it for me?"

I took the plunge.

"Why not?" I said. "Of course I will."

"Will you write that love and trust are the most important things in the world?"

"Yes, I will," I said.

She seemed delighted.

"Thank you, Andrew. And by the way, if you're ever having one of those processions again"—she was trying not to smile—"you know: your Monstrous Regiment of Women? Will you put me in it? Put me in it holding a banner with two words on it: LOVE and TRUST. Will you do that?"

I tried not to smile, too; but I couldn't help it.

"Yes, all right. I will," I said.

"And so that you never forget," she said, "will you make them the last words in your notebook?"

Yes, Maria. I will. I will and I have. The last words in the notebook are LOVE and TRUST.